The Body in the Hayloft

Also by Catherine Dilts

Survive or Die

The Rock Shop Mysteries:
Stone Cold Dead
Stone Cold Case
Stone Cold Blooded

The Rose Creek Mysteries:
The Body in the Cattails
The Body in the Cornfield

The Ninja Grandparent Placement Mysteries:
Grandpa's New Year's Relocation

Writing as Ann Belice

The Tapestry Tales:
Frayed Dreams
Broken Strands

The Body in the Hayloft

~A ROSE CREEK MYSTERY~

CATHERINE DILTS

Top Hat Cat Publishing LLC

Cover art and illustrations by Merida Bass

Author photo by Winston Foto at https://www.winstonfoto.com

Paperback ISBN 978-1-967578-12-2
E-book ISBN 978-1-967578-14-6
LCCN 2025923161

First Edition: December 2025

Published by Top Hat Cat Publishing LLC

https://www.catherinedilts.com/

Printed in the United States of America

10 9 8 7 6 5 4 3 2 1

Top Hat Cat

Publishing LLC

To Merida – not many mothers are fortunate enough to work with their daughters. Thanks for believing we can do this!

Chapter One

Callie Garcia shook a can of cat treats.

"Here, kitty kitty."

She placed herself inside the mind of a pet going on a secret adventure, and imagined the purebred Persian cat hunting for mice.

Would the pampered house cat even know what to do with a mouse?

She walked slowly toward the old barn, scanning for any glimpse of poofy white fur. Even with splashes of orangish fur on his muzzle, tail, and paws, Winston should stand out against the beige straw bales, green late-summer grass, black rubber feed bucket, and brown wood fence posts.

"Uh oh."

Callie noticed an owl pellet under one of the trees shading the old barn's paddocks. The barn owls ate pesky rodents, then regurgitated the undigestible fur and bones. Callie nudged the pellet with the toe of her cowgirl boot. The bits of fur were grayish-brown, not the long white of the missing cat. In addition to that evidence, the owls' digestive process took longer than the hour or so the cat had been missing.

That didn't mean the owls weren't feasting on Winston right now, though.

"Here, kitty. Here, Winston."

When Callie and Clint bought the Oklahoma ranch three and a half years ago, they'd debated tearing down the original horse barn. The weathered building was a couple decades older than Callie's twenty-eight years, rich with the scent of livestock, grain, and leather gear. The bones were good, and recently installed faux wood siding had breathed life back into the six-stall barn. The raised center roof covered a handy hayloft used for storage.

Winston's owner Marcia Bentworth-Fallows had already commandeered wranglers and unwitting bystanders to search the larger new barn. The woman seemed to think the cat, like herself, had elevated tastes and would hide in the "horse mansion," as Callie's friends called it.

The cat's owner was more temperamental than the twitchy Thoroughbred she rode. Or so Callie had heard. She didn't know the woman personally, but the rumor via the equine grapevine was that Marcia had a reputation for being driven and intense. The horses and riders she trained frequently made it onto the Olympic dressage and jumping teams.

Not the crowd typically found on the Double C ranch. Callie and Clint had offered their facilities as an emergency alternate location when the scheduled venue had been hit by a late summer storm that tore half the roof off the Oklahoma lakeside resort's arena. The Equine Excellence Event, or Equi X for short, had to find a place fast to hold the Labor Day weekend workshop. With nearly fifty visiting horses and their accompanying riders, trainers, owners, and staff, not to mention the expected hundreds of spectators, the ranch was bursting at the seams.

The Double C wasn't set up to be a B&B. Sure, they boarded horses and hosted riding classes. Dr. Sam Grady, the famous horse whisperer, drew crowds for his training workshops. They even had an outfitter who arranged rental horses for trail rides.

But the people parking their trailers for Equi X were a fussy group. Playing cat wrangler was just one more indignity heaped onto Callie's attempt to lend a helping hand to the equine community. How did the saying go? No good deed goes unpunished?

And now Marcia's cat had escaped her luxury fifth wheel parked in the cow pasture.

"Here, kitty kitty. Winston!"

Cats were helpful for hunting mice and other grain-eating vermin, but predators higher on the food chain hunted cats. Callie would have been broken-hearted if ranch cats ended up being dinner for coyotes or owls. She didn't have any pets at the moment. Her horses were more than enough.

Three horse trailers were parked along the side of the old barn. Callie unlatched the doors of each and looked inside. The squeaky hinges should have scared any animal out of hiding. If not, the heat should send them running. The late morning was toasty, and the trailers were basically metal boxes. No horses, no cats. She knelt to peer underneath the last one.

"Callie, is that you!" a man yelled.

Startled, she raised her head, bumping against the metal-framed bottom of the third horse trailer.

"Ow!" Callie stood, pressing a hand to the back of her head. Her long blonde ponytail had cushioned the blow, but it still hurt. "George, did you have to holler?" She blinked away the stars dancing in front of her eyes.

"I am so sorry, Callie." Clint's cousin was nearly three months sober after a murder earlier that summer had scared him straight. Unfortunately, he wasn't showing any signs of wanting to leave the ranch. "Here. Up you go."

George Garcia offered a hand to Callie, helping her stand. Going alcohol-free had done him good. He'd shed some of his paunchy gut, and his deeply tanned skin and brown eyes were clear. He resembled his cousin, Callie's hot husband, although no man looked as good as Clint Garcia.

She rubbed her head. "Did they find that darn cat yet?" she asked.

"No," George said. "I came out here to see if you and Marcia'd had any luck."

"Marcia isn't with me," Callie said. "The last I saw, she was tearin' up the tack room in the main barn."

George shook his head. "She left. Her husband's looking for her. He thought she headed to the old barn."

"She must have gone somewhere else," Callie said. "I've been huntin' out here by myself."

"I'll let Alistair know." George turned to rush off, but paused, looking back at Callie. "Don't worry. We'll find that cat."

Chapter Two

Makenzie Selkirk walked into the breakroom Thursday. She was a frequent patron of The Stockman's Café, but today had been a brown bag day. Well, she actually carried her lunch in a purple and pink polka-dotted soft-sided cooler. Makenzie grabbed the top strap and pulled it from the industrial-sized refrigerator.

One more day.

The Brieswell Pottery Works factory would be closed Saturday through Monday for the Labor Day weekend. Once upon a time, Makenzie had dreaded holiday weekends. Now she had a busy social calendar.

And a kitty.

Usually, coworkers sat in the breakroom with their faces plastered to their cellphones or the local newspaper as they munched their lunches. Today, everyone clustered together in groups of three or four. Voices were whispers, and people glanced frequently at the breakroom doorway.

Makenzie sidled up to Wanda, the chemistry lab tech. The woman's messy short hair smelled faintly of cigarettes. Wanda's red hair color came from the hair care aisle of a pharmacy. Makenzie's flame-red curls, hanging below her shoulders, were one hundred percent natural.

"What's going on?" Makenzie asked.

"There's a rumor going around," Wanda said, keeping her raspy voice low.

"Layoffs," Quiana Red Bird, a factory floor supervisor, hissed.

Makenzie's mouth dropped open in shock. She clamped her lips together. Not Brieswell. The Oklahoma pottery factory was world famous. It had been in operation since 1909.

"Layoffs?" she asked, her voice squeaking. "As in reduction of staff? They're not thinking of closing the doors entirely?"

Quiana brushed a single black braid over her shoulder to drape down her back. "I doubt they'll shut us down completely. We're on the historical register. But I've noticed things have gotten sluggish on the floor."

That's the sort of company Brieswell Pottery Works was – employees were so strongly attached and loyal, they thought of themselves as an integral part of a family. Could the company violate that trust by abruptly closing?

"When is this supposed to happen?" Makenzie asked.

"I hope they announce something soon," Wanda said. "I can't afford to lose my job. I'm a single mom supporting a teenager. I don't want to move, but what else is there to do in Rose Creek?"

"Besides work at a barbecue joint," Quiana said. "Maybe they'll just outsource part of the work here. Buy the clay already mixed."

"But that's part of our fame," Makenzie said. "The local clay."

"Makenzie, you know we'll be the first to get cut," Wanda said. "Our chem lab work can be sent to Tulsa or Oklahoma City. Maybe I should apply to one of the big test labs."

"I'd hate to work in a regular factory," Quiana said. "What we do here is art."

"Wait," Makenzie said. "You two are giving up already? We don't even know what the plan is. Who started this rumor, anyway?"

"I heard it from someone in the front office," Quiana said. "I can't reveal my sources. There was a big meeting. My break is over. Gotta get back out on the floor. See you gals tomorrow. I hope."

Quiana waved and hurried out the breakroom door.

"I can't believe this is happening," Makenzie said.

She had just adopted Pat Pat. Her relationship with Deputy Dustin Sage had accelerated from dating to serious intentions since early summer. How could she support a kitten and get married if she didn't have a decent job?

All Makenzie's rosy future plans were in jeopardy.

* * *

Shanice watched as a new classmate, determined not to use steps or a helping hand, scrambled to swing herself onto her horse's saddle. Just a few months ago, one especially awkward dismount had nearly soured Shanice on horseback riding. Now she looked forward to the exercise, fresh air, and camaraderie with large hooved animals.

"It gets easier," Shanice told the new student.

"I sure hope so," the woman replied. Her mom jeans and cowgirl boots looked new. The helmet provided by the riding instructor, required for students, smashed short brown curls threaded with a few silver hairs. "Right now, I'm wondering what I got myself into."

"Give it a few more lessons," Shanice said. "Linda is a great teacher."

Pepper had slightly terrified Shanice at first. Sitting on the back of a horse seemed a long, dangerous way from the ground. Now the dappled gray mare was her trusted friend. Shanice fastened the chin strap of the helmet she had bought herself, with a washable cap underneath to protect her hair. The struggle was real for Black women athletes. Shanice wore a tiered ponytail in her wavy hair. She could enjoy horseback riding without totally wrecking her style.

The class moved their horses to one end of the Olympic-sized arena. The covered space, sixty-five feet by nearly two hundred feet, seemed huge. But when two classes and three individual riders occupied the arena, it wasn't so crazy large.

Linda, a lean cowgirl in her early forties, directed her

students into a line facing her bay gelding Sparky. Shanice hoped to advance to the next level class this fall. She had a lot to learn, but felt like an old hand compared to some of the newbies struggling with their posture and how to hold the reins.

"Just a reminder, this will be our last class until next Thursday," Linda announced. "There's no way we can squeeze in our Saturday lesson with the big workshop going on. You're welcome to come watch the events. There's no entry fee for spectators. The schedule's on both the Equi X and the Double C websites."

Shanice sat up a little taller in the saddle. Linda had selected her, along with five other students, to help demonstrate training techniques. Of the human rider, not the horse.

"Let's get going," Linda said. "We're gonna start with the game Ride a Buck. Roger here will hand you slips of play money to place under your knees. Then we'll go through our paces. The last rider to still have their money wins."

"What do we win?" the new woman asked.

"You can keep your play money," Linda said.

The class laughed. Roger gave each rider two bills. Shanice tucked one under each knee. Then they were moving. First, walking in a large circle. Then trotting.

Riding was a great way to destress. With her flexible schedule, Shanice could get away for a midday class. Shanice loved her job teaching mathematics, but dealing with university students, coworkers, and boring administrative tasks could wear on one's nerves.

Especially one annoying female coworker.

A new instructor had arrived for the fall semester. Already, it was obvious she was going to be a pain. Gemma Lopez was a perky, pretty woman probably close to Shanice's age of twenty-seven. She came on board the faculty of the Rose Creek branch of the University of Oklahoma ready to change the world.

The problem was, most people working for the university were quite content the way things were. Shanice had seen changes in her four years there, generally for the better. Gemma proposed sweeping changes before even getting to know the university culture.

Thinking about work messed up Shanice's concentration. As they began to canter, her fake ten-dollar bill escaped from under her left knee and fluttered to the floor of the arena. Fortunately, Linda used only the calmest horses for her students. No one's mount shied from the falling bits of paper.

By the end of class, the new student was the only one with both bills under her knees.

Shanice unsaddled Pepper and carried the equipment to the tack room. The new student struggled to heft her saddle onto its post.

"Thanks for your encouragement." She stuck out a hand. "I'm Cheryl Paisley."

Shanice grasped her hand. "Shanice Hailey. I'm glad you hung in there. I almost quit after my first lesson, but I'm happy I stayed."

They stepped out of the tack room and into the wide hall of the new barn. Shanice had teased her friend Callie that it was more like a horse mansion. The many extra-large stalls were immaculate.

"I'll see you next week," Cheryl said with a wave.

"You'd better be there," Shanice mock-scolded, with a smile.

Cheryl headed for the main entrance to the huge stables. Shanice had a different destination. Dr. Sam Grady had returned from Japan two months ago. After her initial love-at-first-sight reaction to the handsome horse whisperer, Shanice was deliberately taking things slow. What began quickly often burned out just as fast. A relationship with a guy like Sam was worth taking time to cultivate.

She snapped a picture with her cellphone of Sam's Appaloosa mare, Andromeda, then patted her velvety black nose.

"Where's Sam?" she asked. The mare nibbled Shanice's fingers. "I don't have a carrot this time. And you can't talk. Not in human, anyway. Well, I'd better find Sam."

Shanice walked past the Olympic-sized indoor arena to the other wing of stalls. The ceiling was lower here, but still high enough to accommodate a rider sitting on a horse. The wide aisle was crowded. Three people faced each other in the hall dividing rows of stalls. One held a lead rope attached to a gorgeous chestnut gelding with white socks.

"I was told I had stall fifteen." The young woman in formal dressage wear stood with her knee-high boots spread wide and one fist on her narrow hip. "Ladybird requires a stall adjacent to her companion Sir Maximus. Stalls thirteen and fifteen. She's in thirteen, but there is some strange beast in stall fifteen. That belongs to Sir Maximus."

The gelding shook his head.

"Fourteen is right across the aisle from thirteen, Miss Byron," Mike Kolczynski said. The stable manager's bushy, drooping mustache didn't hide his mouth quirking up in an amused grin. "Your horses can see each other better than if they're side by side."

"We chose stall assignments on our registration forms," a ruddy-faced man with thinning red hair said. "Marcia specifically wanted fifteen for Moonstone." A dapple-gray Thoroughbred poked its nose against the metal bars framing the stall's upper wall. Hardly a beast, the horse was beautiful. "It's his lucky number."

The woman stomped her foot. Her dark hair trimmed in a pixie-style cut emphasized her childlike features. "Thirteen and fifteen. That is non-negotiable."

"Or what?" the red-haired man asked. "You'll file a complaint with the Equi X committee? I don't think stall assignments are at the top of their priority list, after this unexpected change of venue. Nor mine. Has anyone seen a white cat?"

"A cat?" the woman asked. "This is far more important."

"See, that's the real problem." Mike held out an electronic notebook with a screen the size of a paperback book. "You registered for Equi X at the other location, which didn't exactly translate into the Double C barns." He attempted to show his screen to the two equestrians.

Shanice debated interrupting to push her way through, but the argument was educational. These were the type of elites and their pampered horses Sam had to deal with on a daily basis.

Speaking of whom . . .

"Hey folks." Sam walked up the aisle. He dipped his black Stetson briefly Shanice's way to indicate he'd seen her, then turned his attention to the two horse owners. Her heart never failed to beat a little faster in the veterinarian's presence. Tall, dark, and handsome was an accurate description of Dr. Grady. He was five years older than Shanice, and verified to be very single. Until they met, and began dating exclusively. "What's going on?"

Both the woman and the man pelted Sam with their complaints. When they began raising their voices and waving hands, the whites of Sir Maximus's eyes showed. Sam placed a hand on the chestnut horse's neck, calming it with his touch.

"Slow down," Sam said to the humans. "Mike, can we do some rearranging to place Maximus and Ladybird next door to each other? And leave Moonstone where he is. Does that work, Alistair?"

The red-haired man nodded. "That's all I wanted from the beginning."

"I reserved stall fifteen," the dark-haired woman said.

Mike shook his head, returned his electronic notepad to his generous shirt pocket, and placed his hands on his hips. He was great with horses. People seemed to give him difficulty.

"Sydney, you're just causing trouble because you're angry with my wife," the red-haired man said. "And you're taking it out on poor Moonstone." He reached up to pat the horse's nose through the metal bars of its stall.

"I don't abuse horses," Sydney said, with a chill in her voice. "Unlike the illustrious Marcia Bentworth-Fallows."

Whoa. That was one of the big-name instructors at the

weekend workshops.

"That is a serious allegation, Ms. Byron. One I refuse to dignify with a response."

Shanice suspected that Sydney Byron might have flung herself at the man and scratched his eyes out, if he weren't twice her size. Instead, her tone became even more frosty.

"If only Sir Maximus could speak, he would have tales to tell."

"Marcia had nothing to do with that," the man said. "You need to let it go."

"Oh no I don't, Mr. Fallows. But don't worry. I don't believe in holding grudges. I believe in getting even."

"Is that what this nonsense is about?" Mr. Fallows asked. "A pathetic effort to get revenge? Marcia's horse was here first. Marcia wants Moonstone in stall fifteen. He's not moving." He folded his thick arms over a barrel chest. It might be more difficult to move the man than the horse.

Sam tried again. "We could move your horses to the other wing," he told Sydney. "Then you two won't be working side by side all weekend. Are there stalls available, Mike?"

"Every stall on the ranch is booked up," Mike said. "Even the old barn. Full up."

"I'd be happy to move my horses," Sam said. "Heck, they'd be content to hang out in a pasture for the weekend, if worse comes to worse."

Shanice knew Sam's horses were valuable animals. Every bit as valuable as the three in contention for stalls.

"I would consider any stall far from this animal. As long as my horses are side by side."

Shanice wasn't sure whether Sydney was calling the gray horse or its owner an animal.

"Okay, let's see what we can arrange." Sam waved to Shanice. "If you're available, we might need a hand. If you don't mind?"

Shanice smiled. "I'd be glad to help." She could play ranch hand for a few minutes. Especially when she was placed in charge of a horse worth thirty thousand dollars or more. Pepper, her lesson horse, probably cost a mere thousand.

A horse is a horse, right?

She followed Sam past the arena to the other wing of the stable, where stalls one through twelve faced each other across an aisle. Sydney led the chestnut horse.

"My horses have stalls seven and nine," Sam said.

Sydney seemed to encourage Sir Maximus to examine stall seven. She jerked on the lead rope before he could touch noses with the black Appaloosa mare with a white blanket of spots over her rump.

"Let's see the other."

Stall nine held a chestnut stallion with a spotted white blanket covering him from tail to withers. Sam had a thing for Appaloosa horses.

"These will do," Sydney proclaimed.

Shanice didn't like the way the woman spoke to Sam. But she seemed to have a nasty attitude toward everyone.

Leading Sam's horse out of the barn, Shanice felt relief from the human tensions. She held the lead rope for Andromeda, the black mare. She was a little terrified of Ulysses, the huge chestnut stallion, even though he was gentle.

When they had released the horses into paddocks, she turned to Sam.

"Wow, you're good at handling people as well as horses."

Sam tipped his Stetson back, revealing black curls trimmed close to his brown scalp. "It was touch and go. Whew!"

"What's the conflict between those two?" Shanice asked. "The humans, that is."

"I don't know," Sam said. "Marcia seems to be a responsible trainer. I've never heard any stories about her abusing horses. Sydney is playing with fire. A trainer's reputation is their most important possession."

Chapter Three

Spirit twined herself around Uncle Tobias's ankles and purred.

"Does your cat do that all the time?" Drew asked. *Like when you're going up and down that narrow staircase?*

"Only when I'm seated," Drew's great-uncle said. "Spirit is quite affectionate." As if to prove his point, the orange and white cat with the torn ear and scarred face launched herself onto Tobias's lap.

Drew hadn't been convinced getting a cat was a good idea. Eighty-seven-year-old Uncle Tobias had lived alone since his wife's passing six years ago. He occupied the second floor of the Victorian-style house, above his first-floor law office. Drew's friend Makenzie had insisted he needed an animal companion. The rescue cat seemed as smitten with Tobias as he was with her. Spirit's kittens had just been weaned, and the cat had only become a permanent resident days ago. Already, Spirit and her great-uncle were inseparable.

Choose your battles.

"So, to business," she said, ignoring the loud purring. "What do you think about the family's insistence Mr. Nibley was mentally incapacitated at the time he sold his farm's mineral rights?"

"That's a slippery slope," Uncle Tobias said. "The first issue is proving Putnam was too feeble-minded to sign a legal document, and frankly, being taken advantage of by a slick predator like Ted Fulson doesn't require senility. I suspect there are dozens of victims in this part of the state."

"Who don't even know they've been victimized," Drew added, brushing a hand through her shoulder-length dark curls.

People who preyed on the elderly and naïve deserved to be removed from society, Drew thought darkly.

"The second issue his sons obviously haven't taken into consideration," Tobias continued. "If he was incompetent last November, everything he's done since then is suspect. And his family is under a moral obligation, if not a legal one, to take over his care. At the very least, they need to have power of attorney paperwork in place for the day that does happen."

"They don't sound prepared to do that," Drew said. "The sons don't agree about what would become of the family farm if Putnam goes into a retirement home. Neither mentioned moving him in with them."

"I suspect moving their families to the farm to care for Putnam isn't an option for either son." Tobias shook his head, sending his flyaway white hair dancing. "And Putnam is adamant he won't leave the farm to go 'mooch off my sons' as he terms it. Caring for an elderly relative is a heavy burden. I don't blame the sons for avoiding that responsibility."

"I wouldn't consider it a burden," Drew said, reaching across the desk to pat Uncle Tobias's hand. "I would consider it an honor if you moved in with us."

"That's a kind offer, but where will you two kids be? Are you staying here or moving back to Boston? This deal seems to be dragging on, if you don't mind me noticing."

Everyone noticed. Including her book club friends. Drew had moved to Rose Creek in March to help out Uncle Tobias after a health scare. He recovered quickly, but Drew fell in love with the small town. Her eight-year-old son Parker had blossomed from a houseplant of a kid addicted to video games into an outdoorsy boy with a tight-knit group of friends.

Drew's priorities shifted away from climbing the career ladder in her Boston law firm, just as her husband Joel's career was taking off. They might be living 1,500 miles apart, but they were still very much in love. And now Drew was four months pregnant. Complicated didn't begin to describe Drew's life.

"We'll figure something out," Drew said. "Joel's flying in for the Labor Day weekend."

"For my great-nephew's birthday." Tobias smiled. "I've got a big surprise for him."

That was the last thing Drew wanted. More surprises. Hopefully, Uncle Tobias's gift was a new collar and leash for Boomer, the basenji puppy they had adopted, or an old-fashioned game or toy for which Parker had cultivated an interest. She had an uncomfortable feeling a present larger than a puppy might have hooves. But no. Giving a child a horse without consulting with his parents was beyond the pale, even for Uncle Tobias.

Drew glanced at her cellphone screen. "Speaking of Parker, I've got to pick him up. He and his class have a practice session for the Equi X opening parade." She stood.

"I look forward to seeing my cowboy nephew in action." Tobias began to lift Spirit off his lap.

"Don't disturb her," Drew said. "I know the way out."

They shared a laugh. The Falk law offices were two jam-packed rooms on the first floor of the old house, connected by a narrow hallway. Drew exited the building and trotted down the stone steps to her car.

The grade school was only in session a half day Thursday and Friday. Then Monday was the Labor Day holiday. The schedule didn't make much sense to Drew. Why not have school all day today, and give the kids Friday off, for a four-day weekend? No one had asked her opinion. Maybe if she stayed in Rose Creek, she would get involved with the school board.

Parker waited outside the red brick building. Drew had finally become accustomed to her son walking home from school, but today he needed to change for his horseback riding practice session. He hopped in and slammed the door.

"Hi Mom. Can we take Boomer?"

The basenji puppy was five months old. He went everywhere with Parker where dogs were allowed. Socializing was important, the breeder, Drew's friend Hannah Esselberry, assured her. Training a dog was a twenty-four-hour-a-day project.

"Yes, Boomer can go with us," Drew said.

After a quick stop at the house, a huge old farmhouse the small town of Rose Creek had grown around, they headed for the Double C Ranch. Boomer wiggled and squirmed in Parker's lap.

Callie had assured Drew that bringing their new family addition to the ranch was okay, as long as he was on a leash and wasn't being a nuisance. Adult basenjis rarely reached a foot and a half tall at the shoulder. The short-haired, leggy dogs were trim, weighing in at around twenty pounds. Boomer was less than half-grown, only nine pounds, and Drew could carry him if he got in the way of horses and humans.

As they neared the ranch, Drew saw eight people milling around at the front gate. Each held a sign mounted on a stick.

"What are those people doing?" Parker asked.

"Directing guests into the ranch?" Drew asked.

The Equi X event was supposed to be a big deal, drawing two dozen workshop presenters, fifty horses with riders, trainers, and grooms, and hundreds of spectators. Callie had been worried they might not have the capacity for such a large crowd. The event managers and local riding clubs had pitched in to make sure there were portable toilets and washing facilities, and enough outdoor prefab corrals to accommodate the participants.

As they drove closer, Drew realized the people crowding around the entrance gate weren't friendly volunteers. Except for Aster from the Red Cedar Meadow farm. *Isn't she dating Clint's cousin George?* The hippie girl with the colorful braided hair held one of the signs.

Posterboard flapped in the air, reading "End the Subjugation of Equines," and similar messages implying the horses were being treated cruelly. The organization's name was printed in large block letters. Red Alert Organized Rescue. RAOR.

When had people moved past protesting actual animal

cruelty, factory farms, and puppy mills, and into imagining the animals' states of mind? Drew tried to reserve judgment. She was a city girl, born and raised in Boston. *For all I know, the grievances are real.*

Drew rolled down her window and slowed as she turned into the ranch driveway. Maybe Aster could tell her what was going on. The Audi's air-conditioning was instantly overwhelmed by a wave of hot summer air pushing inside. One woman darted in front of their car. Drew slammed on her brakes.

"Ahh!" Parker clutched Boomer tight to his chest. The puppy yelped as both he and Drew's son jerked forward. The seatbelt snapped taut across Parker's chest.

The tires skidded on gravel as Aster dropped her sign and grabbed the woman's arm. Drew managed to stop in time to avoid hitting the woman, but only because Aster had pulled the woman to the side.

"Sorry, Drew," Aster yelled.

Drew didn't hesitate. She pressed the gas and hurried through the gate. In her rearview mirror, she watched Aster and her fellow protestor squaring off in a heated discussion.

*   *   *

"The barbecue starts soon," Sam said. "We can clean up in my trailer."

"I do need to wash my hands," Shanice said. "And maybe change my shirt."

She had been inside Sam's fifth wheel a few times since his return from a two-month assignment treating racehorses in Japan. Her sisters in Chicago had thrown a fit when she described the veterinarian's living situation, but they had never been inside one of the luxurious homes-on-wheels.

Shanice followed Sam up the steps and into the relief of air-conditioning cooling the living room/kitchen. A full-sized refrigerator, oven and stove, and sink island made the interior feel more like an efficiency apartment than a trailer.

"You can change in the bathroom," Sam said.

Shanice had made it clear she wanted to take things slow. Sam respected her boundaries. They'd cuddled and kissed, but Shanice wanted to be certain their relationship was solid before opening the door to a more intense physical relationship.

The small bathroom had all the necessary amenities. She washed off the dust sticking to her sweaty face, then refreshed her makeup. She changed from her T-shirt to a sleeveless blouse in a southwest print. The jeans and cowgirl boots should be appropriate. The lunch barbecue was supposed to be casual. Shanice wondered what that might entail for the wealthy equestrians. *Business casual jodhpurs?*

"All ready," she said as she stepped out.

Sam smiled and gave her a chaste peck on the cheek. "You look terrific."

"You're not too shabby yourself," she replied.

The star of a television program about training horses using his method of understanding horse psychology, Sam was handsome, dark-skinned, and athletic, with a full head of thick, black curls trimmed close to his scalp. He looked good in jeans, boots, and a fitted short-sleeved Western shirt that showed his well-developed biceps.

"Shall we?" he asked.

"Yes," Shanice said. "I'm ready to hobnob with the rich and famous. In the horse world, anyway."

The barbecue was located in a pasture behind the new barn. When Callie had explained the layout, Shanice envisioned a picnic in a field. She understood Callie's wish to have the food tent far from her house. The cowgirl didn't want strangers assuming they could wander into her home. But as Shanice and Sam walked around the barn, it was clear this was beyond a picnic. The large white tent had the upscale look of an outdoor wedding venue.

Callie's husband stood near the entrance. He was taller than Sam by several inches. Taller than anybody Shanice could see in the tent, which wasn't surprising. Clint was six foot six, lean, tanned, with dark wavy hair.

"Hi Clint," Shanice said. "Is Callie inside?"

"I haven't seen her since she went looking for that cat." Clint's words were flavored with a mild Spanish accent. "And now the cat's owner is missing."

"Marcia's not in the tent." Alistair, the man who had argued over stall assignments, approached Clint, appearing a little breathless. His ruddy complexion was flushed an even deeper red than when he'd been about to do battle with Sydney. "She vanished around eleven or so. Have you seen her yet?"

"No," Clint told Alistair. "My wife is also searching for your cat."

"Marcia's cat," Alistair said, wrinkling his nose in distaste. "I swear she treats that hairy creature like it was her baby."

"If Callie finds Winston, perhaps Marcia will be close by," Clint said. "Callie was supposed to be here thirty minutes ago for the welcoming lunch." He glanced at his phone. "She hasn't answered the text I just sent."

"Sam and I can look for Callie. I'll send her a text too." Shanice tapped on her phone.

"If we find either of them, we'll call," Sam said.

"Thank you, Dr. Grady," Alistair said. "I'll check our trailer again. Maybe she found that goofy cat and decided to lock him up in his playpen."

Shanice and Sam walked through the new barn. The aisles were crowded with horses and people. A few riders practiced in the arena on horseback, but more seemed to be heading to the barbecue. Callie was not in the tack room or Mike's office. Apparently, neither was Marcia, because Sam kept scanning faces.

"Maybe Callie's at the house?" Shanice asked.

"Worth a try," Sam said.

They headed for the two-story house. The deceptively simple design disguised a lush interior with state-of-the-art everything. It was a forever house whose style wouldn't be outdated anytime soon.

Before they reached the paving stones to the front door, they saw Aster leading a procession up the ranch driveway. The rag-tag group carried protest signs.

Free the Horses
End Animal Oppression
Only Dopes Dope Horses

"What's that all about?" Shanice whispered to Sam. "The horses here live better than most of the human population."

"Hey, Aster." Sam held up a hand like a traffic cop stopping a bus. "Where do you think you're going?"

"To end the oppression of show horses." Aster pushed her round-framed glasses higher on her sun-pink nose with the hand not holding a protest sign. Her long skirt and tie-dyed tank top made her look like a modern-day refugee from Woodstock. Long, thin braids interwoven with colorful hair extensions draped down her back.

"Now's not a good time," Sam said.

"Aster, don't you harness goats to haul wagons at your place?" Shanice asked.

The apparent leader of the dozen people tilted her chin up. Her face was painted like a leopard, complete with spots and whiskers. Even her clothing of snug leggings and a t-shirt was in the pattern of leopard spots. Shanice couldn't imagine what that had to do with horses.

"Show horses are regularly drugged," the leopard woman said. "The Red Cedar Meadow farm has received our stamp of approval for humane treatment of their animal companions."

"Is that true?" Shanice asked Sam. "Are show horses really drugged?"

"Strict regulations make that unlikely," Sam said. "Show horses are randomly tested for illegal substances."

So it was true. Show horses were sometimes drugged. Why else would drug testing be done unless it were an issue?

But this wasn't a high-stakes horse show. It was a workshop and a training demo. Problem-solving classes for a variety of riding styles, from Olympic-level jumpers and dressage horses to kids' recreational saddle horses in Western tack.

"Why don't you put down your signs," Shanice asked, "and check out how these horses live? The ranch owners would probably be happy to give you a tour."

"But not now," Sam said, "and not with you carrying those signs. They could spook the horses. You wouldn't want any of them to be hurt, would you?"

One protester placed her sign on the ground. Her face was painted like a dog. A headband with puppy ears arced over her short, ratty, brown hair. While Sam and the leader argued, the dog-girl bolted for the new barn.

"Hey!" Shanice chased after her, but the girl had a destination in mind.

"Stop, Josie!" the leopard woman yelled. "Wait for the rest of us."

Josie dog-face reached the barn before Shanice could grab her, the puppy tail pinned to her backside wagging with every step. With a flash of metal and a click, she fastened a handcuff to the barn door latch. The handle of the latch had a decorative horseshoe attached, making it easy to use with gloved hands. The door was wide open, so the action seemed ineffective. But it made for a great photo op, apparently, as the rest of the protesters raced up to snap pics and livestream the event.

Sam spoke into his phone. "Mike, we've got an incident at the front door to the new barn."

Mike Kolczynski, the Double C ranch foreman, was a military veteran and a genuine cowboy. He had no patience for nonsense. Things could escalate quickly.

"Sam," Shanice said, "I'm going to see if Callie's at the house."

The tough ranch foreman versus the animal-costumed intruding protestors. *This could be entertaining.* But Shanice tore herself away. This was her friend's ranch. Callie needed to know what was happening.

Chapter Four

Callie was in the middle of returning texts from Clint and Shanice when she heard the sound.

"Mew."

"Kitty?" She tucked her phone into her jeans pocket, the texts unsent. "Here, kitty kitty."

"Meow!"

That had to be Winston. The mewing came from inside the old barn.

The six stalls, open to individual fenced paddocks, were occupied by visiting horses. The ranch was so crowded, Clint had moved their cattle to pastures far from the center of activity.

Inside the old barn smelled pleasantly of hay and horses, leather and wood. The animals were sluggish in the afternoon heat despite the ventilation fans drawing off hot air. Callie paused inside, waiting for her eyes to adjust to the dim light after the bright sun outside.

"Winston?"

The cat yowled, sending a shiver up Callie's spine. The sound came from overhead, in the small hayloft above the center aisle of the barn. She imagined the poor Persian hemmed up in a corner by an owl or a rat. Cat wrangling wasn't her job, but Callie could make an exception to save a defenseless pet from danger.

Callie climbed the wooden ladder. She peeked into the loft cautiously. There was no sense in hopping into the middle of a predator-prey situation.

Winston scrabbled backward, tugging against his red collar. It seemed to be caught on something.

Then she heard the groan. A human sound.

Callie scrambled the rest of the way into the stifling heat of the loft.

Marcia Bentworth-Fallows lay sprawled on her back across loose hay. Her brown hair, streaked with blonde, was in disarray around her unnaturally pale face. Marcia was a mature equestrian with an athletic build just a bit thick through the midriff. Winston pawed at the sleeve of her dressage jacket, grumbling and mewling in distress.

Callie couldn't stop herself from asking, "Marcia, what's wrong?" even though the woman was obviously in no condition to answer.

Callie hit George's number. "I found Marcia," she said when he answered. "She's hurt. Or something. The cat's here, too. In the old barn." She clicked off without answering his questions and dialed 911. *Should have done that first.* She chided herself for panicking.

Callie stumbled through the dispatcher's questions, trying to remain calm while she knelt beside Marcia's prone form.

"She's alive," Callie said. "Breathing. I don't know how long she's been here. Age? I'm not sure. Mid-sixties?" She grasped the trainer's hand. Marcia squeezed back. "Marcia, it's gonna be okay. Help is on the way." The dispatcher pried for more information Callie didn't have about Marcia's medical history, or whether there were any visible injuries. The woman didn't seem aware of her surroundings, but then her lips moved. "Hold on," Callie told the dispatcher. "She's tryin' to say something."

Callie leaned closer to Marcia as the woman's lips moved. Marcia moaned and clutched at Callie's arm. She uttered an odd word in a whisper. It sounded like kebrasheen, followed by xyla-something. Callie had no idea what that meant.

Her words were slurred. Maybe she was having a stroke.

"Help is on the way," Callie said, trying to keep the

desperation out of her voice.

Marcia exhaled softly. Callie couldn't tell whether she took another breath.

No, no, no. This can't be happening.

"Your kitty is here," Callie whispered. "You have to fight . . . whatever this is. Stay with me, Marcia."

She didn't answer. Winston yowled.

*   *   *

"Hey folks." Bob Pierpont, the Brieswell laboratory manager, rapped his knuckles against the door jamb to the test lab. "Heads up."

Makenzie tore her eyes from the screen where she studied the results of recent colorant testing. The Fourier Transform Infrared Spectroscopy instrument, or FTIR, would reveal whether the proposed new colors were chemically compatible with the ceramic glazes already used on the art pottery.

That hardly seemed important now, compared to whether her job was being eliminated. She held her breath, waiting for Bob's announcement.

"This is it," Wanda murmured, as she tugged nervously at one sleeve of her white lab coat.

"No news on the topic everyone's anxious about," Bob said. "Yes, I've heard the rumors, too."

Milo, a heavyset lab tech with a thin fringe of brown hair circling his head, raised both blue-gloved hands. "No news? We're dying here, Bob."

"I know, and I wish I could help. They aren't telling me anything, either. Considering the stress we're all under, and that this afternoon is dragging, let's call it a day. With pay. Go home. I'll see you in the morning."

Makenzie took that as a very bad sign. Wanda and Milo didn't waste time pressing for answers. They hung their white lab coats on their hooks and escaped before Bob could change his mind. She made her exit a little slower, taking note of all the details of the lab and her work cubicle as she shut down her computer and left.

Is this the last time I'll see the lab?

Bob avoided any questions by closing the door to his office.

Driving home, Makenzie grasped for optimism. Having the afternoon off meant she had more time to get ready for her date tonight with Dustin. She parked beside her little house on the back corner of her parents' property.

"Mew!"

Patrick Patches, aka Pat Pat, greeted her as she entered. Makenzie's cozy home was a converted garage. Larger than a tiny house, which was typically 400 square feet or less, her living quarters were definitely smaller than a full-sized house.

Staying here for the ridiculously low rent her parents charged meant Makenzie could save up a hefty down payment for her own home. Now that Dustin was in the picture, she had slowed her house hunting. Considering her job might be going away, that hunt might be on hold indefinitely.

"I felt bad about leaving you alone tonight after being at work all day," Makenzie told Pat Pat. "But now I get to spend an entire afternoon with you before my date."

Patrick Patches sat on the bed, watching Makenzie search her closet for just the right outfit to wear. He must have become bored with her activity, because he flopped onto his side and began grooming himself. With swipes of his raspy tongue, his gray stripey patches, tail, and hind legs, and contrasting white fur, soon glistened.

"I haven't told anyone about the layoff rumor," Makenzie told the kitten. "Well, besides you. Should I tell Dustin? Or wait until I know something certain?"

Pat Pat cocked his head to one side, as though letting her know he didn't have an answer. He was in a dignified mood for the moment. At twelve weeks old, Pat Pat was still very much a kitten, prone to bursts of frenetic energy. He might be calm now, but Makenzie had more than once returned home from work to a shredded house plant and spilled potting soil. Fortunately, she had gotten rid of her beloved, but mildly toxic, Ficus before adopting the kitten. Shanice's landlady had gladly added it to her collection of houseplants. Maybe houseplants weren't going to be part of Makenzie's life until her kitten matured.

"Do you want to visit Peaches?"

"Mew!"

Pat Pat knew the name of his sibling. The mother cat and the rest of litter had only recently gone permanently to forever homes. Peaches lived next door with Makenzie's parents. It seemed natural for the kittens to have play dates. Makenzie picked up her phone to call her mother, but it buzzed with an incoming text.

Makenzie was learning that disrupted plans were going to be part of her future life with her deputy boyfriend. The Rose Creek police department was small, and when the sleepy little town had an emergency, it was often accompanied by an all-hands-on-deck call. But the text wasn't from Dustin, cancelling a date at the last minute.

"Oh, good. It's one of my book club friends."

Shanice texted, *Dustin asked me to tell you he's at the Double C.*

Makenzie frowned. What did that mean? Was she supposed to meet him there for their date? Callie had said there was a barbecue scheduled for the opening of the equestrian workshops. But that began at noon. It was now nearly two.

Okay, she answered, then added three question marks.

There's been an accident. He's responding to a 911 call. He'll call you later.

Makenzie tamped down the urge to rush to the ranch. People and horses. There were dozens of opportunities for accidents. Dustin could handle the situation better without her adding to a crowd of looky-loos.

"Well, Pat Pat. It might be just you and me tonight. Again."

Chapter Five

"The dispatcher wants to know if you have diabetes. A heart condition?" Callie asked, holding the woman's hand gently. "Marcia, can you help me?"

She didn't answer. But her chest rose slightly. She was still breathing. Winston sniffed her face, then swiped his pink tongue across her sweat-damp cheek. Marcia didn't react.

"I think she passed out," Callie said into her phone. "It's really hot up here." She wiped the sleeve of her t-shirt across her own face, mopping up a rivulet of sweat trickling from her blonde hair to her collarbone.

A voice came from inside the barn.

"Callie, the EMTs are here." For once, the sound of Cousin George's voice didn't grate on her nerves. "And the police. Where are you?"

"I'm in the hayloft."

She heard thundering feet and loud voices. Winston skittered behind a hay bale, straining against his red collar.

"I'd better get you out of the way."

Callie began to lift the cat into her arms, but was halted by a sharp tug. Twine tethered the cat's collar to one of the dozen beams angling from the ceiling to the loft floor, supporting the roof.

That's weird. The cat's claws dug into her shoulder. The animal felt like more fur than body. He shivered. Callie ran a hand down his back, trying to comfort the terrified cat.

Makenzie's boyfriend Dustin poked his head above the

ladder and glanced around the hayloft. His reddish-brown hair was covered with a baseball-style black cap with POLICE and the Rose Creek Police Department logo.

"Hey, Callie. You might want to come down now, while you have the chance. Give these folks some elbow room."

"Do you have a knife?" she asked.

"Huh?" Dustin climbed the rest of the way into the loft. He was a couple inches taller than Callie, maybe six foot one, with a lean build.

The EMTs didn't wait. The hayloft was soon crowded with three people in light-blue, short-sleeved shirts covered with official-looking patches. Each carried a duffel-style bag. They went right to work on the prone woman.

"This is Marcia's cat," Callie told Dustin. "He's tied up. He can't stay here or the owls will eat him."

Dustin examined the twine, then snapped a photo of the arrangement with his cellphone. Finally, he handed Callie a pocketknife. She cut the twine near the cat's collar, freeing Winston. Dustin held the cat while Callie got on the ladder. As she neared the bottom rungs, she held out her arms. Dustin handed the cat to her.

George gave her a hand, steadying Callie as she stepped onto the barn floor.

"You found it," George said.

"Winston was tied up in the hayloft," Callie said, her voice quavering.

"No wonder we couldn't find him," George said. "Whoa. Why would someone—"

"Please move outside." Chief Holloway pointed to the open barn door.

Callie let George steer her past stalls where restless horses shifted and nickered softly. They stepped outside, under the shade of a large oak tree. George's hippie girlfriend Aster trotted up, reaching for Callie. Winston didn't seem to mind being squished between the two women as Aster wrapped her arms around Callie. The girl could be annoying, but Callie was grateful for the hug at the moment.

"What happened?" George asked.

"Give her a minute," Aster scolded. "Callie's shaking."

It was true. Callie was shivering like she was freezing cold, even though it must have been over ninety degrees in the hayloft. It wasn't much cooler in the shade of the tree. Shanice and Sam walked quickly to their huddle.

"We saw the ambulance," Sam said. "What's going on?"

"We're not sure yet," George said.

"Let's sit over here." Shanice motioned to a bench tucked under the oak tree.

George and Aster guided Callie to the seat. Winston clung to Callie, burying his flat Persian face in her shoulder.

"What's taking so long?" Callie asked.

"The EMTs must need to stabilize Marcia before they take her to the hospital," George said. "She's alive, right?"

Callie felt sick. "Y-yes. She spoke to me."

"Did she say what happened?" Aster asked. "Is she sick?"

"No. I couldn't understand. Her words were slurred. Strange. Like a foreign language. But not Spanish. I've been married to Clint long enough to be able to pick up on when people are speakin' Spanish."

"What did it sound like?" Sam asked.

"Kebrasheen," Callie said. "And another word. I thought she was trying to say xylophone, but that wasn't it."

"Xylazine." Sam turned away abruptly, marching inside the barn. "I'll let the paramedics know."

"What's that all about?" George asked.

"Sam recognized the words," Shanice said. "That's my guess, anyway."

Aster spoke the first one into her cellphone. "Is this it?"

Aster turned the phone screen to face Callie. Quebrachine. Derived from an African tree's bark. Also called yohimbine. A stimulant.

"Like amphetamines?" Callie asked. "Was Marcia trying to tell me she overdosed on drugs? Do people her age abuse drugs?"

Marcia was in her mid to late sixties. She and her husband owned a ritzy horse farm. Over the years, some of their horses and her students had been on the Olympic equestrian team. Junkie just didn't seem to fit.

"Um, can you say opiate epidemic?" Aster asked. "People any age and socioeconomic group can be drug addicts."

Callie glanced toward the barn, anxious for news. Clint ran toward the open door, skidding to a halt when he saw Callie on the bench. He joined Aster and Shanice, standing beside his cousin George.

"Callie! Are you okay?"

"I'm fine. We're waitin' to hear how Marcia is."

"You do not need this stress," Clint said.

He wasn't just referring to the current situation. Callie's doctor had suggested her unexplained infertility issue would go away with enough rest and relaxation. There was nothing as annoying as somebody telling a person to calm down. That just flipped a tension trigger in Callie. Selling the security software Callie developed had enabled her very early retirement and purchase of the ranch. Things couldn't be much lower stress in her life. Until she found Marcia in the hayloft.

She hugged Winston, pushing her face into his long white fur, dusted with pumpkin color on his ears and flat muzzle.

Sam returned, followed by Henry Holloway. The chief of the Rose Creek Police Department was built like a bulldozer. A cowboy hat covered his short bristle of hair, and his uniform shirt strained to contain his broad chest and generous belly.

"Hi folks," the chief said. "I understand Mrs. Bentworth-Fallows' husband is around here somewhere?"

"At the barbecue," Clint said. "He was searching for his wife, but decided to wait in the tent, hoping she'd turn up there."

"Can you fetch him over here?" Holloway asked.

"Right away," Clint said.

"I'll go," George said. "You stay with Callie." Cousin George sprinted away.

"You didn't happen to see a cellphone?" Chief Holloway asked.

"You mean Marcia's?" Callie asked. "That's the first thing a person does when they're in trouble, right? Call for help?"

"I often don't carry my phone when I'm working on the ranch," Clint said.

"True enough," Chief Holloway said. "Not everyone is glued to their phone, although it seems that way most of the time. I was hoping to make short work of contacting the husband."

"You need him to give permission for medical treatment?" Callie asked. "Is it that bad?"

The woman had seemed incoherent when she muttered the strange words, but now Callie knew those meant something.

Chief Holloway didn't answer Callie's question. He exhaled heavily. "Send the husband inside as soon as he gets here." He walked back into the barn.

"What is quebrachine?" Callie asked Sam. She turned to Aster, who scrolled through her phone. "And that other one. What are they used for?"

Aster looked up from her phone screen. "Quebrachine sounds like it's kind of a little blue pill. You know. For treating erectile dysfunction?"

"That makes no sense," Shanice said. "Why would Marcia talk about that?"

"She was weak," Callie said. "Maybe confused. The words might not mean anything—"

"The other one," Aster said, "let's see, xylazine."

Sam crossed his arms. That was the word he had said right before racing inside the barn to let the EMTs know about the two drugs, but now he was silent.

"Oh wow," Aster said. "It's an animal sedative. I knew it. Horse doping. RAOR is right."

"You're part of that animal rights group," Callie said. Her earlier gratitude for a comforting hug faded as she recalled Aster's involvement with the disruptive protesters. "Why aren't you with your merry band of mischief makers?"

"The police already cut the cuffs off Josie," Aster said. "Mike ran them off. I didn't see any reason to leave with the rest of the group. I belong here."

"Really?" Callie asked. "After trying to shut down a ranch event, you think you're welcome here?"

"Callie," Clint cautioned.

Of course he'd defend Aster, his cousin George's girlfriend. Voices and scuffling sounds from the hayloft interrupted the brewing argument. Callie strained to hear what the paramedics were saying. What was taking so long?

After a moment's pause, Aster started in again. "Marcia must have been trying to warn people about horse doping. Right, Dr. Grady?"

"Both are used by humans, too," Sam said. "Xylazine is a dangerous drug when used illegally. Drug dealers mix it with fentanyl. They call it 'tranq.' It's deadly. I agree, Callie. It seems unlikely Marcia would be using a street drug, but we can't jump to conclusions—"

Alistair jogged to the oak tree, followed by George.

"Where is she?" Alistair asked, out of breath.

Callie pointed to the open barn doors. Alistair rushed inside.

After an agonizingly long time that might have been less than fifteen minutes, Chief Holloway approached the bench.

"You folks can go about your business." He waved a hand. "Go on now. But Clint and Callie, I need to talk to you."

Shanice, Sam, Aster, and George reluctantly moved away, but stood at a distance.

"Who's your friend?" Holloway asked, nodding at Winston.

"Marcia's cat. Did Deputy Sage tell you how the cat was tied to a beam?" She looped a finger through the red collar, showing the Chief the remains of the twine. "Why would the cat be tied up in the hayloft?"

Chief Holloway folded his arms across his broad chest. He didn't answer.

"Why haven't they loaded Marcia in the ambulance yet?" Clint asked.

"We're waiting on Stanley."

The coroner. Callie felt lightheaded.

"Marcia," Clint said. His tanned face went pale. "She's dead?"

Chief Holloway nodded. "I don't need to tell you folks the harm spreading rumors and half-truths can cause to a case."

"Was she murdered?" Callie blurted out. "You said case. A police case?"

She had heard about Marcia's reputation as a difficult person. Had someone disliked her enough to kill her?

"Any unattended death of a seemingly healthy person has to be treated carefully," Chief Holloway said. "We don't know anything yet. And you know even less. So keep your lips zipped."

"We should never have agreed to host the workshop," Clint said, running a hand through his dark, wavy hair. "I'm sending everyone home. This event is over."

"Whoa whoa whoa," Chief Holloway said, holding both hands up. "That's exactly what you don't need to do. Supposing there is foul play involved? I'm not saying there is, but we can't make any assumptions until the autopsy is done."

"You want any potential killers to stick around," Clint said, nodding.

"For all we know, Mrs. Bentworth-Fallows had a stroke, or a heart attack," Holloway said. *Or a drug overdose*, Callie thought grimly. "Mr. Fallows indicated his wife would want the workshop to continue. Her horse and rider are participating." He shrugged his broad shoulders. "The show must go on? Proceed with your original plans. That'll keep people calm."

"What about us?" Clint asked. His Spanish accent became more pronounced when he was distressed. "How are we supposed to stay calm when someone died on our property? In our barn?"

"Unfortunately, this isn't the first tragedy we've had occur in our little town." The chief met Callie's eyes. "Once again, you and your book club friends are the first people on the scene. The best we can do for now is to take our time figuring out what happened in the hayloft." He touched a hand to Winston's head between the pumpkin-colored ears, giving the cat a gentle pat. He seemed to eye the red collar with the bit of twine. "I'll need this."

He hollered through the open barn door for Deputy Sage. In just a few moments, the collar was gently removed and placed in an evidence bag.

The deputy peeled off his plastic gloves and scritched Winton's head. "What're you going to do with this little guy?"

Callie looked up at Clint. "Take him to the house? Just until Alistair gets things settled. He's in no condition to worry about a pet right now."

"I'll get the things cats need from him," Clint said. "Litter? Food? Chief, we'll be at the house or around the ranch if you need us."

Clint practically carried Callie to the house. She was in no condition to attend the barbecue. After getting her and Winston settled in their spacious bedroom suite, Clint stood in the doorway.

"You have your cellphone?"

"Yes. I couldn't answer your text earlier because . . . of all that happened."

"Keep it on you," Clint said. "When I leave, I am activating the alarm system."

"That's a bit extreme, isn't it?" Callie asked. "We don't even know how Marcia died."

"I'm doing as the chief requested," Clint said. "The barbecue is already underway. I'll attempt damage control. I can only hope rumors are not already flying."

"What did Marcia mean?" Callie asked. "Her dying words were the names of drugs."

"Who knows?" Clint asked, spreading his arms wide in an expansive shrug. "You told the police what happened. You don't need to be involved any further."

As he left, Callie kept her response to herself. Marcia died on their ranch. She had trusted Callie with her dying words. And now Callie had the woman's cat.

Well, that little detail would be remedied when she gave Winston back to Alistair.

As for the rest, Callie was involved, whether she wanted to be or not.

Chapter Six

Shanice had not met the woman who died in the hayloft, so she listened with interest to the chatter she overheard in the food tent.

"—chasing after that ridiculous cat," came from the table next to Shanice and Sam's. "Marcia probably fell out of the hayloft snockered to the gills."

Marcia hadn't fallen, but how did this woman even know she'd been in the hayloft? Did news travel that fast?

"I'm not surprised," a woman said in a snide tone. "Although I would guess it was pills, not booze."

That detail touched a little too close to the situation. The police, Callie, Clint, Sam, and Shanice would not spread information about a questionable death. But George and Aster had been there, too. Shanice didn't know them well enough to be certain how they'd behave with sensitive details.

"You're right," the first woman said with conviction. "Marcia wasn't a booze hound, but if she'd drug horses, she'd take drugs herself. Right?"

Oh, so that's it. Pure snarky gossip. These women must not have heard the Latin phrase, *De mortuis nihil nisi bonum* - "of the dead, say nothing but good." Or as Shanice's grandmother would say in plain English, don't speak ill of the dead.

"Poor Alistair," the second woman said. "This must be quite the shock."

"Oh, he'll be okay," the first woman said. "Probably

relieved to be rid of the harridan."

Shanice was itching to see if the speakers matched her imaginary image of vicious gossips. She glanced over her shoulder. Sydney was the first voice she'd heard, her dark hair in a pixie cut. The other woman was older. Both were dressed like they were attending the Kentucky Derby, but without the fancy hats. Sydney's violet dress had frilly shoulder straps. The other woman's highlighted hair was drawn to the back of her head in a chignon.

Awfully fancy for an afternoon barbecue.

When a hand touched her bare arm, Shanice jumped.

"I asked whether you like the coleslaw," Sam said, repeating a question Shanice had obviously not heard.

"It's delicious," Shanice said. Sam raised one black eyebrow. "Okay. Honestly, I've barely tasted the food. I'm a little bit distracted by what happened."

Sam reached for Shanice's hand. "You should be. Neither of us is in the business of dealing with death. Although it seems to be happening with alarming frequency this year."

Shanice had become involved with two murder cases after joining the Rose Creek Reads book club. She hadn't been on the scene of the death in either case. Two, in the space of a few months. After a peaceful summer, she had hoped that was the end of the book club's amateur homicide investigations.

"Chief Holloway said suspicious death," Shanice said, lowering her voice, "not murder. But a woman at the next table suggested Marcia's husband might be glad to be rid of her."

"Marcia had plenty of enemies," Sam said. "I don't believe Alistair was one of them. Marcia was one of the top dressage trainers in the country, and a tough competitor. Some might call her ruthless." He placed his hand over Shanice's and gave it a gentle squeeze. "But isn't it too early to be compiling a suspect list?"

"You're right," Shanice said. "I need to calm down. Not jump to conclusions just because I overheard a snippet of nasty gossip." But one of the women had mentioned pills. Shanice lowered her voice to a whisper. "Could Marcia have been a drug addict who accidentally overdosed? You said xylazine could be mixed with fentanyl."

"The cause of death hasn't been declared," Sam said. "Marcia's death could have a simple explanation." He looked across the crowded tent. "The dessert buffet is calling my name."

"I did notice a peach cobbler," Shanice said. "That might take my mind off things."

*   *   *

After a few texts from the book club loop, there was no more news about Marcia's death. Friday morning, Shanice tried to shake the memory of the previous day from her thoughts. The beginning of fall semester was still fresh. She needed to focus on getting her classes smoothly underway.

Stepping into the foyer of the old brick university building, Shanice saw Mrs. Venetia Torley-Parr, the front desk receptionist. This semester, her short hair was white with pink highlights. She leaned out of the alcove where her desk guarded the entrance to the administrative offices.

"Shanice!" Venetia glanced up and down the hallway above the cat-eyed lenses of her sparkly framed glasses, then waved a hand. "Quick!"

What was so important it could pry the woman off her desk chair? Venetia had worked at the branch of the University of Oklahoma since it opened fifteen years ago, but her career was rumored to have begun shortly after statehood.

"What is it?" Shanice asked. She suspected Venetia might be seeking information about Marcia's unexpected death.

"That new instructor." Venetia's nose wrinkled. She moved back behind a desk cluttered with trinkets and knick-knacks. "Gemma Lopez. 'Pronounced like a gem,' she tells everyone. She's a real gem all right. She's taking over the homecoming committee. We need a person strong enough to stand up to her to explain the way things are done around here."

Shanice could see where this was going.

"Maybe she has some good ideas," Shanice said. "Sometimes it takes fresh eyes to see a new way to do things."

"We don't need a new way. The first homecoming of fall semester from time immemorial has had a cowboy theme."

The fifteen years the university branch had existed hardly required the vast time frame of tradition Venetia suggested.

"It is fun," Shanice said, "but sometimes a change can be refreshing. What does Gemma have in mind?"

Venetia rolled her eyes. "Instead of our traditional Western theme for the homecoming, Gemma wants to call it New York, New York."

That did strike Shanice as a drastic change. And challenging. Most of the students could scrape together a ranch hand-style shirt or hat, maybe even boots. The dress code for the Western homecoming dance was hardly a costume for most of their students. What did a New York homecoming entail? Business attire? High fashion? Clothing appropriate for panhandling in a subway tunnel?

"That's up to the committee, isn't it?" she asked. "They decide what the theme will be. It actually doesn't sound too bad. It could be a fun stretch for our students."

"But you've lived in Rose Creek for years," Venetia said. "You understand our culture."

"I'm coming up on my fifth year," Shanice said, nodding.

"See? You'd be a stabilizing influence on the students, as a faculty advisor."

"Gemma is faculty," Shanice said. "I'm sure she'll do fine."

Venetia sniffed. "Well, I'm a little disappointed. I thought you'd take more of an interest."

"I'm hesitant to take on another task," Shanice said. "The students deserve someone with the time to devote to the committee."

"It's a one-time deal," Venetia said. "Once the homecoming events conclude, you're free. I've volunteered in the past, but it's clear my input isn't appreciated." She waved her manicured bright pink fingernails in front of her. "I understand. I can't imagine how busy you must be, dating a celebrity."

Dr. Sam Grady was a minor star compared to mainstream television personalities. Yet his show on the *All Equestrian Today* channel touting him as a horse whisperer was hugely popular among the horsey set. News that Shanice was dating Sam had spread through the university grapevine with as much enthusiasm as if she'd been dating a mega movie star.

"It's really not as time-consuming as you think," Shanice answered wryly.

Her tone completely blew past Venetia.

"Then you'll do it?"

Shanice sighed. "Okay, I'll attend one committee meeting. But if it's not my cup of tea, I make no promises to continue."

"Wonderful," Venetia said, beaming. "I know you'll do a wonderful job."

"When's their next meeting?" Shanice asked.

"Tomorrow morning," Venetia said.

"I can stop in for a few minutes," Shanice said. "But I'll be at the Equi X workshops all weekend."

She hurried out of Venetia's alcove. If the receptionist hadn't yet heard about Marcia's death, there was a chance Shanice could enjoy a normal day of teaching.

* * *

When Joel arrived at the old farmhouse on Friday at midday, he spent the first five minutes playing with Boomer. The African "bark-less" dog didn't bark like ordinary dogs. It made noises called yodeling. Boomer attempted the puppy version of the yodel, which made Drew grateful the dogs were not constantly vocal. The basenji puppy was in ecstasy, wriggling and wagging his curly tail as Joel petted and played with him.

"I think I'm jealous," Drew said.

"Who knew having a dog in the family would be so fun?" Joel asked.

When the idea of adopting Boomer first came into serious discussion, Drew had hoped the puppy would offer an anchor, keeping them tied to Rose Creek. But puppies were portable. The only problem was their Boston condo's no pets rule. That could be easily remedied by moving to a different Boston location, where dogs were welcome.

Joel seemed reluctant to give up his position in a prestigious Boston law firm. Drew had wrangled a remote, part-time job with her firm, but it was obvious the position would stall out career advancement. The assistant theater manager job at the Rose Creek Natural Amphitheater did little more than help pay the bills, and that was only when the theater had an active production. While Uncle Tobias's law firm provided stability, Drew felt she was cobbling together a life.

"Where's Parker?" Joel tore his attention away from the dog for a moment. He dressed formally for plane travel, in a button-down shirt and tie, slacks, and polished dress shoes. With dark, curly hair and a perpetually intense look in his brown eyes, Joel was handsome whether in a suit or jeans and a cowboy shirt.

"Upstairs, resting," Drew said. "Between school and a trip to the ranch, he wore himself out."

"How's that going?" Joel asked. "School, not the riding. Is he keeping his grades up?"

Joel had agreed to the Oklahoma experiment for the fall school season. Parker's continued progress from withdrawn video game junkie and couch potato to an outdoorsy boy with actual friends had convinced Joel to let him stay longer.

"He's thriving," Drew said. "His scores are the equivalent of a B average."

That was an improvement over his former below-average academic performance. Parker was just eight. Turning nine on Monday. It wasn't like he'd be applying to colleges next week. But in their academically inclined extended family, he was seen as a slacker.

Unfairly, in Drew's mind.

"I'm glad the firm realized they could live without you for

a long weekend," Drew said, steering the conversation in another direction.

"I'm looking forward to relaxation," Joel said. "I should have time to look over Uncle Tobias's case. If you don't mind?"

"Working?" Drew asked with a smile. "You used to complain about me being a workaholic."

"It's really interesting, though," Joel said. "There are law firms devoted to nothing but mineral rights."

Drew had hoped the Nibley case would open Joel's mind to the idea of relocating to Rose Creek, although the business drawn to Uncle Tobias's tiny law office wasn't enough to support a family. The only firms dealing exclusively with mineral rights anywhere near were in Tulsa or Oklahoma City. Drew had checked. And that was too far to commute to Rose Creek.

"The sons are pressuring Mr. Nibley to claim he was mentally incapacitated when he signed over the rights to that buyer," Drew said. "Tobias doesn't want him going that route because of the mess it will create. And Mr. Nibley's not mentally feeble. He was talked into something by a slick salesman."

"I want to comb over that contract," Joel said. "See if there's a way to nullify it. That would be the best path for Mr. Nibley. I hope the case is finished before the baby comes."

Drew was a little over four months along. The baby was a welcome surprise.

"Hannah had her baby at the local clinic," Drew said. "The staff is wonderful. I think we should consider having our baby here."

"We should go to Boston," Joel said. "To be closer to excellent medical care. Drew, we're in our mid-thirties."

"That's not old to have children," Drew said. "It wasn't even considered old in our parents' generation. There's no reason to expect age-related complications."

"I'd like to be closer to family," Joel said. "Have you talked to your folks?"

Joel was much closer to his family. Drew's relationship with her mother was problematic.

"As long as Mom has my pediatric geneticist sister Fallon, her brain surgeon husband, and their perfect children, she doesn't need me and my embarrassing JD degree around."

In some families, having a child in possession of a doctorate in law, or *Juris Doctorem,* with a career as a lawyer, would be something to brag about. In Drew's overachieving family, being a lawyer was sadly unimpressive.

Joel laughed. "It's not that bad. Your mother loves you."

"I'd rather be far away," Drew said. Her heart pained her a little as she realized the truth of her statement.

"What about my family?" Joel asked. "And your extended family. You're close to your cousins. Your aunts and uncles."

Closer to them than her own mother and father. *How sad.*

"Uncle Tobias would be devastated if we left," Drew said. "Parker is doing so much better here. My mother's influence is obviously not a contributing factor in his well-being."

"And you think living in a small town is."

If Joel couldn't see it now, what hope was there he'd ever change his mind?

"A boy and his dog," Drew said. "It's so wholesome. Parker belongs in the country, not a big city where you can't let kids or dogs roam. And where horses are a hobby for the wealthy."

"There are stables in the Boston area," Joel said. "Parker can continue taking lessons."

"At a much greater expense," Drew said. "I checked. Anything related to horses near the city is twice the cost we have here. And then there's Uncle Tobias. He said he had a big surprise for Parker's birthday. He's been building up to it for days."

"It can't be a dog," Joel said. "Parker already has one." He rubbed Boomer's head. The curly tail wiggled wildly.

"What if it's larger than a dog?" Drew asked. "Like a horse?"

Joel chuckled, then stopped. "Wait. Seriously? You can't just give a kid a horse."

A horse. That would be an excellent anchor. More realistic than a dog.

"Why not?" Drew asked.

Joel shook his head. "The baby, Drew. We can come back to Rose Creek. Maybe spend a few weeks here every summer. You talked me into Boomer because we can manage a dog in the city. But this talk of horses is entering into a, a, I don't know. Some fantasy world of small-town America. I'm not sure I'm ready for this. I imagined our baby growing up near expert medical care and the best schools. That's in Boston—"

Drew heard a stair creak. She held a finger to her lips. Boomer hopped off his seat on Joel's feet and ran to the staircase.

"Hey, buddy," Joel said.

Parker rubbed a fist against one eye and yawned. Drew wondered how much he'd overheard.

Chapter Seven

News of the death on the Double C ranch had spread all over town before nightfall. For once, Makenzie hadn't been on the scene of the body. She was grateful she had no eyewitness report to give her coworkers on Friday.

"I wasn't even at the ranch," she told Wanda for the third time. "I was home with Pat Pat."

Getting ready for a date that didn't happen because Callie found a body.

"You and that kitty," Wanda said with an indulgent smile.

She turned her attention away from Makenzie and resumed chopping a tiny color pellet for testing in the FTIR. The lab techs did sample prep, while scientist Makenzie did the testing and analysis of results.

When Makenzie had started working here right out of college, the Brieswell Pottery Works lab testing equipment was verging on outdated. Maybe that was why there was talk of closing the lab. It could be cheaper to outsource testing than to spend the hundreds of thousands of dollars required for an upgrade.

"I told you a pet would liven up your life," Wanda continued as she weighed the pellet. "Do you want another kitten?"

"Wanda. You didn't get your cat fixed yet?" Makenzie shook her head. She had struggled to get Spirit and her six kittens placed in safe homes. After a cat had produced a litter, the sensible thing to do was shut down the kitten assembly line.

"I take my mind off her for a minute," Wanda said with a

shrug, "and she ends up full of kittens."

Makenzie planned to be a responsible pet owner. Tobias Falk had already gotten Spirit spayed. Her kitten-making days were over. One or two in her final litter might be allowed to produce a litter. They were such great cats, it was hard to resist the idea of letting more be created. But every cat deserved a safe and loving home.

"I might start a collection for you," Makenzie said. "A can to collect coins by the breakroom coffee maker." Makenzie made air quotes. "'Contribute to the fund to spay Wanda's cat.' I'll need a picture of her."

"If only you could take up a collection for my kid," Wanda said. "For a bus ticket to send him far away."

"Is he in trouble again?" Makenzie selected the program on the FTIR to test Wanda's sample.

In late spring, the boy had come home reeking of marijuana smoke. He'd tried to blame his buddies for maliciously blowing smoke on him to get him in trouble. But Wanda had used a home drug kit to prove he'd been partaking.

"He started going to Pastor Foster's youth group."

"That's a good thing, right?" Makenzie asked.

Wanda rolled her eyes. "From stoner to holy roller. I don't know which is worse."

"I hope you're kidding," Makenzie said. "Getting religion improves anyone's life."

She couldn't imagine not having her safe haven. The church ladies. Sunday sermons. Church was a big part of Makenzie's happiness.

"Aiden nags me to quit smoking," Wanda said. "The kid who spent his grandparents' birthday money to him on marijuana. He gives me the evil eye if I have a glass of wine after work."

"Maybe he's overreacting a little bit," Makenzie said. Although she agreed with the boy about Wanda's cigarette smoking. "He's new to the faith. He'll calm down with time."

"Not if he goes on that youth retreat," Wanda said. "He'll

be twice as bad after spending a weekend with those kids."

Makenzie gave up. Wanda just wanted to complain. How could she be upset about her son turning from drugs to religion? It made no sense.

In the texts flying back and forth with the book club, drugs had been mentioned as a possible cause for the horse trainer in the hayloft's death. Drugs were dangerous. They ruined people's lives.

At the end of the workday, Makenzie drove to Rose Creek Reads. Dustin had already let her know he would be occupied with the new case. Which might mean Marcia's death wasn't from natural causes. She was close to finishing the book club selection, and she couldn't risk running out of reading material at the start of a long holiday weekend. Sure, she could order an e-book online, but going to the bookstore supported a local business. Plus, there was the sixty-four-year-old bookstore owner Emily Crockett, whose sweet exterior hid a shocking depth of knowledge about murder and mayhem.

The waterwheel hugging the side of the building spun slowly, droplets of water glistening in the late afternoon sun. Over a hundred years ago, the brick building had operated as a grain mill, but for the past forty-five years, it housed a bookstore. A place that had become nearly as important to Makenzie as her church, where new friends had unknowingly helped her overcome crippling shyness.

She opened the door and paused, inhaling the scent of rose potpourri, books, and homemade cookies.

"Meow." Mitch bumped his head against Makenzie's shin.

"Hi, boy. How are you doing?"

She reached down to rub the butterscotch tabby's head. Mitch purred. Agatha, the other bookstore cat, did not trouble herself to climb off an upholstered chair.

"Mew," she said with a regal air. After the greeting, she returned her attention to grooming the white neck ruff that contrasted with her black and gold calico fur.

"Hello, Makenzie." Emily pulled her into a brief, pillowy

hug. Emily's white-streaked hair was pinned into a tight bun on top of her head. She wore a bright summery housecoat with buttons in the shapes and colors of various fruits. "It's nice to see you outside of book group."

"I've almost finished our group read," Makenzie said. "I need something to read this weekend. When I'm not at the ranch."

"I'll be there, too," Emily said. "My son is participating in a workshop about training miniature horses to pull carriages and wagons."

Makenzie was barely aware that Emily had grown children. She and her older husband had moved to Rose Creek six years ago, but he had passed away unexpectedly only two years later. Their son and two daughters were scattered across the country.

"Tiny horses," Makenzie said. "That sounds fun. I'm going to watch Shanice. She's in a workshop. Drew's son is riding in the parade. They're so excited."

"I read the text messages this morning," Emily said. "It sounds like there was a bit of excitement at the ranch already."

"That woman dying?" Makenzie asked. "You've heard as much as I have."

The book group had begun a text loop, originally only intended to stay informed about meetings. It had quickly turned into a way to share real-time notes as they discovered clues in two murder cases.

"Of course, a cat was involved," Makenzie added.

"Of course," Emily added, casting a glance toward Agatha.

She had once expressed her theory that cats and mysteries went together. Makenzie had to agree. So far, a cat had been on the scene of every body discovered under suspicious circumstances in Rose Creek.

"I imagine there was so much commotion at the ranch," Emily said, "so many people, it may be difficult for Henry and his officers to sort things out. Unless there's a simple explanation for what happened to Marcia Bentworth-Fallows."

"The strange thing is the cat being tied up in the hayloft,"

Makenzie said.

"What happened to the cat, by the way?" Emily asked. "Returned to Marcia's husband, I would assume?"

"Alistair's in shock. And he thinks the cat escaped their trailer somehow. He asked Callie to keep the cat until he can sort things out."

"Hmm. Callie doesn't strike me as a cat person," Emily said.

"She likes them okay," Makenzie said. "She just doesn't think the ranch is a safe place for outdoor cats. Of course, Winston is strictly indoors. We'll see how that goes, with all his long white fur shedding in their beautiful big house. Well, it shouldn't be for very long. The equestrian event ends Monday night, and everyone rolls out after that."

"Maybe we can meet Winston this weekend," Emily said. "I would like to see the hayloft, too, if Henry has removed the crime scene tape."

So far, Chief Holloway and the Rose Creek Police were investigating Marcia's unexpected death. The Oklahoma State Bureau of Investigation might step in if local resources weren't adequate to solve the case.

"If Winston is the only witness," Makenzie said, "Chief Holloway might have a tough time solving this case."

Emily brought up the local news service on her countertop computer. The screen showed angry faces of protesters guarding a girl handcuffed to the barn door. "I have to wonder whether those animal rights activists protesting the equestrian event might have been involved in Marcia's death. They seem rather energetic."

"Callie and Shanice didn't mention them," Makenzie said. "Have those people actually seen the Double C Ranch? They treat their livestock great."

"Some people believe horses should be left to live their lives without human interference," Emily said. "I happen to know firsthand that my son's tiny horses love pulling his cart around."

"Some of those activists look unhinged," Makenzie said,

studying the article over Emily's shoulder. "Do you think they could be mad enough to kill a horse trainer?"

"It's too soon," Emily said. "We need more information. As Sherlock says, 'Data, data, data . . . I can't make bricks without clay!' But I'm guessing you didn't come here to discuss a case that might not even be a case."

"Right," Makenzie said. "I need a book."

Emily made her suggestions and let Makenzie browse the shelves. After paying for her selection, Makenzie sat in her car. She debated calling Shanice, but she and her boyfriend were busy with Equi X events all weekend. Makenzie called Emiko.

"Hey, want to get some dinner?" Makenzie asked the engineer.

"I'm scrambling with the beginning of the semester," Emiko said. "Maybe another time?"

"Sure," Makenzie said. "Are you going to Callie's ranch this weekend? Shanice is going to be in a training demo."

"I should be able to," Emiko said, "but only if I get some work done tonight."

"I'll leave you alone then," Makenzie said. "You've got to make it on Sunday. Emily just told me her son has a team of tiny horses that pull a cart."

"That sounds adorable," Emiko said. "What time?"

Makenzie sent Emiko the event schedule link. Then she faced an evening alone. With Pat Pat, which made everything better.

As she drove down the cobbled main street, Makenzie looked at the hardware store. Tools, flats of autumn flowers, and plastic lawn chairs crowded the sidewalk. They were open late for the Labor Day weekend sales.

Makenzie parked. She might be acting prematurely, but maybe it was time to get fresh materials. Already, information was floating around about the body in the hayloft. She needed a new murder board. Just in case.

*   *   *

"Time for dinner. The timer went off." Callie leaned through the doorway to the office. "I pulled the casserole out of . . ."

Clint had three monitors going, and piles of papers strewn across his oak desk.

"What are you doing?" she asked.

He looked up, obviously startled. Releasing his grip on a mouse, Clint leaned back in the leather chair.

"Just doing research."

Callie padded across the thick carpet in her sock feet, moving a chair closer to his desk. Winston, the fluffy white Persian with pumpkin highlights, followed on her heels. The traumatized cat was Callie's perpetual shadow whenever she was indoors.

"For what?"

"The barn does not have enough stalls for this event," Clint said.

"This is a one-time deal," Callie said. "I thought. Things don't even officially begin until tomorrow, and people are already drivin' us both crazy."

Trainers, riders, and spectators had begun arriving Thursday morning, with fancy rigs pulling onto the ranch. Friday things just got crazier. People demanded immediate attention to their picky requirements. Neither Callie nor Clint had anticipated the clamoring for arena space for informal workshops and training sessions. Riders asked for directions and access to trails. A television crew needed electrical hookups and space to set up their cameras. There were stall assignment snafus. The giant food tent took up an unimaginable amount of space, displacing a herd of cattle from their pasture. The electrical and water demands strained the resources of the Double C. Sure, the Equi X organizers were in charge of event logistics, but none knew the layout of the ranch. Clint was running his tail off, assisting with the setup. Callie was afraid he was enjoying the chaos.

"Do you really ever want to invite this many people to the ranch again?" Callie asked.

"That's something we need to discuss," Clint said.

Winston meowed until Callie picked him up and set him on her lap.

"Considerin' how things have gone so far," Callie said, "I vote no."

Clint's tanned forehead creased as he eyed Winston. "How long is that going to be with us?"

"He," Callie corrected. "Just until Alistair Fallows leaves. He's terrified the cat will escape his trailer again. I thought you didn't mind cats?"

"Cats are fine," Clint said. "Are you certain there's a cat under all that fur?"

Callie didn't have an answer. She squeezed Winston gently. He felt skinny under the fluff.

"Back to our original discussion," she said, "twenty-four stalls is plenty. Plus the six in the old barn." She paused as the image of Marcia flashed through her memory. Callie shook her head. "Once we can use them again." They'd moved horses out of the old barn to keep people away during the police investigation. "We don't need more stalls. Besides, we're hostin' this workshop out of kindness. We're not making any money off this. Are we?" Callie was sometimes embarrassed by how little interest she had in the financial workings of the ranch. She trusted Clint, and he seemed to enjoy managing their substantial assets.

"The event was going to pay the original venue a decent rental," Clint said. "I told the workshop organizers I would cut them a deal, considering their losses due to the last-minute location change. Normally, there is a profit to be made." He tilted a screen in her direction. "If we install RV hookups, we can make back the expense of the construction in a summer. Two at the most."

"Whoa, cowboy. This sounds like a major expansion of the ranch facilities. Is there somethin' you're not telling me? Do we need the extra income stream?"

Clint looked at Callie. "What? Oh, no. This isn't about money."

"Then what?" Callie brushed away a white hair that had drifted onto her shoulder.

Clint's eyes were on the cat as he spoke. "Both Sam and Mike told me about a disagreement over stall assignments. Marcia's horse was in a stall that Sydney Byron thought one of her horses was going to use." Clint stood, shoving his hands into the pockets of his jeans. "What if Sydney killed Marcia because we didn't have enough stalls to place horses where owners wanted them?"

"First off, Honey, we don't know why or how Marcia died yet. And even if your theory is true, how can people behavin' that crazy be the ranch's responsibility?"

"There's another theory. If I allowed drug users and dealers on our ranch," Clint said, "I bear some responsibility. What were the words Marcia said to you?"

"Quebrachine and xylazine."

Clint nodded.

"You heard Sam. They're animal drugs. And then Aster blew up, claimin' those were show horse doping drugs. Nobody's in competition here. There's not even any drug testing required because who'd drug their horse for a training workshop?"

"Sam said humans use the drugs, too. Is that why those were her final words? I looked them up." Clint sat in his office chair and waved a hand for Callie to come around the desk.

She stood and set Winston on her chair. Callie placed her hands on Clint's broad shoulders and leaned closer, inhaling the subtle scent of his aftershave. Looking at the three monitor screens was like seeing Makenzie's murder board. One screen showed barn blueprints, another RV hookup installations, and the third pharmaceuticals.

"Quebrachine is a stimulant," Clint said.

An article on problematic performance enhancers listed names for the drug derived from tree bark. Yohimbe. Yohimbine. Quebrachine. Multiple name brands.

"Caffeine is a stimulant, too," Callie said. "And it's legal.

Are you sayin' Marcia was taking quebrachine to, I don't know, stay awake?"

"It could be as simple as her husband Alistair using it to enhance his bedroom abilities," Clint said. "On the other hand, perhaps she had a drug problem? And then there's xylazine." Clint brought up another page. The alarming article told of the illicit use of the animal sedative. Horrifying photos showed drug addicted people with hideous open sores and rotting flesh where they had injected street drugs mixed with xylazine. It was also called tranq. "Troubling. A guest on our ranch names a drug that has both veterinary uses and is used illegally by addicts."

"With devastatin' results," Callie said. "So which is it? Unfortunately, Marcia didn't give me any details."

"Maybe she was able to tell the EMTs or police more," Clint said. "Before she passed."

"Okay. I agree that's weird. But what does it have to do with expanding our barn and invitin' more of these events, which I will say again is drivin' us both crazy?"

"Marcia's death made me realize the dangers of opening our ranch to outsiders," Clint said. "Building a formal RV park would give us better oversight and control. If there are dealers pushing drugs on visitors, we may need to set up surveillance cameras. Post a guard."

Clint was nothing if not vigilant.

"Marcia was a senior citizen," Callie said. "In her sixties. Not the druggie type."

"You never know," Clint said. "We can't demand drug tests from everyone who sets foot on the Double C."

Callie laughed. "No, you can't do that. We need to have a serious discussion about your plans."

Clint's phone chimed. "I'm needed at the arena."

"Hey, dinner is gettin' cold," Callie said.

"I'll be right back." He paused in the doorway. "Go ahead and eat."

Callie picked up Winston and held him at arm's length. "I guess it's just me and you, fur puff." The cat dangled from her hands, its huge blue eyes unblinking. "You are a pretty boy."

Callie's phone chimed. She tucked the cat into the crook of her arm and pulled her phone from her jeans pocket.

Book club.

Drew texted, *I thought you gals would like to know, my uncle's connection with the coroner's office learned the official cause of death. Homicide.*

Chapter Eight

"How does he know?" Joel asked.

"Once upon a time, Uncle Tobias helped out a woman who is the aunt of a man who assists the coroner," Drew said. "She hears things and passes them along to Tobias."

"I'm sorry I asked," Joel said, chuckling. "But a coroner's finding of homicide doesn't necessarily mean Marcia was intentionally murdered."

"I realize that," Drew said. "I tried to explain it to the book club, but this conversation is too complicated for text messaging. Thanks for understanding."

"Parker and I need father-son time," Joel said. "There are still a couple of hours of daylight. He's so wound up about his parade tomorrow, we need to burn some energy throwing a ball around. Enjoy your meeting."

After a quick hug and a kiss, and then a longer kiss, Drew grabbed her purse and tote bag and drove to Rose Creek Reads. It wasn't very far from her house, but the sun might set before she came home. Even in sleepy little Rose Creek, Drew didn't feel comfortable walking alone in the dark.

She and Shanice arrived first. The recently promoted Associate Professor wore a skirt in a sea foam green print, with a cream top. The thin sweater draped over one arm was necessary for the inevitable transitions from summer heat to indoor air conditioning.

"Deck or shop?" bookstore owner Emily asked them. "Although I'll warn you, it is quite warm this evening."

"Indoors," Shanice said.

She headed for a cozy corner filled with well-worn antique chairs reupholstered with materials in book-themed prints. Drew followed, choosing a high-backed chair with padded armrests.

"I'll be back with refreshments," Emily said, disappearing behind bookshelves loaded with paperbacks and hardcovers.

"How are you feeling?" Shanice asked. "If that's okay to ask?"

"Perfectly okay," Drew said. "I'm just starting to have a baby bump." She ran a hand down the loose waistline of her sleeveless summer dress. "I had Parker so long ago, pregnancy is like a whole new experience. Back then, both Joel and I were building our careers. This time, I hope to be able to enjoy pregnancy, since we're certain this will be our last child. I'm just thirty-four, but we weren't expecting a new baby when our son is about to turn nine." Drew paused. "The only negative is how badly I feel for Callie."

The tall cowgirl and her husband Clint had been trying unsuccessfully for over two years to conceive. Callie was being gracious about Drew's unplanned pregnancy, but it had to sting.

"Life can be hard," Shanice said. "But situations can change in a hurry, and so will hers. Until I met Sam, I was mentally preparing for the eternal single life. Now, I'm hopeful."

"It must be nice," Drew said, "spending time with him over the long weekend."

"It's a working weekend for him," Shanice said. "But I am enjoying seeing what he does for a living. The worst part is not unruly horses. It's dealing with problem people. And now there was a murder?"

"That's why I wanted to meet in person," Drew said. "To define homicide, and what it means concerning Marcia's death. Maybe we should save discussion of her situation until the rest of the club arrives. When are you riding in the workshop?"

"Tomorrow afternoon." Shanice brought up the schedule on her phone. "And Parker will be in the noon parade?"

"Yes," Drew said. "His class is carrying flags. Parker is so excited to be playing cowboy in front of an audience."

Shanice laughed. "I'll have to admit, I'm a little terrified!"

"Joel and I will be at the ranch for Parker's ride, of course," Drew said. "We'll stick around to watch your class demo."

"I didn't realize what a big deal Equi X is. I think Linda was included mainly because her classes are held at the ranch." Shanice leaned forward on her chair. Her brown eyes shone with excitement. "There are going to be Olympic contenders showing off their stuff."

"Will you be riding one of Sam's gorgeous Appaloosas?" Drew asked.

Shanice and Drew had both arrived in Rose Creek with the same level of horse knowledge – none. Drew was quickly learning her way around a stable. The equipment used, the terminology, the different horse varieties – it was a learning curve.

"I'm using my lesson horse, Pepper," Shanice said. "Sam offered Andromeda to me for the workshop, but I'm not confident I could handle her in front of a crowd."

"You'll do fine," Drew said. "We'll all be there to cheer you on."

"That's the scary part. If I mess up, all my friends will see."

All my friends. That sounded so nice. Drew had friends in Boston she stayed connected with, but her girlfriends in Rose Creek had developed in a more organic way.

"We'll all be there to pick you up," Drew said.

"Hopefully not literally." Shanice laughed.

*   *   *

Callie held the door for Makenzie. The chemist carried the makings for a murder board. Two more members of their book club waited in a cozy reading nook furnished with well-worn antique chairs and a love seat.

"Hey, ladies." Callie waved a hand. "Inside tonight?"

"It's cooler indoors," Shanice said.

Callie sat on a club chair covered with a fabric print that looked like a jumble of old books. "I'm guessing your murder board means this emergency meetin' isn't about a plot twist in our newest reading assignment. Did you squeeze some information out of your boyfriend?"

"Dustin would never compromise an investigation." Makenzie unfolded the thick tri-fold foam project board. She unwrapped a pack of sticky notes. "I bought this before Drew called the meeting. I just had a feeling."

Emily carried a tray, placing it on a coffee table at the center of the chairs.

"Callie, I see your cat-sitting experience is going nicely," Emily said.

Callie glanced up at the bookstore owner. "Winston is a nice cat. Needy, but he's kinda growin' on me. How did you know?"

Emily plucked a long white hair off Callie's shoulder. "This indicates to me that you've been holding the cat close to your face. In the cradling position." She lifted Agatha from the floor and held her against her shoulder. "There's my pretty kitty."

Agatha mewed softly.

Callie brushed her shoulders, looking for more Winston hair. "Well, he's goin' home Monday. Tuesday at the latest. I'm just being a good hostess."

*   *   *

Makenzie had never thought of herself as a take-charge kind of person. Since joining the Rose Creek Reads book club back in April, she had gained confidence. Especially when she was a subject matter expert. Like in chemistry. Kitten care. And murder boards.

"Are we waiting for Emiko?" Shanice asked.

"She's busy tonight," Makenzie said. "We can go ahead without her. Drew, you have the update. You start."

"A little birdie told Uncle Tobias the cause of death listed on Marcia's death certificate is homicide," Drew said. "That doesn't mean she was murdered."

"I need an explanation," Shanice said.

"Every murder is a homicide," Drew began, "but not every homicide is a murder. Murder is a specific type of homicide."

She went on to say that both involved a human killing another human, the difference being intent.

"Like manslaughter," Makenzie said. "A person doesn't approach a situation with the intention to kill a person."

"Manslaughter often involves a heat-of-the-moment incident," Drew said. "The killer is triggered and acts without premeditation. Negligent homicide is when a person causes the death of another human through their own carelessness."

"Like drunk driving?" Callie asked.

"Or other reckless behavior," Drew said. "The point of my explanation is that listing homicide on Marcia's death certificate is only a starting point. With the choice of listing natural causes, suicide, or accident, homicide leaves the legal question open. Now it's up to the police to determine whether there was intent."

"Whether it was murder," Makenzie said. Her instinct to create a new murder board might have been correct. It was one of those times she didn't want to be right.

"This creates more questions than it answers," Shanice said.

Emily touched a finger to her chin. "In order to list homicide as the method of death, the coroner must have had evidence that another human was involved."

"Winston was tied to a beam in the hayloft," Callie said. Her fair skin, which had a bit of a summer tan, went pale. "Marcia wouldn't treat her kitty like that."

Was Callie becoming smitten? Winston had to be returned to Marcia's husband soon, but Wanda's cat was pregnant. There would be cats in need of a home. Makenzie filed away that thought for later.

"Let's start filling in the board," she told the group. "First, method of death."

Makenzie spelled out the word on a sticky note, then placed it at the top of the board. *Homicide*. She felt a chill crawl up her spine.

"Back up," Drew said. "Let's list Marcia's full name and age at the top of your board. It would be nice to have a photo of her, to keep us focused on Marcia's humanity."

"There's a nice one in the newspaper," Shanice said. "Otherwise, we can print one off of a news site."

"I'll get the paper and scissors," Emily said, standing. "Do we need tape?"

Makenzie smiled. Her last murder board had been a mostly solo project. She preferred this group effort. Soon, a flurry of sticky notes in different colors listed potential causes of death and suspects. It was a jumbled mess now, but patterns would organize it all into a coherent story. Like images of chemical formulas, murder clues would be meaningless until they were properly connected.

"Chief Holloway asked Clint to keep the Equi X workshops going," Callie said. "He didn't want suspects takin' off."

"Clint wanted to shut it down?" Shanice asked.

"He can be a little overprotective," Callie said. "He's upset that I found her. I'm the one she mumbled those words to, which made no sense to me. Sam knew right away what they were. Marcia sayin' the words quebrachine and xylazine sent Clint on an online research frenzy that scared the pants off him." She described the illegal use of the animal sedative, to the groans and gasps of the book club ladies. "I thought her words were garbled because she was havin' a stroke, but what if illegal drugs and addicts are on my ranch?"

"I overheard an unpleasant conversation at the barbecue tent," Shanice said. "News gets around fast. The gossips were already at it, but they didn't have the story right. They thought Marcia died falling out of the hayloft. It was believable to them because they assumed she was drunk, although one woman thought it more likely Marcia took pills."

"That's sad," Emily said. "It sounds like Marcia was not well-liked. And the horse world is a tight-knit group."

"Sam would agree," Shanice said. "He said a trainer's

reputation is their most important possession. In the stable, Marcia's husband argued with a horse owner who claimed Marcia was abusive to horses."

"I find that hard to believe," Callie said. "I didn't know her well. Really, just knew of her. But people who abuse horses get run out of business quick."

"Slow down," Makenzie said. She scribbled on sticky notes, trying to keep up with the conversation.

"What about the activists?" Drew asked. "That girl who chained herself to the barn?"

Makenzie had seen the photo on the front page of the newspaper.

"What a mess," Callie said. "The story they told the reporter was all wrong. This isn't even a horse show. Who's gonna drug their expensive horse for a workshop?"

"For a small town," Makenzie said, "we sure attract a lot of crazies. I'll bet most of those RAOR people are from Tulsa. Out of state, even."

"Aster was part of the protestors," Shanice said.

"Oops," Makenzie said. Then she placed her hands on her wide hips with a frown. "Hold on. Aster's mixed up with them? On their website, RAOR says any use of animal products is cruel. Aster's farm sells eggs and milk. There's a disconnect here."

When she first visited the Red Cedar Meadows farm, Makenzie thought it was a drug-hazed hippie commune. They had gained her respect when she learned the residents were serious about providing organic produce, humanely raised eggs, and goat milk and cheese.

"Interesting," Emily said, nodding.

"Do people really drug their horses for shows?" Drew asked. "Horse races, I can believe. There's a lot of money involved."

"Sam said show horses are regularly tested," Shanice said. "For the elite competitions. Not local gymkhanas, or the smaller horse shows. But high-level dressage and jumpers?" She nodded.

"That's terrible," Makenzie said. She wrote "Motivation" in large block letters on a sticky note and slapped it near the top of her murder board. "So, motivations might include a disagreement over stall assignments, concern about drugging horses, or an accidental or deliberate drug overdose. Anything else?"

"Not yet," Emily said. "Who might be involved?"

"Apparently, Marcia had a lot of enemies," Shanice said. "Competitors? Other trainers?"

"A drug dealer upset because she owed them money?" Makenzie asked.

"The obvious motivation," Emily said. "A love affair gone wrong. Or a husband wanting to get rid of a difficult wife."

Makenzie struggled to keep up. "Drug dealer. Husband. Lover. Trainer. Maybe a client? Someone Marcia trained to ride? Or trained their horse?"

"Angry activist," Drew said. "Sometimes people can go off the deep end pursuing their causes."

"A person with access to the drugs," Shanice said. "Other than a drug dealer. There could be legitimate routes for Marcia to have acquired them."

"That's assuming Marcia was using drugs," Emily said. "We won't know that until the autopsy report is released, with the specific results."

"The cat tied up in the hayloft seems key," Makenzie said. "Someone lured Marcia up there using her cat. They had to know she owned a cat."

"And how to steal Winston," Callie said.

Silence settled over the group.

Drew glanced at her watch. "I didn't realize it was so late. I need to run."

Emily stood. "We're not going to solve this tonight. It's entirely possible the police will bring the case to a swift conclusion without our assistance."

Makenzie had faith in the Rose Creek Police Department. But it never hurt to lend them a hand.

Chapter Nine

"Parker, are you ready?" Drew called up the stairs on Saturday morning.

"We're going to be late to temple," Joel said.

"I'll go see what's keeping him." Drew climbed the staircase to his bedroom. She tapped on his door. "Parker. We're leaving."

"I'm not going," was his muffled reply.

"Are you feeling ill?" Drew asked.

Joel hurried up the stairs and stood behind Drew. "Open the door, Parker."

The bedroom doors in the old house were hardly secure. Rattling the doorknob hard would unfasten the lock. But Drew and Joel wanted their son to enjoy his own space, with the understanding that ultimately he couldn't deny entry to his parents. There was a balance in there. One which Joel was preparing to breach.

The door opened. Parker held the puppy in his arms.

"I can't take Boomer to temple," he said.

"No, you can't," Joel said.

"I was explaining that to him." Parker seemed a little old at nearly nine to carry on conversations with a dog. He swiped his face across his shoulder.

"What's wrong?" Drew asked.

"We can talk later." Joel trotted down the stairs, his dress shoes loud on the wood.

"Let's put Boomer on the porch," Drew said.

After the puppy was secured on the screened-in back porch, they drove in silence to the small Rose Creek synagogue. The normalcy and routine of the service were comforting. Afterward, Parker went outside eagerly to play with the rest of the congregation's kids on the tree-bordered lawn. They weren't staying for the informal oneg, a casual potluck lunch, because Parker's parade started soon. Drew glanced out the window of the community room.

Malki touched her arm. "Are you okay? You seem a little out of sorts."

"Pregnancy hormones?" Drew said.

"Okay," Malki said. "I get that." She was the mother of two boys. She and Gary had been talking about trying for a girl. "Are you sure that's all it is?"

Drew turned to her friend. "Parker's the one who seems hormonal, although he can't be hitting puberty yet."

"He's been an only child for the past eight years," Malki said. "Parker might be having trouble adjusting to the idea of a sibling."

"I would think the age difference would make it easier," Drew said.

"A cute new baby?" Malki asked. "That's already the center of conversations? He might be feeling left out."

Drew wanted to snap back that having two kids didn't make Malki an expert on Drew's son, but she bit back that reaction. *What is wrong with me? Is it really hormones gone wild?* She took a breath. "You could be right. Partially. But I think something else is going on. It was hard getting Parker out the door this morning because he was clinging to the puppy."

"I hope I'm not being nosey," Malki said, "but maybe he's afraid you'll leave the dog behind if you move back to Boston."

Drew shook her head. "If we return to Boston, the dog goes with us. Although that may not be clear to Parker. I've been avoiding talking about whether we're returning to Boston in front of him because I want to stay here. In Rose Creek."

But not if it leads to the end of my marriage.

"That's understandable," Malki said. "You and Joel need to present a united front. It's stressful for kids to see their parents disagree."

"That sounds so much worse than it is," Drew said. "I'd describe it more as Joel and I having different visions for the future. City life, or country life."

"I hope you stay in Rose Creek," Malki said.

The conversation felt awkward. Maybe even intrusive. But it did open Drew to the fact that she and Joel needed to include Parker in their discussions about a return to Boston. He was not old enough to make that choice for the family, but he deserved to be heard.

When they got home, Parker changed into his cowboy clothes for the parade. Then he ran to release Boomer from the porch and give him some puppy time in the backyard. The puppy yodeled once. The African dogs with the curly tails had probably been successful hunters because they were typically silent.

"Joel, while we have a minute," Drew said, "I want to make a suggestion."

"Sure," Joel said.

"We need to sit down with Parker and discuss with him the pros and cons of moving back to Boston."

Joel smiled and placed his arms around Drew's waist. "Are you ready to head home?"

"I would prefer staying here."

"After two murders and a suspicious drug-related death?" Joel asked. "Rose Creek isn't the safe haven you thought it was when you came here in March."

"Parker has the idea that returning to Boston would mean leaving Boomer behind."

Parker burst into the kitchen. The screen door to the porch slammed shut as he skidded to a stop. "Dad! Boomer chased the ball—"

"We can't have a dog in the condo," Joel was saying to Drew. "But I guess we haven't—" He stopped, an alarmed look on his face as Parker's smile melted.

"We have a dog." Parker picked up the basenji puppy, snuggling his face in its short fur. "Boomer. I love him."

"We need to talk about Boston," Joel said.

"I don't want to move," Parker said. "I want to stay here."

"Your mother and the new baby need to be close to family and medical care. Sit down."

"No! I don't want a baby. I want Boomer. I'm not going to Boston." Parker bolted up the stairs to his room. Drew heard the door slam.

Joel started after him, but Drew grabbed his arm.

"Let him calm down, then we can explain about the puppy."

"Boomer's part of the family," Joel said. "The dog might be even more important for Parker once the baby arrives. But I can't tolerate his attitude." Joel ran a hand through his thick, dark hair. "First this morning, and now this. I'm thinking of grounding him from the parade."

Drew felt tears filling her eyes. *Baby hormones*. Her shoulders shook with the sudden onslaught of tears.

"Hey." Joel pulled her into a hug. "I didn't know the parade was so important to you."

"It's not," Drew sniffled. "It's what it represents. Parker having friends. Going on adventures. He's a really good rider. Uncle Tobias is thrilled Parker is turning into a cowboy. Do people even ride horses in Massachusetts?"

"Of course they do," Joel said.

"Rich people," Drew said. "We couldn't afford a house near a riding stable."

Drew continued her whining, feeling ridiculous. She surrendered to the sobbing. Joel held her, rubbing her back, until she was done.

"I'm making a mess of things," Joel said.

"No," Drew said. "You're my rock. I'll get cleaned up, and we can have that talk with Parker."

"Too late," Joel said as his cellphone alert pinged. "It's time to head to the ranch."

*　　*　　*

Shanice glanced at the clock on the wall. The homecoming committee Venetia had talked her into attending was far from reaching any conclusions. She had to leave soon if she wanted to eat before heading to the ranch. The two donut holes she'd had weren't enough fuel for the day.

"You aren't listening," Professor Chapelle said. "The homecoming dance has always had a western theme."

"With barbecue," Gemma said in a weary tone. "Isn't anyone else tired of barbecue? Plus, several of our students are vegetarians. They'll be left out."

"We always offer vegetarian options," Chelsea, one of the student committee members, said.

"The student survey proves the New York theme is popular," another female student said.

"Your survey was unscientific," Professor Chapelle said. "Asking your friends what they want doesn't capture the sentiment of the entire student body."

The room erupted with impassioned arguments for the New York theme versus the Western theme. This was going nowhere fast.

"Let's take a break," Gemma said.

"I have to leave," Shanice said. "Email me any decisions made."

Gemma followed Shanice to the door. "I hope this hasn't soured you on being on the committee. We need three faculty advisors."

"I plan to hang in there," Shanice said. "I don't mind volunteering for a good cause, but I never expected the discussion to be so lively."

"Change comes hard for the old guard," Gemma said.

"Professor Chapelle is completely on board with new ideas," Shanice said. "He's just expressing concern about preserving the unique flavor of our branch of the university."

"What about you?" Gemma asked. "You sound open to the

New York theme."

"Absolutely. But maybe it would work better for the winter homecoming. The western theme is better suited for outdoor events, while the New York theme could be held mostly indoors. Plus, we'd have more time to plan for the completely new décor."

Gemma scrunched up her face like Shanice's suggestion was distasteful.

"Think about it," Shanice said. "I'll be at the next meeting, but I need to leave now."

"Hot date with the television doctor?" Gemma asked.

Shanice ignored her prying. "I'm participating in a training workshop at the Equi X event," Shanice said.

"That's open to the public, right?" Gemma asked.

"Yes," Shanice said reluctantly.

"Great. I want to watch the hunky doctor in real time. His show is amazing."

Hunky? Shanice stifled a gag reaction at the thought of Gemma lusting after Sam.

"Do you have a horse?" Shanice asked.

"No. You don't need to have a horse to admire that particular horseman." Gemma winked. "I would love to invite Dr. Grady to be a guest lecturer for the School of Veterinary Medicine. Maybe he'd be open to mentoring students?"

"I can't answer for him," Shanice said. "He might be interested."

"I'll try to wrap up the homecoming meeting so I can watch you ride. And maybe you can introduce me to the doctor?"

Shanice frowned. She hoped she wasn't being paranoid. It sure seemed like Gemma had more than a professional interest in meeting Sam.

"Sure," she said. "Although he'll be busy with his workshops."

"I'm sure he'll want to talk to me," Gemma said. "I heard about that woman dying at the ranch where Dr. Grady works."

Shanice struggled to hold back the obvious question. How

did a newcomer to Rose Creek find out about Marcia so fast?

"She OD'd on drugs, right?" Gemma folded her arms across her chest, seeming to wait for a reaction from Shanice.

"Wow. Did you see an autopsy report?" Shanice asked. If it had been released, Tobias Falk's little birdie would have heard, and therefore the book club would have known.

"Word gets around," Gemma said. "It doesn't take a genius to connect the dots. Quebrachine. Also known as yohimbine. Not something you'd expect a woman to use, if you catch my drift."

Does the book club have a leak? How could Gemma know about the quebrachine? The police and Shanice's friends were the only ones who knew. *And Aster.*

"That's a stimulant, right?" Shanice asked.

Gemma nodded. "I checked the Veterinary Medicine school's drug safe as soon as I heard about it. There isn't any in our inventory. But it's pretty readily available. It's used by prescription to reverse sedation in animals, but you can get it over the counter for human use."

Sam had mentioned the drug was used by both humans and animals.

"Did you happen to hear whether Marcia had prescription or over the counter quebrachine in her system?" Shanice asked. *Since you seem to have all the information. Except about Marcia's mention of xylazine.*

Gemma shrugged. "I don't know the specifics. I'd better get back to the meeting. If I give them too long a break, people might start wandering off."

"Thanks for the info," Shanice said. "I'll see you at the next meeting. Or in the hallways."

"Or at the Equi X event," Gemma said with a grin.

She sashayed back to the meeting.

Shanice didn't like the thought of introducing the woman to Sam. And she didn't know quite what to do with this new information. Gemma claimed quebrachine, used to counteract an animal sedative, wasn't in the university's veterinary school drug safe. Sedatives might be. Maybe Gemma hadn't heard about the xylazine.

A drug safe. Shanice knew how unreliable locks could be. How many veterinarian students had access to the safe? Did Gemma have some connection to Marcia?

Chapter Ten

When Makenzie stepped inside The Stockman's Café, she nearly ducked back out. Her lab coworkers sat in a booth with their manager. Makenzie was here to meet Dustin for brunch, not have a work meeting.

Might as well get this over with.

She walked directly to the booth. "Hi, everyone. I guess I didn't get the memo."

Wanda laughed. "We just happened to run into each other."

"You're welcome to join us." Bob Pierpont, the chemistry lab manager and Makenzie's boss, waved a hand at an empty spot on the booth seat.

Awkward.

"I'm meeting someone," Makenzie said. "Besides, it looks like you're about finished." Plates of crumbs with smears of orange yolk and white gravy sat in front of each of the three people. "But I can sit with you until he arrives."

"Deputy Sage?" Wanda asked.

Makenzie felt her fair cheeks flush. "Yes." There was no keeping a secret in Rose Creek. Not that her dating Dustin was a secret. They had gone public about their exclusive relationship over a month ago. She slid onto the seat next to Wanda.

"We were talking about our plans," Bob said. "If the lab closes."

"There aren't many options in Rose Creek for lab work," Milo, the heavyset tech with a thin fringe of brown hair circling his head, said. "Unless you can land a gig at the university. But those mostly involve teaching, and I'm not interested in teaching."

"That's not an option for me," Wanda said. "I only have an Associate's degree. I'd have to finish a Bachelor's. Kind of late in the game for that."

"It's never too late to pursue higher education," Bob said.

"Is that your plan?" Makenzie asked. "Teaching?"

Bob had a PhD in chemistry. He shook his head.

"I'm close enough to retirement," he said. "I've always dreamed of running a horse B&B. For people traveling with their horses. Or donkeys. Mules, too."

"We're kind of out of the way," Milo said. "I could see that being successful if you were on a major highway."

"With nearby trails," Bob said, "we might be able to present ourselves as an equine vacation destination."

"I didn't know you had horses," Makenzie said. "Half my friends are horse crazy. I'm going to watch one in a workshop this afternoon." She glanced at her watch. "And if I leave here soon enough, I'll see another friend's son ride in the parade."

"The wife and I just have a couple saddle horses," Bob said. "Not like the dressage horses and jumpers going to the Equi X workshops. So Makenzie, what plans do you have if the lab closes?"

"Plans?" Makenzie had never contemplated a different career. The laboratory at Brieswell Pottery Works encompassed the whole of her career ambitions. Before she could dream up an answer, the door opened. "Here's Dustin." She lowered her voice. "I haven't told him about the possible layoffs. The closure. Whatever it is."

"There's no sense scaring people if it turns out it was all a wild rumor," Wanda said. "Although I'll hunt down and choke whoever started it. I'm worried sick."

"Hey, Makenzie." Dustin was dressed in off-duty clothes of jeans and cowboy boots. He wasn't a particularly muscly guy, being on the lean side, but his T-shirt showed off nice biceps.

She slid out of the booth. "Dustin, this is my manager, and

my coworkers." She made the introductions all around.

"I'm just leaving," Bob said.

"You're coming to my folks' barbecue later?" Makenzie asked. "You're all invited."

Mom and Dad had invited half the town of Rose Creek. After assuring her they wouldn't miss trying her father's secret ribs recipe, the Brieswell lab employees vacated the booth.

"I don't want to rush things," Makenzie told Dustin, "but I want to get to the ranch to see the opening parade. Drew's boy is carrying a flag."

"Let's order to go, then."

They were both frequent diners at The Stockman's Café. It didn't take long to decide on breakfast sandwiches. Makenzie sat on a stool at the counter while they waited for the cook to rustle up their order.

"I found out that Emily's son brought his tiny horses," she said. "I didn't even know her son had horses. They're going to be pulling a wagon around."

"I don't want to miss that," Dustin said with a grin. Then he turned serious. "Besides, I want to make sure you and your friends stay out of trouble."

"You warned me to stay clear of the last case," Makenzie said. "And I did. Mostly. You even thought my murder board was helpful."

"True," Dustin said. "Compiling information's not the same as investigating." Emily would certainly disagree with that definition, but Makenzie kept quiet. "We don't know enough about what happened yet to determine whether this is a dangerous situation or not."

"Whether it was a murder?" Makenzie asked.

"It's a weird deal. A middle-aged woman, practically a senior citizen, overdoses in a hayloft while her cat's tied up and meowing."

Overdose! Makenzie wanted to pepper Dustin with questions, but he would be mortified to realize he'd let slip with a critical autopsy detail. Which drug? What method – injection, pills, powder? Self-administered or forced?

One thing Makenzie was certain of was that someone used deception to draw Marcia to the hayloft.

"Callie is babysitting the cat used to lure Marcia to the hayloft." Makenzie watched Dustin's face for any hint that she'd hit the mark.

"That's nice of her," Dustin said with a totally bland expression. "I'd feel a lot better if you were satisfied to learn about the death from the newspaper, instead of picking my brain. The police don't need the help of your book club running all over the county digging up clues."

Makenzie started to defend her friends, but their bagged-up order arrived. Before she could restart the discussion, Dustin ended it.

"It's pointless to try and convince you to stay out of it, I suppose," he said. "I'm beginning to think your book club likes real murders better than the fictional kind."

* * *

Shanice had only eaten a couple of donut holes at the homecoming planning meeting, hoping to have something more substantial before her workshop at the ranch. Later that afternoon, Makenzie's parents were hosting a backyard barbecue. There was food in Shanice's future, but Gemma's information had killed her appetite.

She paused in the hallway of the main building, then turned and headed for her office.

How had Gemma learned details about Marcia's death? She was too new to town to have her own connection to the gossip grapevine. Granted, some people were faster at forming social bonds, but Gemma had only arrived a few weeks ago.

Why had Gemma told Shanice about the drug safe? It felt like an attempt to avoid being blamed for drugs from the veterinary school finding their way into the general public.

Shanice needed to visit the only person in the book club who knew Gemma.

The main door to the engineering school was open. Shanice wandered the maze of cubicles and offices until she found the nameplate for Emiko Nakamura. At twenty-five, she was two years younger than Shanice and had been in charge of a wind energy project over the summer. An avid fan of cats and reading, Emiko had joined the club after meeting the ladies during their last case.

"Knock knock," Shanice said.

Emiko looked up from her computer screen and smiled. Her thick black hair was pulled back in a low ponytail. Oversized computer glasses gave the engineer an adorably nerdy look.

"Hi. I wasn't expecting to see anyone on a Saturday. And a holiday weekend."

"I was here for a meeting of the Homecoming Committee," Shanice said. "I thought I'd see if you were around."

"Yup. Diving into a new semester," Emiko said. "What's up?"

Shanice tried to ease into discussion of Marcia's death. *Start with a little social chit chat.*

"I wondered whether you planned to start the next book club read."

Emiko had joined the group, but so far had been too busy to actually participate much.

"I need to." Emiko pulled off her glasses and set them to one side of her keyboard. "I mean, it's so easy to get caught up in work stuff. I love my job, which makes it harder to make strictly me time, because working feels like the best me time there is."

"I know what you mean." Shanice loved teaching math, but earlier this year had decided a career wasn't the sole source of satisfaction in life. Now she had a book club, new friends, horseback riding, and Sam. "Sometimes you have to schedule personal time. That's what keeps me on track. Riding lessons. The book club." *Dates with Sam.*

"The book ladies are great," Emiko said. "Plus there always

seems to be . . ." She rose from her chair and glanced around the mini cube farm. "You know. Other activities."

"Have you heard the latest?" Shanice asked.

"I read the book club texts about a woman in a hayloft at Callie's ranch."

Did Gemma jump to the overdose conclusion based on Emiko leaking information?

"I wondered how Gemma heard about the drugs," Shanice said, raising one eyebrow.

Emiko placed her fingers against her lips, then lowered her hand. "Oops. Was I not supposed to say anything?"

"The story was in the morning paper," Shanice said. "But not the details about the drugs."

"Okay," Emiko said softly. "I'll admit I told Gemma that Marcia's last word was quebrachine."

"And you didn't mention the xylazine?" Shanice asked.

"I was trying to come up with the word, but Gemma was in a hurry to get to the homecoming meeting. She took off before I remembered what it was."

Shanice felt a little better. Gemma had made a wild assumption based on gossip from a coworker. "Did you know Gemma's department has a drug safe?"

"No, I didn't. But that makes sense. Duh. A veterinary school would have animal drugs."

"I'm curious about that safe." Gemma had claimed the inventory was sound. After Gemma heard Emiko's tidbit based on the book club texts, she might have covered up any discrepancies. If she was guilty of mismanagement. Maybe doling out animal drugs to the public. Or committing murder. "How accessible is the safe to the general population?"

Emiko smiled. "You want to take a look?" she whispered. "Today's a good time, since there's hardly anyone around."

Shanice's heart beat a little faster at the thought of engaging in intrigue. This wasn't breaking and entering. She just needed to see where the drugs were kept. Among which might be one of the drugs mentioned in a dying woman's last words.

"Yes." Shanice glanced around the space, nearly echoing in its emptiness. "There might not be a better time."

Emiko led the way out a back door of the main building to a modern one-story construction that contrasted sharply with the traditional old brick and ivy university.

"Act like we belong here," Emiko whispered.

"We do belong," Shanice said. "At the university. Maybe not here specifically."

Shanice resisted the urge to glance over her shoulder.

The doors were unlocked, meaning faculty were on site. Or perhaps security was so lax, anyone could walk in and steal drugs. The polished tile hallway floor reflected the overhead fluorescent lights. Office doors were closed. Instructors could be taking the holiday weekend off. Or were they planning next week's classes like Emiko had been doing?

"Where would you keep a drug safe?" Shanice asked in a low voice.

"The lab?" Emiko asked.

"Let's try it," Shanice said.

She tried not to think about how it would look, two young instructors entering an area they clearly had no business in. To look for drugs.

It was too late to turn back. They were inside the lab. On one wall, gleaming white cabinets hung above white cupboards with gray countertops. Electronic instruments with glowing red, green, and yellow lights were silent, and racks of glass tubes and pipettes waited for the next tests. In the center of the room were five stainless steel tables.

Shanice strolled past the counters, peering into the glass-fronted cabinets. Emiko pulled two blue nitrile disposable gloves from a box.

"Fingerprints," she whispered.

Although being caught in the lab wearing gloves just might make them look more guilty, Shanice did the same. Now she could open the cupboards under the gray counter.

The building and lab were so new, there was still order to

the arrangement. Clutter was minimal, so it only took a moment to open a door, verify there was no safe, and move on.

At the end of the counter, where the cabinet met the far wall, they found racks of prescription bottles and boxes of drugs. Shanice scanned the labels. Antibiotics, dewormers, and ear lice ointments. Those couldn't possibly appeal to a drug addict.

"Here's the safe," Emiko whispered, holding a lower cabinet door open.

The small safe had a glass door. Shanice could see a notebook inside. Probably the inventory list.

"It has a keypad lock," Shanice said.

"Darn," Emiko said. "We need the code."

"I dabble in cryptography. Ciphers. Code-breaking. Strictly as a hobby." Shanice had few chances to make practical use of her interest. The round face had buttons with both numbers and letters, similar to a telephone keypad. "Randomly punching numbers won't help," she told Emiko. "We need to figure out who has access. That might help us figure out a code."

"Like a word?" Emiko asked. "Or somebody's birthday?"

"If multiple people use the safe, the code won't be too personal."

"How about v-e-t-l-a-b?" Emiko asked. "Maybe with the year."

The safe didn't appear to have an alarm. Shanice punched in 8-3-8-5-2-2. Nothing happened. She tapped in the numbers again, this time with the addition of the four-digit year. Still nothing. Then she tried again, this time adding the two-digit year to the end.

"We're getting nowhere." Shanice snapped a photo with her cellphone. "And I need to change before I go to the ranch." Her stomach grumbled in complaint. Food would have to be whatever she could grab from her apartment. *Protein bar.*

As they neared the lab door, Shanice heard footsteps.

"Yikes," Emiko whispered.

They flattened themselves on either side of the closed door. The steps continued down the hall. Emiko nodded. Shanice followed her into the hallway.

"There's a side way out," the engineer whispered.

As Emiko opened the exit door, they stood face to face with a startled young man. The door slammed shut behind them. Their mutual silence on the outdoor walkway stretched awkwardly long.

"You scared me." Emiko pressed a hand to her chest dramatically. A hand covered with a blue nitrile glove. "I didn't expect anyone to be here on the weekend."

Shanice tried to be discreet as she pulled the gloves off her hands, but they made a loud snapping sound as they released from her fingers.

"I need to feed the mice," the student said. "Professor Dinty gave me the code." He pointed to the keypad next to the door.

"By all means," Shanice said. "Feed the mice. Uh, do you also have access to the medicine for the mice?"

"In the drug safe?" Emiko asked.

"Professor Dinty only told me to feed them," the student said. "He didn't say anything about medicine."

"That probably comes later in the semester," Shanice said. "Well, carry on." She stepped aside.

When the student tapped on the keypad, he made no effort to cover his fingers. Shanice watched intently. 8-6-7-2-5-2-2.

The door lock clicked. The student stepped inside, studied Shanice and Emiko for a moment, then carefully pulled the door closed behind him until the latch mechanism clicked.

"That was a close call," Emiko said.

"I got the code." Shanice tapped it quickly into her phone notes.

"Great. Let's test it to be sure." Emiko punched the keypad while Shance recited the numbers 8-6-7-2-5-2-2. The lock clicked open.

"Are we going back in?" Emiko asked, holding the door open.

"No," Shanice said. "There are too many people wandering around." She walked away from the annex, toward the main building. "Although I'm itching to try the code on the drug safe."

"That would be dumb," Emiko said. "Using the same code for everything?"

"People do it all the time," Shanice said. She pulled out her phone. "8-6-7-2-5-2-2. The numbers correspond to, let's see. I think it's University of Oklahoma at Rose Creek lab. U-O-R-C-L-A-B, maybe."

"That was fast," Emiko said. "You're really good at this."

"We need to come back when there aren't so many people around," Shanice said.

"Who knew veterinary science was so top security," Emiko said. "Not."

Chapter Eleven

Callie felt funny being on the sidelines. The ranch was crawling with people and horses. Equi X organizers directed people to the correct location at the right time, doing an admirable job of keeping the program on track.

She felt . . . out of control. Of her own happy place. Making it stressful.

Never again.

Clint had better not be serious about expanding the ranch facilities to make future large events more inviting. As she stood by the railing to the indoor arena, Callie realized no one knew she was the owner of the ranch. They walked past, in their fancy dressage costumes, or crisp Western wear, like she was a hired hand. Just because she dressed in worn jeans and boots, and a Rose Creek Reads T-shirt.

The Saturday parade would officially kick off Equi X, although non-televised workshops had started as soon as people began arriving on Thursday. No later than Tuesday, everyone would load up their horses and leave. It couldn't end soon enough.

"They finally updated the website," a woman's voice said. "Looks like Marcia's workshops were parceled out to several different people."

"As if it would take multiple people to fill her boots," another woman said in a snide tone. "The aspiring stars fought tooth and nail over the slots, no doubt, what with the workshop being streamed on the *All Equestrian Today* channel."

That was the channel where Sam Grady had his show. Was that good or bad? Maybe spectators would watch the Equi X workshops in air-conditioned comfort from their homes, and leave Callie's ranch alone.

"I for one don't mind seeing a shake-up," the first woman said. "Fresh blood was needed."

"Blood," the second woman said. "I'm guessing more than one of those trainers would have killed for such a high-visibility spot."

Who are these catty women? Callie attempted a casual look-around. They were both in dressage attire of knee-high black leather boots, white breeches, and tailored black jackets. The older woman's highlighted hair was drawn back in a tidy chignon. The younger woman with the dark pixie cut Callie recognized. Sydney.

"I still say she must have broken her neck falling from that hayloft," the older woman said.

"Day drinking," Sydney said. "No doubt."

Callie felt dirty just listening to the harpies. Dealing with people like this might have contributed to Marcia's difficult personality. She debated approaching the women, to tell them exactly what she thought of them.

"Callie."

Saved by Emily. The bookstore owner walked through the crowded aisle. Instead of her usual housedress, she wore mom jeans and an oversized T-shirt featuring little horses pulling a miniature stagecoach. Her crossbody bag, in a colorful cartoony horsey print, looked hand-crafted. Emily gave Callie a quick side-hug squeeze.

"Are you okay?" Emily asked in a lowered voice.

"Just being unpleasantly reminded of why I like being alone on the ranch," Callie muttered. "It's great to see a friendly face."

The woman with the pillowy figure and kind eyes was the owner of Rose Creek Reads and the book club organizer. Or was that instigator?

"I'm looking forward to seeing my son and his tiny team,"

Emily said. "Plus our book club friends. I'm surprised you aren't taking part in one of the workshops."

"Playing hostess was enough stress for me," Callie said. "If my horses need training, Sam's around, and if I need training, we've got instructors."

"I imagine finding Marcia in the hayloft raised your stress level even more," Emily said. "After that incident in April, I couldn't sit on my bookstore deck for weeks without thinking about that poor man washing up in the cattails. It's difficult enough running across a deceased person you don't know. But you knew Marcia?"

It was a question Callie couldn't answer easily.

"I didn't really know her," Callie said carefully. She thought for a moment. "I knew her by reputation. She was a sought-after trainer of dressage horses, jumpers, and their riders. With an intense personality. But aren't some of the best teachers and coaches tough on their students?"

"I'd like to ask a favor." Emily touched Callie's arm. "Could you take me to the barn? Where it happened?"

"I haven't gone there since I found her," Callie said. "Mike's doing his best at keepin' anyone with no business there away. He moved the horses out of the old barn and into a pasture."

"If you don't want to go, I understand," Emily said.

Emily had been involved when the ladies found two other bodies. She knew stuff about murder cases from reading hundreds of mystery novels, and now from real-life involvement. Maybe she would see something even the police had missed.

"Sure," Callie said. "Let's go now, so we don't miss the parade."

As they walked, Emily asked questions, keeping Callie distracted from her dread about returning to the barn.

"Remind me, Callie. What brought you here Thursday? Talk me through that day."

"Winston got out of the Fallows' RV. Marcia was upset. I mean, anything could happen to a housecat on the loose at the ranch. A bunch of us were huntin' for the cat."

"He's still staying with you," Emily said.

Callie couldn't suppress a smile. "Yep. He's a pretty boy. Fluffy white fur with light pumpkin-colored highlights. Feathery tail. Big blue eyes."

"Winston sounds beautiful."

"He's got visual appeal," Callie said. "He's a clingy scaredy cat. But that's understandable. So back to Thursday, Marcia wrangled us into a full-blown search. Then she kinda vanished. I'm the one who found her. And Winston. In here."

Callie stopped in front of the barn. The doors were closed.

When Callie just stood there, Emily asked, "Shall we?"

"Right."

Callie opened one half of the wide double door and led Emily into the barn, across a straw-strewn dirt floor.

The backside of a woman was visible, crouched over a tack box. She dug through grooming equipment, bottles of horse shampoo, spray cans of bug repellent, and neatly coiled lead ropes. They weren't neat now.

"Can I help you?" Callie asked.

The woman's head popped up like a prairie dog emerging from a hole in the ground. Now that Callie could see her face, she looked familiar. Curly, dirty blonde hair framed a face lined from sun exposure. Not a trainer. Not a rider.

"Just looking for my gloves." She grabbed a pair of worn leather gloves. "Found them."

"Aren't you Sydney's groom?" Callie asked. The big-name trainers and horse farms had top-of-the-line everything. It didn't seem like they'd mingle their tack with the general public. "Your gear should be in the new barn." If it wasn't locked up in their fancy trailers or RVs.

"Overflow," she said, then flounced out of the barn like she owned the place. Leaving the lid of the box open.

"Huh." Callie placed her hands on her narrow hips and studied the tack box. Well-worn. More like a heavy-duty plastic storage box with a few trays and drawers. The equipment inside could have come from any feed store or Western outfitter. "That does not look like a tack box used by an Olympic contender."

"A problem?" Emily asked.

"I hope she wasn't tryin' to swipe gear from one of our boarders. Her boss has plenty of money for curry combs and gloves." Callie frowned. "I'd hate to have to tell folks they need to start locking up their tack boxes."

"You called that woman a groom," Emily said. "What's a groom? Other than the partner to a bride?"

"Only rich people hire grooms," Callie said. "Us lowly ordinary people brush our own horses. The Olympic-level competitors usually don't even have their own horses. They ride for ultra-wealthy people. Grooms take care of the horse grooming and tack. They're actually pretty important, 'cause they notice the animal's health and injuries before anyone else." She glanced at Emily. "Not from personal experience. I like takin' care of my own horses."

The interior of the barn was toasty, despite the fan sucking hot air to the outdoors. Callie walked to the base of the loft ladder and looked up.

"They've taken the crime scene tape down?" Emily asked.

"Yesterday," Callie said. "Or so Mike told us."

Marcia had died Thursday afternoon. It was just Saturday, nearing lunchtime, and the yellow tape blocking access to the ladder and the loft was gone. Things seemed to move awfully fast, considering a person had died.

Emily's head was on a swivel as she studied every detail of the barn's interior. Then she looked up the ladder.

"Do you mind?"

"Nope," Callie said, holding an arm out toward the wooden ladder permanently attached to a support beam on one side and the floor of the loft at the top.

For a mature woman of moderately plump girth, Emily was spry. She climbed the ladder with ease, managing the awkward transition from ladder to loft floor without Callie's help. Callie took a deep breath, then followed.

Rays of sunlight beamed through the narrow gaps around the hayloft door. Dust motes floated lazily in the light.

"That's where the hay is loaded?" Emily asked.

"Used to be," Callie said. "Before changing away from the smaller rectangular bales, they loaded hay up here with a pulley. Now most folks use equipment that makes the giant round hay bales. That's about all that's available anymore. Those won't fit through that little door, obviously. We have a steel hay barn to protect the big round bales from the weather."

"May I?" Emily walked to the hay door.

"Sure," Callie said.

She reached for the latch. It wasn't meant for security. Just for holding the door closed. The door swung outward. Callie tensed as Emily held onto the doorframe and leaned out.

"Careful, Emily. A fall wouldn't be any fun at all."

"No, indeed. Although it's not as far a drop as I would have thought."

The bookstore owner peered up at the pulley, then at the ground below. A hill behind the barn made loading hay easier, back in the day of the rectangular bales. Backing a truck to the barn, the pulley was used to haul bales up through the hay door. The sloping hill formed part of the back wall, making the distance from the hay door to the ground maybe a dozen feet. Still far enough to break a bone, Callie thought, especially for a senior citizen.

"When was the last time that was used?" Emily pointed at the pulley suspended from a beam protruding from the barn. Worn rope looped around the pulley and the post.

Callie shrugged. "Not sure. Before we bought the ranch. At least over three years ago, but I'd guess way longer than that."

"Doesn't seem a likely entry point," Emily muttered to herself. "A person could jump to the ground from here, but coming up? That ratty rope and rusty pulley business doesn't look capable of lifting a human." After closing and latching the hay door, she explored the loft, apparently searching for any entry besides the ladder. "Well, it seems the most likely way into the hayloft is the ladder."

"That's my guess," Callie said.

"Where was the cat tied up?" Emily asked.

The bookstore owner was clearly in amateur detective mode. Callie led her to the slanting beam where Winston had been tied.

"Oh, the poor kitty." Emily crouched down and ran her fingers along new claw marks on the beam, bright against the wood's aging patina. She picked up a puff of white fur. "The baby was terrified. For himself. And maybe for Marcia."

Callie had been warming up to the needy cat. She still thought of him as pampered and silly. Now her heart ached for Winston and the trauma he'd been subjected to, helpless to do anything for his mistress.

"Winston was used to lure Marcia up here," Callie said. "It's so obvious, with him bein' tied to the post."

"The police are aware?" Emily asked as she studied the surrounding straw.

"Oh yeah, they know."

Emily stood and dusted her hands together. "And Marcia? Where was she?"

Callie swallowed the lump in her throat. The terror of that day faded into a different emotion. Sadness. For Marcia and her cat. The ugly-hearted women talking dirt about the deceased woman didn't even see her as a human being.

"Marcia was here." Callie pointed to the area where Marcia had struggled to speak her final words. "On her back."

Emily stepped around the space respectfully. Her attention to the crime scene was oddly comforting. Unlike the mean girls who used Marcia's death as an excuse for cruel gossip, Emily sought answers. Clues.

"Her cellphone was never found?" Emily asked.

"Not that I know of," Callie said. "I could ask Alistair." She paused, as emotions washed over her. "Why did someone hate this woman so much they wanted her dead?"

"Did they, though?" Emily asked. "What if it was an accident?"

Chapter Twelve

Makenzie's phone chimed as she and Dustin exited his truck. She waggled the phone at the deputy.

"Mom again. I have to take this."

He nodded and leaned against the truck. The improvised pasture parking lot was filling up.

Makenzie's father Clyde had completed his backyard gazebo and barbecue extravaganza, with Dustin's help, a couple of weeks ago. Mona, her mother, had planned their "grand opening" party well before Callie and Clint agreed to host the last-minute Equi X horse workshop. Now the two events presented a scheduling conflict.

"Mom, I promised Shanice I'd watch her workshop," Makenzie told Mona. "And Drew's boy is in the parade, carrying a flag or something."

"Well, we do seem to have everything on our end arranged," Mona said. "Your father put the meat in a marinade last night. He won't fire up the grill until a couple of hours before the party starts. I can manage without you for a little bit longer."

It was going to be tricky timing, but Makenzie had made sure her side dishes were prepped and ready for the late afternoon barbecue. No one came to a Rose Creek party without a dish of some kind. There would be plenty of food.

"How is Pat Pat doing?" Makenzie rarely left the kitten alone if her mother was home to watch him and his sister. And vice versa. Peaches was a frequent visitor to Makenzie's house.

"I'm keeping them both in the guest room," Mona said.

"That's safer, with all the people going in and out of the kitchen and bathroom. You told your book club about the party?"

Yes, for the tenth time.

"They'll be late," Makenzie reminded her mother. "They're coming after their workshops."

"Your father wants to talk to Drew and Joel about the legalities of starting a business."

This was news.

"It's not polite to talk to people about business at a party," Makenzie said.

She motioned to Dustin, mimicking a person chattering with her hand. He stood and offered her his arm. They walked slowly to the open pasture gate.

"There's no better place than at a party," Mona said, as though she were a high-powered entrepreneur. "Just to pick their brains about basics. If Clyde needs to incorporate or create an LLC, of course he'd go through the formality of making an appointment and paying the Brauners for their time."

This was the first Makenzie had heard about a business plan. Her mother had worked for two decades as a hygienist for the local dentist, sometimes doing office work to fill in for the receptionist. Dad had operated heavy equipment for the county road crew until earning a desk job doing scheduling. Maybe both were tiring of their jobs and yearned to expand their horizons.

"Mom, what business are you talking about?"

"A barbecue hut," Mona said. "Your father wants to ride the wave before the market is too glutted."

"It's already glutted," Makenzie said. "Everyone and their Aunt Harriet has opened a barbecue hut in Rose Creek."

She glanced up at Dustin. He raised his eyebrows and shrugged.

"Tell that to your father," Mona said.

"I will," Makenzie said.

"Before he takes out that second mortgage."

"What? Isn't opening a restaurant a huge risk? I didn't think you and Dad were the risk-taking types."

"In pursuit of his dream?" Mona asked.

Makenzie almost blurted out that her career might be balanced on a knife's edge. Her own home, rented from her parents for a pittance, would be in danger if Dad risked their property on a whim. But hours before they hosted half the town at the party of the summer was not the time to tell her parents she might lose her job.

Or Dustin. This was Makenzie's burden to carry until she knew what was actually going to happen to Brieswell Pottery Works. She stepped carefully across the uneven ground to the graveled area in front of the new barn.

"We're just in the discussion phase," Mona said. "I would have thought you'd be excited for your father."

"It's just . . . a surprise."

"Even us old folks can be full of surprises."

"You're not old. I didn't mean anything by asking questions. Restaurants are a risky business to go into when neither you nor Dad has ever even worked in one."

"We'll have a ready-made manager," Mona said. "Your father ran into Jacob Caine at the hardware store. Do you remember his daughter Candy?"

How can I forget? Although Makenzie had never actually met Candy Caine, she had been mistaken as her sister last May. That led to Makenzie's unexpected friendship with Jacob, a whiskered hillbilly who made moonshine. His pregnant daughter had gone into hiding after having a disagreement with some scary criminals.

"I haven't talked to Jacob in weeks," she said. "Did he finally hear from Candy?"

Dustin focused on Makenzie. She could tell he knew instantly Makenzie wasn't referring to a confection.

"She's moving back to Rose Creek," Mona said. "Her baby is due soon, and she wants to be home with family."

Makenzie cast a sideways look at Dustin. Had he heard, and neglected to tell her the infamous Candy was coming back to town? The Deputy didn't exactly approve of her association with the Caines.

"What does this have to do with Dad's barbecue dream?"

"Candy is managing a restaurant in Tulsa."

"Mom, you don't know anything about Candy."

"You shouldn't hold her past against her," Mona said. "Judge not, the Good Book says."

A stripper who ran afoul of Tulsa criminals. Makenzie thought there was plenty of room to judge. Or at least be cautious. Extremely cautious.

"It's never too late to take a new career path," Mona continued. "Of course we'll examine all the pros and cons. You're right. We haven't been risk-takers. Maybe we've been a little too stodgy. It's time to step out on that limb and spread our wings."

As Makenzie ended the call and placed the phone in her small purse, she told Dustin about her mother's unexpected revelation about wanting to open a barbecue hut.

"There are too many barbecue huts in town for that to be a sure thing," he said. "If it was me, I'd go into some business dealing with the infrastructure needed by all these restaurants. You know. Like equipment, or plastic forks and food baskets. During the California gold rush, the people who got rich ran hardware stores, hotels, and bars. But that's not the part that concerns me. Did I hear you mention Candy Caine?"

"Mom said she's coming back to have her baby in Rose Creek. And she and Dad want Candy to manage their restaurant."

"Oh, boy." Dustin frowned. "I'd better let Chief Holloway know. That girl leaves a path of destruction in her wake."

"She claims to have begun a new career," Makenzie said. "Being pregnant had to end her days as a stripper. For now, anyway. Mom says Candy's been managing a restaurant."

"I'll bet," Dustin muttered.

A new career path. Makenzie had zero interest in being part of her parents' barbecue hut scheme, but if Brieswell closed the lab, she might not have a choice. A career change might be in her future.

Her phone pinged with an incoming text.

"You sure are popular," Dustin said.

"We're invited to a late lunch," she told him as she read her phone screen. "Clint is making something non-barbecue at their house after the parade." Makenzie sent a return text accepting the invitation.

"It's a good thing we only had sandwiches on our way here. Today's gonna involve a lot of eating."

Makenzie hardly considered the hearty sandwiches they'd eaten in the truck light fare, but Dustin was one of those people who could eat a ton of food and still stay trim.

"Where are we going first?" Dustin asked.

"The opening parade. I want a good seat."

"Lots of nice-looking horses here today," Dustin said.

When Dustin noticed Sam, he veered toward an outdoor corral to meet the veterinarian's pretty spotted Appaloosa horses.

Dustin asked Sam questions that sounded like he was considering buying a horse for himself. Makenzie's mind wasn't on animals. She took a couple of steps away from the men to read an incoming text from the book club.

That morning, Shanice's coworker Gemma claimed that Marcia died of a quebrachine overdose. Shanice and Emiko had attempted to investigate the veterinary drugs at the university, but had nearly been caught. They planned to return later.

Less than an hour ago, Dustin had let slip confirmation that Marcia died of an overdose, but he didn't reveal which drug. Drew's reliably sourced nugget that Marcia's death was a homicide made for an interesting development.

Now that was a career option Makenzie could get excited about. Private investigator.

She sighed. Creating a murder board with her book club friends was entirely different than becoming a PI. What she really wanted was to continue her dream job, working in the chemistry lab at Brieswell.

* * *

"An accident." Callie tried out Emily's words. "But she didn't fall."

"No, of course not." Emily looked around the hayloft. "You said Marcia died right here, soon after saying the names of a stimulant derived from tree bark, and an animal sedative. Did you notice anything indicating a violent death?"

"Not really," Callie said, feeling queasy. "She was out of it. Just about incoherent. But I didn't notice any obvious blood or bruises."

"That's a blessing, anyway," Emily said. "Still, it couldn't have been pleasant. Death is death."

The grandmotherly bookstore owner caught Callie off guard with her morbid observation.

Both their phones pinged at the same time. Callie and Emily read the text message on their phones.

"Hmm." Emily returned her phone to her colorful crossbody bag. "Overdose from quebrachine?"

"Drew told us the cause of death listed on the death certificate. Homicide," Callie said. "But no one's seen the autopsy report yet. That Gemma gal can't know. Unless she saw the autopsy report before Tobias's connection."

"We must consider that Shanice's new friend at the university could be right," Emily said. "How could this Gemma person learn something of this nature before our book club? A newcomer to town?" Emily sounded baffled and a little upset.

"It's just gossip," Callie said. "A lucky guess. People come up with these ideas. The gorier, the better. I overheard some ladies here talkin' about Marcia, like they weren't surprised she was a drunk, or even a druggie. Do you think she could have taken the drugs deliberately?"

"A self-administered overdose?" Emily grimaced and rubbed her nose. "I can't imagine. Realizing she'd taken too much, via whatever route, Marcia alerted you to her condition with her last words. Hoping for rescue."

"That doesn't explain Winston." Callie pointed to the beam where the cat had been tied. "Marcia was lured up here. If she overdosed, maybe someone forced the drugs on her."

"I agree," Emily said decisively. "In examining all the possible angles, the cat seems to be a clue to a more nefarious situation than unintentional self-overdose. Besides which, homicide indicates another human was involved."

"Why leave Winston?" Callie asked. "If a person wanted to murder Marcia and used Winston to lure her up here, it seems like they would've untied the cat afterward, to cover up."

Emily gazed at the hay door. "Here's a thought. Trapped when you entered the barn, the perpetrator leapt out the hay door. Was it latched when you came up here?"

Callie closed her eyes. "I wasn't payin' any attention to the door." She opened her eyes. "The police might know."

Emily headed for the ladder. "If only cats could talk."

Callie agreed. They'd all be saved a lot of trouble if felines could tell humans what they had witnessed at murder scenes.

Her phone buzzed with another incoming text. This one was from Makenzie.

"Hold up, Emily. It's another text from book club."

Emily paused at the edge of the hayloft with one hand on the ladder railing. "More news?" She reached into her horse-themed crossbody bag and studied her phone screen. "Oh my."

Makenzie relayed Deputy Sage's slip of the tongue.

"He said overdose," Callie said in a soft voice. "I think he'd know."

"More than Gemma," Emily said.

"An overdose." Callie looked from her phone screen to Emily. "Does that make it murder?"

"Not necessarily," Emily said. "If it was self-administered . . ." She trailed off, looking thoughtful. "The cause of death being homicide means another person was involved. But if Emily willingly accepted pills or a drug injection . . ."

Callie shook her head. "Drugs. In Rose Creek. And I thought Cousin George's drinking problem was the worst substance abuse issue I'd come in contact with."

Emily placed a hand on Callie's arm. "We don't have enough data. We need to keep an open mind about this case. Things may not be as they seem."

After ending the text conversation, Emily climbed down the ladder to find her son and his miniature horses. Callie headed to the new barn, hoping to find Clint. She needed a hug after revisiting the site of a murder.

Homicide. Not a murder. Yet.

Clint was at the center of a cluster of excited people. The parade began in less than thirty minutes. Callie was already exhausted. The throngs of people, all their chattering, drained her introverted self.

She walked down the wide aisle past stall fifteen. Someone was murmuring. A human. Talking to a horse. Callie paused. She didn't want to interrupt, but she strained hard to listen. The stall door latch jiggled open. Alistair Fallows stepped out, giving the handsome gray horse one last pat on the neck. He closed the door, then turned, startled to see Callie judging by the look on his fleshy, freckled face.

"Mr. Fallows," Callie said. "I was headed to the refreshment tent. Can I bring you back anything? A cold drink?"

"Nice of you to offer." But his tone didn't sound grateful. More like grating. "You won't be back in time. Like you didn't reach Marcia in time. She might still be here if you had."

Callie's mouth hung open. She snapped her mouth closed, then attempted to speak.

"I wish I could have done more," Callie said. "Everything happened so fast."

It's not my fault I didn't find your wife until it was too late. Callie had been struggling to cast off a load of guilt, thinking she could have done more. Now Alistair was piling it on higher and heavier.

"They haven't told me yet how she died," Alistair said. "But in the case of strokes, they say seconds count."

"Stroke?" Callie asked. She couldn't share the rumors of

overdose with Alistair. He might have been the one to give her the drug.

"Heart attack?" Alistair asked. "Brain aneurism? How does a woman go from being alive, vibrant, with so much to look forward to, then suddenly cut down in her prime?" He stepped closer to Callie, lowering his voice. "Please. If you know anything that can help me make sense of this, tell me."

Callie couldn't help him. Alistair might be a suspect in his wife's homicide. *Or murder.*

"Did the police give you information?" Callie asked. "About how Marcia . . . passed?"

"Don't bother with euphemisms," Alistair said. "Dead. That's what she is." Tears filled his hazel eyes, already red and puffy.

"I, uh, I have the cat still," Callie said. Maybe the snowy white Persian cat with the pumpkin highlights, Marcia's precious baby, could offer comfort to Alistair. "You can have Winston back any time."

"I have my hands full dealing with Moonstone." He waved a hand at the gray horse's stall. "He knows something's wrong. I don't have any energy left to coddle that ridiculous cat."

Understandable. But poor Winston.

"I'll keep him as long as you want," Callie said.

"It's the least you can do." Alistair turned to walk out of the barn. He threw over his shoulder, "for letting my Marcia die."

Chapter Thirteen

Shanice walked down the rows of RVs, trailers, and fifth wheels. She felt spiffy in the cowgirl outfit she had pulled together for the training workshop. Nice fitting jeans, polished boots, and a long-sleeved pearl snap blouse. The dark pink fabric had an embroidered yoke.

Linda required her students to wear protective helmets during class. Shanice could only wear her pink straw cowgirl hat outside the arena. She wanted a photo with the handsome horse whisperer before she accumulated a layer of dust and horsehair.

As she neared Sam's luxury fifth wheel, she heard a familiar voice. One she'd had a conversation with very recently. *What is Gemma doing here?* Shanice slowed her steps.

Sam emerged from the space between his trailer and the enormous RV parked across from his steps. Gemma followed on his heels. Was Sam deliberately taking extra-long strides? Gemma gave the impression of a puppy chasing after him. Her shorts barely contained her round bottom, and she risked sunburn on the acre of chest and shoulders revealed by a snug sleeveless top. A brown ponytail anchored a university ballcap to her head.

"Shanice!" Sam smiled. He looked relieved as he pulled her into a quick hug. He kissed her full on the lips.

With a greeting like that, how could Shanice entertain a jealous thought about Gemma? But she wondered. Had Gemma been inside Sam's fifth wheel? Shanice couldn't let the lingering insecurity generated by the cheating fiancé she'd left behind in

Chicago affect her present.

"You really must be in a workshop," Gemma said, looking Shanice up and down.

"Yes," Shanice said. What did Gemma think? She'd made up the story about being an avid horseback rider? Or did Gemma assume Black women couldn't be cowgirls? "What brings you here?"

Shanice hoped Gemma hadn't seen her and Emiko snooping around the lab. She smiled, but waited for an accusation. *Spy. Thief.*

"I told you this morning," Gemma said. "I'd love for Dr. Grady to guest lecture at the School of Veterinary Medicine. You didn't seem thrilled about giving me an introduction, so I introduced myself."

"And I said that discussion will have to wait until after this weekend," Sam said. "I'm juggling too much to feel agreeable about adding volunteer work to my plate." Sam looped his arm through Shanice's and headed for the arena. "I want a good seat for the parade."

"Dr. Grady." Gemma trotted alongside them. "I have a more immediate question. A representative of RAOR called me. Are the horses here this weekend being tested for illegal doping?"

Emiko admitted she told Gemma about Marcia's death, but there might be more than one information leak. Namely, Aster.

"Are you part of RAOR?" Shanice asked.

"I can't join," Gemma said. "You have to pledge not to eat animals. I like eating animals."

"No drug testing is required for Equi X," Sam said. "This is not a competition. It's a workshop."

"But there are drugs around," Gemma said. "Like that lady who died Thursday."

"What does horse doping have to do with Marcia's death?" Shanice asked the annoying woman. "Sam, this morning Gemma told me Marcia overdosed on quebrachine."

Sam stopped and looked at Gemma. "The autopsy report has been released?"

They had been slowly making their way from the impromptu RV park in Callie and Clint's pasture toward the new barn. Soon, there would be too many people around to continue this odd conversation. Gemma was a bit of a loudmouth, and Shanice didn't want total strangers overhearing them. Especially when the talk involved a potential murder case.

"No," Shanice said. "The report hasn't been released. Gemma is just really interested in Marcia's death."

"Like you aren't," Gemma said. "I've heard about your little book club. You and your crew of amateur sleuths are famous at the university."

Shanice was afraid she and Gemma sounded like bickering junior high girls, not education professionals.

"Ladies," Sam said. "We're going to be late for the parade."

Sam tipped his straw cowboy hat back with one hand and brushed sweat off his forehead with a bandana. The day was too hot to stand in the sun arguing about murder clues.

"I've got good cause to be concerned," Gemma continued, as though Sam hadn't spoken. "Our students could be in danger if quebrachine is that readily available in Rose Creek."

Sam pushed his hat firmly back into place. "You think Marcia overdosed on quebrachine?"

"What else could it be?" Gemma asked. "That *was* her dying word."

Callie had told them Marcia uttered two dying words. So far, Gemma hadn't mentioned xylazine. Shanice hoped Sam wouldn't reveal the other drug. Gemma already knew too much, and wasn't shy about sharing her information.

"Quebrachine is unlikely to kill a person," Sam said. "Unless Marcia had a preexisting medical condition."

"Gemma, you said it's not in the university's safe," Shanice said. "Where else would Marcia have gotten the drug?"

"Any veterinarian has access to it," Gemma said. "Right, Dr. Grady? It's used to counteract sedation in animals."

"It isn't a controlled drug," Sam said. "It's sold over-the-counter. Online."

A new factor in the mystery equation occurred to Shanice. Marcia might have wanted the drug because she had sedatives in her system.

Gemma didn't know about the xylazine. Or at least, she hadn't admitted she knew about it. Unless she had been with Marcia. Provided her with the drug. Or forced it on her.

People filed toward the outdoor arena.

"If we want a good seat for the parade," Shanice said, "we need to go."

"I'll talk to you later, Dr. Grady. And Shanice," she said, pointing a finger, "I'll see you at the next homecoming meeting. I know I can convince you to let go of the stuffy old ways and embrace change." Gemma waved a hand like she was dismissing Shanice and Sam, then melted into the crowd.

"Did she just call me stuffy?" Shanice asked.

"Gemma is certainly self-assured." Sam clearly didn't mean it as a compliment.

"Were you talking to her for very long?" Shanice asked.

"She pounced on me when I left my trailer," Sam said.

Good. Gemma hadn't been inside Sam's trailer. *Or so he says.* Shanice chided herself. Sam was a good guy. Not a liar and a cheat.

*   *   *

Joel had agreed not to ground Parker from riding in the parade. Their son's outburst before going to temple, and then declaring he didn't want a baby in the family, had been disturbing, but he had behaved well since then. Drew still felt prickly and oversensitive. She reminded herself she was experiencing pregnancy hormones. It was awful, bursting into tears at the slightest stress.

I am not going to cry in front of complete strangers.

They had arrived early enough to have seats in the shadiest area of the bleacher-style outdoor arena seating. Joel brought her a lemonade.

"Fresh squeezed," he said, handing her the sweating cup.

A sprig of mint floated on top of the ice cubes. She sipped the drink eagerly. Spending the afternoon outdoors at a horse ranch felt healthy. Fresh air and sunshine.

Hard metal bleachers. She shifted in her seat, anxious for the workshop events to be over, longing to put her feet up in air-conditioned comfort at home. And she wasn't even quite five months along. Maybe Joel was right. She would be better off in Boston, with family fussing over her.

Uncle Tobias nearly arrived late. Drew's heart thumped faster when she noticed he was limping. Someone hopped up from their spot on the lowest row of the bleachers and offered Tobias a seat. The old man sat down gingerly.

Drew debated scurrying down to find out what had happened to her great-uncle, but then Parker's class entered the arena. His pigtailed friend Jill led the group, followed by Parker and her brother Bear riding side by side, and then two more pairs of riders. Jill carried an American flag, Parker the flag of the State of Oklahoma, and Bear a tribal flag representing the Seneca-Cayuga Nation.

The kids wore Western or Native attire, depending on their ethnicity. Joel had suggested Parker wear a kippah in recognition of his Jewish heritage. Their instructor insisted the kids wear helmets, so the kippah was covered by the protective plastic dome.

Parker looked at ease in the saddle on Flash, a pinto gelding that was equal parts chestnut and white, with a colorful mane and tail streaked with white, brown, and red. Parker glowed with happiness.

Drew's eyes filled with tears, and despite her best effort to contain them, they overflowed. Joel placed an arm around her shoulders.

"Are you okay?" he asked.

"I'm so proud of our reformed couch potato. Parker looks natural on a horse."

"Uncle Tobias has influenced him," Joel said. "All those

stories about Jewish cowboys and Wild West figures."

And Joel wants us to return to the East Coast. Couldn't he see how important it was for Parker to live in Rose Creek?

The opening ceremony and flag parade went off without a hitch. Joel recorded it with his cellphone, even though they had set the DVR to record the television broadcast. When Parker's group rode out of the arena, Joel went outside to congratulate their son on a job well done. Drew began to climb down to check on Uncle Tobias, but before she could, Shanice's workshop was announced. Uncle Tobias didn't make a move to leave, so Drew settled back on her seat to watch Shanice's class.

Linda took her students through several fun games, explaining to the audience the purpose of each. Humans required training, even more so than horses.

Drew was engrossed in the demo. Her friend Shanice had only been riding since May, but she looked confident seated on the dappled gray mare. Maybe when she recovered from having the baby, Drew would sign up for lessons.

When the workshop concluded, another group prepared to enter the arena. Drew climbed down the bleachers to Uncle Tobias.

"Need a hand?" she asked him. "Let's go find Parker."

Tobias extended a hand. Drew gave him a pull. He didn't need much help to stand, but when he took a step, he grimaced.

"Okay," Drew said, "what happened?"

"In the wee hours of the morning, Spirit alerted me to an intruder."

"Is that why you're limping?" Drew asked. "You tripped over the cat?"

"Spirit was defending hearth and home," Tobias said. "It was a box, not the cat."

Drew had doubted adopting a feral animal was a good idea, even though Makenzie assured her the cat knew how to behave. The orange and white cat had adjusted quickly to the plush indoor life. Uncle Tobias adored the torn-ear, scar-faced girl, claiming she gave him a reason to get out of bed in the morning.

Drew didn't buy him needing a motivation. Uncle Tobias had always been active.

"You'll have to give me the details while we go find Parker and Joel," Drew said.

Tobias waved one hand in a dismissive gesture. "It was nothing, really. Spirit woke me, and I heard a noise downstairs. When I went to investigate, I tripped over a box."

As soon as they started the trip to the kids' staging area, it was obvious Uncle Tobias was in serious pain. They found Joel at a corral railing, watching kids unsaddle their mounts under the supervision of Linda, their teacher.

"Parker has become quite the capable cowboy," Tobias said to Joel. "Soon he'll be roping calves and riding bucking broncs."

"Hi Tobias." Joel glanced at the older man. "What happened to you?"

"Is it that obvious?" Tobias asked. "Spirit heard something. An intruder. I saw a shadow outside, trying to open the window. When I went to investigate, I tripped over a box in the dark."

The additional details fit what he had just told Drew, but the new information was frightening.

"Clint and Callie invited us to lunch," Joel said. "You're included, Tobias."

When they collected Parker, practically having to drag him away from his horse, they started walking to the ranch house.

Tobias paused on the climb up the mild incline to the ranch house. He leaned over, placing his hands on his knees. Drew grabbed his arm.

"Uncle Tobias, stop right there," Drew said. "I'm taking you to urgent care."

"I would argue with you." He looked up at Drew from his bent-over position. "But that sounds like a good idea."

Chapter Fourteen

Callie felt sick at heart after her encounter with Alistair. She didn't even have the energy to offer Clint help.

"I'm glad you tore yourself away from Equi X to fix my book club friends lunch," she told him from her seat at the kitchen table.

"They are my friends, too," Clint said.

"This all looks great."

A casserole dish packed with colorful Cuban-style arroz con pollo rested on the stove top. Leafy green salad with lots of chopped goodies like sweet peppers, fresh tomato, and chopped olives, made for a light lunch.

"A person can only eat so much barbecue." Clint put the finishing touches on the salad. "The local obsession with meats cooked in tomato-based sauces should be balanced with vegetables."

Callie laughed. Clint approached her seat.

"It's nice to see you smile." He placed a hand on her shoulder and squeezed gently. "You can't let Alistair's cruel words bother you. I know," he said when she began to object. "That is easier said than done. The human tongue can cut like a knife."

"He's right in a way," Callie said. "I didn't even know what Marcia was saying. If I had, it might have clicked, and I could have told the EMTs about the drugs."

"We don't know why she chose those as her last words," Clint said. "Has Drew's uncle learned yet what the results of the autopsy are?"

"He'll be here for lunch," Callie said. "If he knows something, he'll share with us."

The doorbell chimed. Clint left the spacious kitchen. In a moment, he returned, his long-legged strides carrying him back into the room. Joel and Parker followed. The boy wore a solemn expression.

"Uncle Tobias had an accident," Joel said. "A fall. Drew insisted on taking him to urgent care by herself."

"I wanted to go," Parker said. "He's my uncle too."

"He'll be fine," Joel said. "Too much of a crowd in these situations only adds stress. They'll patch Uncle Tobias up as good as new. And faster without all of us being in the way."

Parker folded his arms across the front of his Western shirt and frowned. *Little mister attitude*, Callie thought with a smile. She could only hope to have child discipline issues someday. For that, you needed a child.

"Did he fall here?" Clint asked. "On the ranch?"

"No," Joel said. "It sounds like he tripped over that stray cat he adopted."

"Her name is Spirit," Parker said. "And Uncle Tobias said she was helping him. Spirit didn't make him fall down."

Callie had seen older relatives deny the truth behind accidents when they feared their families would use their growing frailties to curtail their independence.

"Hopefully it's just a sprain or a bruise," Callie told Parker. "I'm sure your uncle will be right as rain in no time. How did you like bein' in the parade?"

Parker switched gears quickly from concern about his uncle to ensuring Callie the parade was the best thing that had ever happened to him. Besides Boomer, of course.

"I wish Boomer could be here," Parker said, "instead of locked up on the porch."

"Boomer needs to be introduced to ranch life without the distraction of crowds," Joel said.

"I have heard it's a good idea to assimilate dogs to groups

of humans at a young age," Clint said. "This weekend might be a good opportunity to do that."

The doorbell chimed again.

"I'll get it." Callie hopped up. Makenzie, Dustin, Shanice, and Sam waited at the door. Behind them, Emily walked up the paved walkway. "The gang's all here. Come on in."

Soon everyone was munching on salad and the mildly spicy rice dish.

"Don't eat too much," Makenzie said. "My dad will be heartbroken if you don't try his super-secret ribs recipe cooked on his brand-new backyard barbecue grill."

Dustin patted his flat stomach. "No worries. We'll wear off lunch by then."

"Where's Drew?" Shanice asked.

Joel told the story of Tobias's accident, and the older man's claim the feral cat had been playing the role of guard-cat.

"I understand the Garcia household is now in possession of a cat," Emily said.

"Temporarily," Callie said. "I'll see if I can find him."

Winston had claimed a sunny window in the first-floor family room. She lifted him from the blanket she had placed on the sill.

"Come on and meet the gang," she told Winston.

The book club ladies fawned over the fluffy white cat with the pumpkin highlights, who seemed oblivious to the flattery. Well, maybe a little nervous. He clung to Callie's shoulder with his claws.

"Such big blue eyes," Emily said. "Is he yours now?"

"Oh, no," Callie said. "Alistair will take him back at the end of the workshop."

The man who had practically accused Callie of murder. Or at least neglect, letting his wife die because she didn't act quickly enough. She gave Winston a hug. He needed to go home before she became too attached to the silly animal.

Lunch wasn't exactly leisurely. Everyone had workshops to attend, participate in, or run in the afternoon. Sam, the famous horse whisperer, planned demos on his technique for gently training horses. Everyone wanted to see Emily's son in the mini-horse demonstration. When Joel and Parker left to watch a workshop, Callie brought up her latest news.

"This wasn't appropriate to share in front of a kid," she told the group, "but Alistair basically accused me of letting Marcia die."

Emily threw her arms around Callie, while Shanice and Makenzie joined the bookstore owner's protests. In theory, Callie knew she'd done nothing wrong. Alistair's words still stung, and sowed seeds of doubt. Was there something Callie could have done to save Marcia's life?

"People often feel guilty when they're on the scene of a death," Dustin said. "Even an expected passing, like of an elderly relative. There was nothin' you could do to change the outcome of that situation."

"That is what I've been telling Callie," Clint said, "but I think it will take time for the experience to fade."

She had selfishly hoped Tobias would have autopsy information that might ease her feelings of guilt. Although that might be tricky to discuss in front of the deputy.

"I don't suppose you can tell us anything?" Callie looked hopefully at Dustin.

"You know I can't give details of an active case."

Makenzie pounced. "Has Marcia's death shifted from a homicide to a murder investigation?"

Dustin held up his hands. "See what happens? I say anything, and you blow it up into way more than it is."

"I wouldn't have to speculate if you gave us actual facts," Makenzie said.

The chemist had texted the book club about Dustin letting it slip that Marcia's death was an overdose. There was a lot of room left for speculation.

"Callie, you told us Marcia's last words were quebrachine and xylazine," Shanice said. "I heard through the campus rumor-mill that Marcia OD'd on quebrachine." Callie admired the smooth way Shanice had deflected attention from Makenzie. "But Sam, you said that's unlikely to cause a fatal overdose."

Sam held up a hand. "Hold on. Unlikely doesn't mean could never. As a stimulant, quebrachine could have aggravated an existing condition."

"The xylazine is a whole 'nother deal," Callie said. "It's a sedative. Clint looked it up. Fine for some animals, but it's a dangerous drug when people are stupid enough to use it."

"But no one's saying the victim had any drugs in her system," Dustin said. "Don't go leaping to conclusions. The tox tests are still being run."

Makenzie looked like she was ready to speak, but Dustin gave her a look. She must have decided it was a good idea not to tell him she'd shared his slip-up about Marcia dying of an overdose with the entire book club.

"So we're missing critical data," Emily said thoughtfully. "How do we solve this mystery without knowing the autopsy results? In particular, the toxicology?"

"Right," Dustin said. "Slow your roll until we get a clearer picture."

"If these test results aren't completed before the end of Equi X," Clint said, "the person responsible may get away."

"If there's a person responsible," Dustin said.

"Homicide," Callie said. "According to Drew, that implies someone else was involved."

"And then there's Winston," Emily said.

"Tied up in the hayloft?" Shanice asked. "The two questions are, did Marcia tether her own cat in that barn, or did someone use Winston to lure her there?"

"Winston was definitely Marcia's cat," Callie said, holding the fluffball protectively. "Alistair doesn't seem much interested in him."

"Making the cat expendable," Makenzie said. "He knew Marcia was attached to her cat. And aren't spouses the first suspects police question?"

Dustin ignored her as he helped himself to another scoop of

arroz con pollo.

"Is Alistair's presence accounted for during the timeframe of Marcia's demise?" Emily asked. Callie almost laughed at how she stared pointedly at Dustin, while he studiously concentrated on his plate.

Callie shook her head. "Alistair seems genuinely broken up about Marcia. If he had anything to do with her passing, he's sure a great actor."

Dustin was silent as a sphinx.

"You're not going to give our private investigators even a hint," Clint said with a smile.

"The ladies are doin' pretty good all on their own," the deputy said.

Which Callie figured might mean they were on the right track. Or that they were so far afield, there was no way the Rose Creek Reads book club could interfere with the police investigation.

Emily placed her napkin on the table. "It's obvious we won't make any more progress at the moment. I'm going to the mini-horse demo. Do you need help cleaning up?"

After Clint assured everyone he had the kitchen duties well in hand, they hurried off to the workshops. Callie bused dishes from the table to the counter. Clint took a stack of plates from her hands and set them down, then grasped her hands in his.

"I will take care of this," he said. "Go talk to your horses."

"Honey, you're the best." Callie kissed his cheek.

Clint always knew how to restore Callie's mental well-being, and it typically involved horse time. She headed for a small pasture behind the old barn where she and Clint had moved their horses.

Callie finally had a moment of relative solitude. She leaned against the top railing and watched as Big Mama plodded slowly toward her. The large gray mare's face and lower legs were a darker shade of gray. She rested her whiskery chin on the railing.

This was the reason she'd wanted a ranch after unexpectedly making a fortune developing a security software.

Not for some sort of prestige, but for the space. Being able to escape into the acres of pasture and woods. The riding trails.

Maybe that's what she needed right now. A trail ride with her favorite mutt of a mare. Get away from the pretentious, neurotic upper crust types, both human and equine.

"Hello."

Great. Some folks just can't stand to see a person enjoying a moment of peace and quiet. She turned to face a stranger. He thrust out a hand.

"I'm Ted Fulson."

Callie reluctantly shook hands with him. His grip was firm, but his hand was soft.

"Callie Garcia."

"This is a nice spread you have," Ted said. "Eight hundred acres?"

"Um, yeah." That was a matter of public record.

"You own the mineral rights."

It was a statement, not a question. Clint and Callie had made sure the mineral rights were attached to the land before buying the ranch.

"What was your name again?" she asked.

Ted reached into an interior pocket of his tailored jacket and extracted a business card. "Ted Fulson. With Fulson Minerals Acquisition."

Callie glanced at the card, then slid it into a back pocket of her jeans. "You here for the Equi X events?"

"I do love horses," Ted gushed. "I'm told some of these ponies are worth a pretty penny. That's a nice-looking piece of horseflesh."

Is this guy for real? Callie patted Big Mama's nose. The mare was of unknown parentage, a rescue horse, with draft horse in her bloodline giving her the solid build. Big Mama had been owned by a guy back east who wanted to go off the grid and farm using draft horses instead of tractors. Knowing nothing about either farming or horses, he'd swiftly gone belly up. Callie had bought Big Mama for five hundred dollars eight years ago.

This Ted guy knew nothing about horses. Big Mama was both worthless and priceless.

"So what are you after, Ted?" Callie asked.

"I can tell you're a gal who likes to get straight to the point. Mineral rights, ma'am. My firm purchases rights from folks who have no use for them. Drilling for oil or natural gas is an expensive proposition. Few people have the resources to invest in mineral exploration and extraction."

"I'm not interested."

Callie turned away, heading to the new barn. The guy followed her.

"Perhaps you aren't aware of the potential value, just sitting underground. Even if no one ever chooses to extract the minerals, you can make a small fortune selling the rights. You get paid while my company takes all the risks."

Callie stopped, turning to face the man. His face brightened at the prospect of a potential sale, until he noticed the expression on her face.

"There are a lot of wealthy people here this weekend," Callie said. "I know you couldn't have picked me out of the crowd as a woman of means, in my ratty jeans and scuffed boots. Who set you loose here?"

"Alistair Fallows pointed you out," Ted said, "after I approached him, thinking he might be the ranch's owner."

Of course. Alistair had that look. Money. Some people exuded it like a cologne. The way they dressed. Their mannerisms. Polish acquired from prep school, maybe. Callie knew serious money often looked remarkably ordinary. But most people were suckers for appearances.

"I'm not interested," Callie said. "And if I have to tell you a third time, I'll let my ranch foreman do the talkin' with a shotgun full of birdshot."

Ted's eyebrows lifted. "A simple no would suffice."

He spun around on one heel of his way-too-new and clean cowboy boots.

Yeesh. Callie was glad she had somewhere to go later.

Makenzie's small-town backyard barbecue would be the perfect antidote to all the snobbery and phony people invading her ranch.

Chapter Fifteen

Dad's backyard barbecue had turned out better than either Makenzie or her mother expected. He had done a terrific job creating an attractive outdoor living area. And without sustaining injuries. Dustin had convinced Clyde it wasn't cheating to hire a professional to put the roof on the gazebo. The project was worth celebrating.

The party was in full swing by the time Makenzie and Dustin arrived midafternoon. It seemed like half of Rose Creek was crammed onto the Selkirk's neatly trimmed lawn.

"Good," Mona said when Makenzie walked into the kitchen. "I need a hand. Can you slice this cake? People seem to do better when dessert is ready to serve."

"Are we late?" Makenzie asked. "We're already at dessert?"

"The party is open-ended," Mona said. "Some people came in time for lunch. Others haven't arrived yet."

"Like my friends." Makenzie grabbed a knife and began cutting a sheet cake into squares. "They're still attending workshops, and they'll need to clean up before coming over."

"There's plenty of food," Mona said, "no matter how late they arrive."

"Are Peaches and Pat Pat doing okay?"

"When I peeked in earlier, they both wanted to join the party. But I can't bear the thought of them getting hurt, tangling up in someone's feet who's more focused on a plate of food than on a little kitten playing on the floor."

"I agree," Makenzie said. "Speaking of cats, it sounds like

Spirit might have saved Tobias Falk from a burglar. But she couldn't keep him from tripping over a box and falling."

"Oh, no. Falls are dangerous for the elderly. Was he hurt?"

"Drew took him to urgent care," Makenzie said. "I haven't heard a report yet."

"I knew Spirit would make a good companion for Tobias," Mona said.

"Me, too," Makenzie said. "Tobias adores Spirit. I hope he recovers quickly, and can still care for the cat. She can't return to the barnyard life after a taste of indoor living."

Spirit had inserted herself in Makenzie's life this May, demanding help for her litter of trapped kittens. Makenzie and her mother had found homes for the feral litter. Placing Spirit had been a challenge.

"If Drew makes it to the party," Makenzie said, "we can find out exactly what happened."

A guest stepped into the kitchen from the backyard.

"Where do you want salads?" Clarice Weddell asked. The elderly church lady balanced a plate with a wobbly lime green mound filled with carrots and celery.

After attending to the gelatin mold, Makenzie tiptoed to the guest room. She didn't like crowds. Being at the ranch had just about drained her sociability quota, but her folks would be disappointed if she didn't participate in the party. *Just a little kitten time will refresh me.*

Mom and Dad showered the fur balls with toys. Makenzie dangled feathers, rolled crinkle balls, and tossed felt mice until the kittens seemed satisfied. She snuck out, closing the door carefully. No escapees.

Clint and Callie arrived at the late end of dinnertime, dressed in cool casual wear. Callie cleaned up nice, when she wasn't in her usual jeans and boots. They loaded sturdy paper plates with food. When Drew and her family walked into the backyard, Makenzie hurried to welcome them. Parker had brought his puppy. Joel steered him to the kid corner of the yard, where lawn games like corn hole, croquet, and foam darts were in use. He joined Clint in an attempt to organize kids in a state of sugar overload into playing games.

"How is your uncle?" Makenzie asked Drew in the kitchen.

The lawyer placed modest portions of salads next to a barbecue beef slider. Her bright sundress was way different from the tailored designer suits she used to wear. But those suits couldn't accommodate the little baby bump the loose folds of the sundress flowed over.

"He'll be fine," Drew said. "The urgent care doctor took X-rays. Nothing's broken. He has a big bruise on his right hip and thigh."

"Poor guy," Makenzie said. "What happened?"

"Uncle Tobias told the doctor a story so strange, it might be true. He said someone tried to open a window in his office late last night. He wouldn't have noticed, except Spirit made a fuss. Downstairs in the dark, he tripped over a box of legal briefs sitting on the floor. He credits the cat with saving him from an intruder. Now Uncle Tobias is more attached to Spirit than ever."

"That's a relief," Makenzie said. "Oh, I didn't mean it that way. It's just that it was difficult to find Spirit a good home. She and Tobias seem to get along so well."

"I'm afraid I might need to ask a big favor," Drew said.

"Anything."

"We're bringing Tobias to my house for a few days," Drew said. "Just until he isn't hobbling so badly. We can't bring Spirit because of Boomer. It would be too chaotic."

"And you need someone to keep her," Makenzie said.

"I was thinking more of someone to drop by to feed her and change the litter," Drew said. "I don't want things to be inconvenient."

"It would be easier to bring her here," Makenzie said. "My place is kitten-proof. Mom can watch Pat Pat for a few days. Probably not a good idea to put my boy with his momma so soon after weaning."

"Good point," Drew said. "Will tomorrow morning work? After your church service?"

"Before would be better. I'm going to the ranch with Dustin after church."

"Terrific," Drew said. "My uncle will be relieved Spirit is in good hands."

"I realize you were preoccupied with more important things at the clinic," Makenzie said, "but did your uncle happen to mention whether he heard anything about an autopsy report?"

Drew shook her head. "It hasn't been released. He's certain his 'little birdie' would have clued him in by now. Of course, our book club questions weren't a priority for Tobias today."

"Did you call the police?"

"About his fall?"

"No, about the window," Makenzie said. "If someone was really trying to break in," Makenzie began, then hesitated. "Um, I mean, he's not showing any signs that his mental faculties might be slipping?"

"None that I've seen," Drew said. "Uncle Tobias runs a law office. He's sharper than most people half his age. He doesn't show any signs of dementia."

"Why didn't he call the police last night?" Makenzie asked.

"He was in a lot of pain," Drew said. "That may have distracted him. When I took him to the urgent care clinic today, my only concern was getting him medical care."

"Half the police department is here," Makenzie said. "I know just who you should talk to."

*   *   *

Drew knew Officer Chandler. The curvy blonde had answered Drew's call for help when her home had been burglarized in April. After relaying Uncle Tobias's story to her, Sarah encouraged Drew to report the potential break-in attempt at Tobias's combination law office and home.

"It happened late last night," Drew said. "I hope we didn't wait too long."

"It's not too late." Sarah waved a rib bone to emphasize her point. "Other people in the neighborhood could be in danger. Tobias could be in danger if the person comes back."

"I'll bring him around tomorrow morning. Will anyone be available to take a report on a Sunday morning?"

"Yes, we're staffed twenty-four seven," Sarah said. "Is Tobias at home alone now?"

"No," Drew said. "The doctor doesn't want him climbing stairs. So he's at my house. His house, actually. We rent it from him. There's a bedroom on the ground floor."

"Yeah, I remember the layout," Sarah said. "That's good. Just in case there was an attempted burglary. An eighty-something year old man with a bum leg doesn't need to be home alone. Although I guess he's alone right now?"

"We're not staying much longer," Drew said. "We've had a busy day."

Not long after her conversation with Officer Chandler, Drew rounded up her family. Parker played croquet with the Esselberry kids while Boomer chased after a tennis ball thrown by Suzie.

"I'm not tired," Parker protested. "I want to stay."

"We're in the middle of a game." Jill swung the croquet mallet idly by her side.

The day had begun on a sour note when Parker tried to weasel out of attending temple. Then he'd said hurtful things about not wanting a baby in the family. Drew had argued against Joel grounding their son, and not allowing him to ride in the parade. Parker seemed emboldened by escaping punishment for his attitude. Now he was attempting to write the script again.

"We're leaving." Joel reached for Parker's hand. "Now."

"No." Parker jerked his hand away. "I'm finishing the game."

"Parker."

"It's okay," Jill told Parker, her freckled face looking serious. "We can finish later."

"Put the mallet away," Joel said. "It's past time to go."

When he reached a second time for Parker, the boy jerked

the wooden mallet to the side. The handle slipped from Parker's hand. The mallet flew past Tommy Esselberry, just missing him. Jill screamed as the mallet hit the cedar fence with a solid *thunk*.

A stunned silence followed the scream. Then Tommy launched himself at Parker, fists circling in a frenzy. After Tommy landed a couple of punches, Joel and Jim Esselberry pulled the boys apart.

"Hey, guys." Jim held a struggling Tommy by the shoulders. "That's enough. Parker wasn't trying to hit you on purpose."

"I'll whack you!" Tommy yelled.

Parker's face was white. Drew was certain he wasn't afraid of Tommy hitting him again. They tussled often enough. Maybe she was making excuses for her son, but he appeared to be stunned by the mallet's near miss. Still, it was shocking to see Parker so out of control.

"Parker is obviously overtired," Joel said. "He's having an attitude problem."

"Kids," Jim said. "They're always testing the boundaries."

"Apparently, Parker's boundaries have stretched too far," Joel said. "Getting into a fight is the last straw."

Parker's face crumpled as he struggled against tears. "No." He gathered Boomer into his arms. "I'm sorry, Dad."

"It's too late for apologies," Joel said. "Get your hat. We're leaving."

"We need to make sure Uncle Tobias is settled in," Drew said. "And it's way past Boomer's bedtime."

"Okay," Parker said.

When Parker trudged slowly to a picnic table to fetch his cowboy hat, Jim put a hand on Joel's shoulder.

"Giving kids a little free rein once in a while doesn't hurt," Jim said. "You know. Boys will be boys."

"I appreciate the parenting advice," Joel said, but his tone of voice clearly indicated he didn't.

Drew's hormones chose that moment to go into override. She tried to hide the tears filling her eyes as they left the party.

*   *   *

Makenzie glimpsed Drew and her family hustling out of the yard. They didn't appear to be enjoying themselves. The day had been hot, and Drew was almost five months pregnant. Maybe she'd gotten over tired.

Finding out whether something was wrong would have to wait. Makenzie was learning how chatty Dustin's friends in the police force could be in social situations.

"You wouldn't believe the things people do to themselves," night desk receptionist and police dispatcher Gracie Arnold said. She was one of those women with such a pretty face and flawless, deep brown skin, she could wear her tight black curls shaved extremely short and still look feminine. "Night shift is the craziest."

Makenzie glanced around. Dustin was talking to Henry and his wife. The Holloways were wearing cute matching blue-checkered Western shirts. Well, maybe cute wasn't the word to use for the barrel-chested, bristle-haired chief of police. While Dustin was distracted, she needed to get some answers.

"Is it true people take drugs meant for animals?" Makenzie asked Gracie.

The receptionist grimaced, then nodded toward Dustin and the Holloways. They had joined the kids at the corn hole game.

"I can't give you any information about an active case," Gracie said. "The boss would not be happy with me."

"I respect that," Makenzie said. "But I already have information. My friend Callie found Marcia, and heard her say the words quebrachine and xylazine. Aren't those animal drugs?"

"A Google search would give you this info, so I suppose it won't hurt to tell you. Keep in mind, I haven't seen an autopsy report, so this may not apply to Marcia at all. But yes, they are both animal drugs."

"The quebrachine can be used by humans, too," Makenzie said. "People, or specifically men, use it to help with, uh, bedroom issues?"

"Right. Available over-the-counter. But it's also used by veterinarians to bring animals out of sedation."

"The xylazine could be used as a sedative if an animal has an operation?" Makenzie remembered how groggy Spirit had been after her spaying procedure.

"That, and you might need an animal kept calm for other reasons. Unfortunately, people have been known to take animal sedatives."

"Like for fun?" Makenzie asked.

"It takes all types." Gracie rolled her eyes. "Xylazine is incredibly dangerous for humans. The dealers mix it with other stuff like fentanyl, making overdose deaths more likely. But stupid knows no bounds."

"Marcia didn't sound like a drug addict," Makenzie said. "She was a senior-aged lady who owned a horse farm."

"You never know," Gracie said. "Some of the most respectable people have the ugliest skeletons in their closets."

Makenzie felt a hand on her shoulder. She yelped, startled, as she turned. Dustin did not look happy.

"Hi Dustin. Finished with your game?" Makenzie asked.

"I hope you weren't prying for clues," he said, turning his glare from Makenzie to the receptionist. "Gracie, my girlfriend's not on the staff, you know."

Gracie fixed her own formidable look on Dustin. "I would never divulge information about an active case. Or even a closed one. I know the rules."

"You can trust Gracie," Makenzie said. "She didn't tell me anything." *Nothing I hadn't already figured out, anyway.*

"Makenzie, you know better." Dustin steered her away from Gracie. "How about you quit playing detective long enough to have some cake and ice cream with me?"

"Why waste time on cake?" Makenzie asked. "I know the hosts. They purchased three kinds of pie from The Stockman's Café."

"What are we waiting for?" He reached for her hand and

gave it a squeeze.

Makenzie breathed a silent sigh of relief. Dustin didn't seem upset. Makenzie hadn't learned much from Gracie. But the conversation had strengthened one of the book club's theories.

What if Marcia were a closet junkie who accidentally overdosed on street drugs?

Chapter Sixteen

Lunch at Callie's had been hours ago. Shanice regretted saving her appetite for Makenzie's barbecue. Her stomach growled as she waited for Sam to turn his gorgeous black and white Appaloosa mare into a paddock.

"Finally done," Sam said, latching the gate securely. "I'm ready for dinner."

"I'm starved," Shanice admitted. "I hope they left us something."

"I need to wash up first," Sam said. "Let's take the shortcut."

All day, the new barn had been crowded with trainers, participants, and spectators. The summer sun was low in the sky. Only a few people lingered. Most had gone to the big white tent for their dinners.

Sydney Byron led her chestnut gelding toward his stall. After overhearing her ugly gossip in the tent Thursday night, Shanice wasn't anxious to engage in casual chit-chat with the woman. Instead, she focused on the tall thoroughbred.

"Good evening," Sam said.

"Hello, Dr. Grady." Sydney glanced at Shanice, a question in her eyes, so Sam made introductions. Then the conversation was all about horses. As expected.

"Sir Maximus flew over the jumps like he had wings," Sam said. "He should be ready for any competition."

"That's kind of you to say, Doctor," Sydney said. She tugged off her helmet, revealing her dark pixie-cut hair, flattened and messy. "Unfortunately, I'm afraid he passed his peak last year. He was ready to take every cup. We lost the entire season due to the disqualification. And now he's fifteen years old."

"Don't count him out," Sam said. He turned to Shanice, cluing her in on the facts. "Olympic jumpers don't enter competition until nine years of age. They tend to peak by age eleven, but some compete until the ripe old age of twenty. I believe Sir Maximus has what it takes to be in this for the long run."

Sydney shook her head. "His heart isn't in it. Or maybe it's my heart. I don't expect him to do well this winter. I'm training his replacement, but I doubt Ladybird is at a level to beat the competition."

"I hate to be the one to tell you," Sam said, "but your attitude is what could sink your chances."

Shanice agreed, although she kept her opinion to herself. Sydney struck her as a young woman as pampered as her show horses. When everything came easily to a person, their sense of appreciation for the little successes in life seemed to fade.

"Spoken like the famous horse psychologist," Sydney said. "But I ask you this. How could I not be devastated? My once-in-a-lifetime opportunity was crushed by Marcia Bentworth-Fallows."

Sam laughed. "How old are you, Sydney?"

"A gentleman is not supposed to ask a lady her age," Sydney said with a mock haughty air. She smiled. "Twenty-six."

A year younger than me.

"There it is," Sam said. "You're way too young to count yourself out. People many decades older than you still participate in the equestrian Olympics. And win."

Shanice had learned that, unlike most Olympic sports, dressage and jumper equestrians often competed as senior citizens.

"Thank you for the reminder," Sydney said. "I do have a future. I've allowed myself to be angry too long about losing an entire year due to an incompetent trainer. Imagine my shock, though, when I see her at this ranch, facing no consequences for causing my Sir Maximus to be disqualified. It stirred up the old resentments."

A woman dressed in jeans and a long-sleeved T-shirt walked up to Sydney. With barely a glance to acknowledge her, Sydney handed the reins to the older woman. Curly, dark-blonde hair framed a weathered face that was past the preventative effects of sunscreen. Shanice thought the woman's presence would end the conversation, but Sydney continued talking as though she wasn't there.

"I'll agree with you, Doctor," Sydney continued, "that perhaps I have many more years to spend in athletic competition, but a horse's lifespan is much shorter."

The careworn blonde woman began the unsaddling process, handling Sir Maximus like a pro. She must have been a horse groom, as anonymous in the elite equestrian world as a butler in an English estate of yesteryear. Or maybe butlers were still in vogue amongst the wealthy?

"Was Marcia your horse's trainer?" Shanice asked.

"Was, yes, until she gave him an injection to calm him for trailering. Sir Maximus was randomly tested." Tears welled in her eyes. "And banned from the sport for a year."

Bitterness was a poison too many people carried in their hearts.

"Marcia is dead," Shanice said a little more abruptly than she intended. The woman's tears didn't fool her. Sydney was the queen of snarky gossip. "That should settle your disagreement with her. Very permanently."

Sydney didn't seem phased in the least by Shanice's tone. But Sam looked uncomfortable.

"My father had been considering speaking with his lawyer about suing Marcia," Sydney said. "Now I suppose we'll have to sue her estate."

When the groom led her tall chestnut horse into his stall, Sydney closed the gate. The equestrian version of slamming a door in a person's face, Shanice guessed. Sydney walked away, never having so much as said "hello" to the groom.

When Sam had guided her out of the barn and to the field where his trailer was parked, Shanice stopped.

"Sam, I am so sorry. I should have kept my mouth shut. I was angry about the things she and that other woman said about Marcia."

"No need to apologize," Sam said. "You're new to this world."

"Horses?"

"The horses are the reason I stay in this business," Sam said. "What causes me the rare occasional doubts are the ultra-wealthy who treat their horses with more respect than they do their fellow human beings. It's been a long day. Let's go spend time with normal people."

*   *   *

By the time Shanice and Sam arrived, the Selkirk's barbecue was winding down. Callie was sorry to miss a chance to compare notes with Drew, and neither Emiko nor Emily had attended the barbecue. The book club would need to hold a catch-up session at Rose Creek Reads soon.

Callie joined Makenzie on the covered swing in a quiet corner of the yard. Shanice dragged a canvas camp chair closer. The men sat under the gazebo, yakking about whether barbecue sauce without tomatoes should be outlawed, or was the hottest new thing.

"I didn't talk to Drew," Callie said. "We still don't know the autopsy results?"

Makenzie glanced around, probably checking to make sure her boyfriend or his police coworkers weren't listening in on their conversation.

"Paranoid?" Shanice asked with a smile.

"You know how Dustin feels about me being involved in investigations," she whispered.

"We know. It's not okay," Shanice said, "until your murder

127

board reveals the connections that solve the case, and then it's okay." She raised her hands when Makenzie began to object. "I'm glad we have someone on our team to keep us from interfering with the police."

"Agreed," Callie said. "I'd hate to be responsible for messin' things up, and lettin' a killer walk free." She carried a heavy enough burden of guilt, thinking maybe she could have done more for Marcia.

"Drew said her uncle hasn't heard anything about the autopsy," Makenzie said. "She doesn't think it's been released, because his contact is very reliable."

"That would sure help," Callie said. "Between that Gemma girl saying Marcia overdosed, and hearin' stories about animal drugs, human drugs, and drug abuse, I don't know what to think. Maybe Marcia accidentally killed herself?"

"That's a consideration," Shanice said. "Just because Marcia had enemies doesn't mean anyone killed her."

"Don't forget, though," Makenzie said. "Homicide means another person caused the death. I mean, it could be an accidental overdose, but there was another person involved."

"That's what I understood," Shanice said. "Some of the elite ladies had a very unlady-like conversation about Marcia."

Shanice reminded her friends about the disgusting and catty conversation she'd overheard. Callie winced at the harsh words the women had shared in public, not seeming to care who overheard.

"Sam and I ran into one of them on the way out of the barn tonight," Shanice continued. "Sydney blamed Marcia for causing her horse to be disqualified from competition last year."

"A motivation for murder?" Makenzie asked as she tapped notes into her phone.

"Over a horse show," Callie said. "That's just sad. I mean, we're talking Olympics qualifications, but still."

"You love your horses for just being horses," Shanice said to Callie. "Sam thinks some humans have horses as extensions of their own egos."

"Or cats," Makenzie said. "I wonder if Marcia's fancy Persian cat was just another status symbol."

Shanice shook her head. "I heard Alistair say Marcia treated the cat like it was her baby. They didn't have human children."

A situation Callie feared she was headed for. Crazy old horse lady. *Maybe I should ask Alistair if I can keep Winston as my starter pack for becoming a crazy cat lady.*

"Winston was well-loved," Callie said. "I can vouch for that. The poor boy clings to me like he's terrified." She felt a twinge of pain for the kitty. "Lost. And Alistair doesn't seem like he's in a hurry to take the cat back. The gossip girls suggested Alistair might be happy to be rid of Marcia." And he might also be happy to be rid of Winston.

"A client of Marcia's is still mad a year later that she caused a horse to be disqualified from competition," Makenzie said, repeating the information. She glanced at Shanice, who nodded. Makenzie kept tapping notes on her phone. "Red Alert Organized Rescue, otherwise known as RAOR, came to the ranch to protest horse doping."

"One protestor handcuffed herself to the barn," Shanice said. "Aster has 24/7 access to the ranch, and she's part of that group."

Clint wouldn't appreciate his cousin George's girlfriend being put on the book club's suspect list, but Callie didn't object. George was still living rent-free at the ranch. Aster should have been sensitive to the negative "vibe" that the protest brought to the Double C, plus the fact that George owed his ongoing recovery from alcoholism, at least in part, to his cousin Clint's patient and caring acceptance.

"Marcia's last words," Callie said, "to me, anyway, was to name two drugs. One to sedate animals, and the other to bring them out of sedation."

"Both are used by humans, too," Makenzie said. "I just received even more confirmation of that fact from Gracie Arnold, the police dispatcher. The same things Clint told you about his research."

The more they learned, the less helpful the information seemed. Marcia thought the two drugs were worth using her last breath to relay to Callie. For what purpose?

"I wish Marcia could have been more clear," Callie said. "Why did she mention those drugs? To tell me somethin' about horse doping? To confess her own drug use? To tell me someone injected her in a murder attempt? It's so frustratin'. Maybe she said something else to the paramedics we don't know about that might explain everything. Before she . . ."

The swing creaked in the silence as Callie recalled her encounter with Ted Fulson.

"Drew and her uncle are workin' on a case about mineral rights, aren't they?" she asked.

"Yes, and Joel is interested, too," Shanice said. "It's the first glimmer of hope Drew has had that he could be lured away from Boston. Mineral rights law is a big business. Lots of lawyers involved. Lots of litigation."

"What does this have to do with Marcia?" Makenzie asked.

"Not sure," Callie said. "This slick salesman type guy approached me before your party." She reached into her skirt pocket and pulled out a business card. "I brought it in case Drew was here. Ted Fulson from Fulson Minerals Acquisition. He wants to buy our mineral rights. So I guess if he was really lookin' to buy, not sell, that makes him a slick buyer? Doesn't have the same ring. Oh well. Anyway, he claimed Alistair sent him my way."

"That's easy enough to check," Makenzie said. "Although this Ted guy could have just used the name of someone with money to get his foot in the door for his sales – er – buy pitch."

"I can't imagine Clint would be interested in selling off something of potential value like that," Shanice said.

"I didn't mention it to him," Callie said. "Yet. Clint's been talkin' of ways to expand the facilities to accommodate more big events like Equi X. Havin' a chunk of money might convince him to make the investment."

"Not to be nosey," Shanice said, "but do you need a windfall like that to be able to expand?"

"Probably not," Callie said. "I just don't want any encouragement for this idea that we could host more of these deals. It's been hard enough just tryin' to make it through this weekend."

Clint walked toward the swing. He probably wanted to leave, so he could get back to planning a ranch expansion Callie was sure would make her life miserable.

"Looks like my ride's ready to go," she said.

"I'll update my board with the new data," Makenzie said. "We need to stay on top of things in case this homicide turns into a murder."

"Then let's schedule a book club meeting," Shanice said. "If everyone can get away for a couple of hours. It is a busy weekend."

"I'll make time," Callie said. "Text me." She stood, heading Clint off at the pass. "Ready to go, babe?"

Clint kissed her cheek. "I'm exhausted, and tomorrow will begin early. We should try to get a good night's sleep."

Callie hoped she could. It might be hard, considering there could be a murderer loose on the ranch.

Chapter Seventeen

Makenzie drove to Tobias's law office early Sunday morning. The plan: pick up the cat, then drop it off at her house before going to church. Mom had agreed to take Pat Pat for a few days. It would just confuse the kittens so soon after they'd been weaned, to reunite with their mother.

A police cruiser sat out front, parked next to Drew's Audi. Makenzie retrieved the cat carrier from the back seat of her late-model Buick and walked up the stone steps.

"Hello?"

The front door was open a crack. Spirit could escape. If she hadn't already.

"Come on in," Drew called. "I'm in the office."

Makenzie stepped inside, closing the door behind her. Officer Sarah Chandler stood next to the window in Tobias's office.

"It doesn't appear the intruder got it open," Sarah said. "We're dusting for fingerprints outside."

"What if we hadn't been in town?" Drew asked. "What if he couldn't reach a phone to call for help?"

Drew was so emotional lately. Makenzie chalked it up to the effects of pregnancy, a situation she'd read about in women's ezines, but had yet to experience herself.

"Tobias was able to drive himself to the ranch," Makenzie said, hoping that pointing out the facts would prevent Drew from spiraling into tears.

"At the clinic, they told us this sort of injury gets worse

before it starts healing," Drew said. "If he hadn't come to the ranch, he might have become too stiff and in pain—"

"But it didn't happen that way," Makenzie said.

She looked around the office, dominated by a huge dark wood desk and tall windows covered by sheer curtains. Boxes towered next to a filing cabinet. Papers cluttered the desk.

"I know," Drew said, following Makenzie's gaze. "This is no environment for an old man. It's a miracle he hasn't fallen before. Or broken his neck on the staircase."

"Where is Spirit?"

"Up those horrible stairs. I'm having nightmares imagining Uncle Tobias tripping over that animal and tumbling all the way down."

"But he didn't." Makenzie's firm statement finally seemed to hit the pause button on Drew's escalation into panic. "Everything is okay."

"You're right." Drew inhaled, then released the breath. "Everything is going to be okay, but only because we were in Rose Creek, not Boston."

Tobias had friends. Half the town would drop everything to come to the octogenarian lawyer's aid if they knew he had a need. But now wasn't the time to point that out to Drew.

"The cat?" she asked, lifting the cat carrier as she raised her eyebrows.

"I locked her in Uncle Tobias's bedroom," Drew said. "Follow me."

The staircase to the second floor was narrow and steep.

"How does Tobias manage these stairs?" Makenzie asked. "I would have a hard time climbing these every day."

"Several times a day," Drew said. "He claims it's what helps keep him young."

Drew pushed open the bedroom door. Makenzie slipped in behind her and pushed the door closed. She knew firsthand how quickly cats could escape rooms.

Spirit sat in the middle of the bed on what looked like a handmade quilt in golds, browns, and greens. The room was tidy.

Makenzie wasn't sure of the significance of some of the artwork and knick-knacks, but she thought they must be related to Tobias's Jewish faith. One framed photo on the dresser showed Mrs. Falk in her forties.

"Your great aunt was beautiful," Makenzie said.

Drew lifted the silver frame. "Yes, in heart as well as appearance. It's a shame they were not able to have children. But the rest of the family made up for it."

"Meow." Spirit stood and stretched.

"I hope this isn't too much of an imposition," Drew said.

Makenzie loaded Spirit into the cat carrier with surprisingly little drama.

"Mom and I have the situation under control. Peaches and Pat Pat will stay at my parents' house, and Spirit will be with me."

"I hope this is only temporary," Drew said. "But my uncle is getting older. I really don't think he can live alone much longer. We have the puppy. The baby early next year." She placed a hand on the noticeable swell of her stomach. "That's if we're here. The thought of trying to convince Tobias to move to Boston . . ."

Tears filled her eyes.

Here we go. Makenzie hoped she didn't act this crazy if she and Dustin eventually got married and were blessed with children. She wasn't a people sort of person, and didn't have a smooth, natural ability to comfort others. Especially a woman in the throes of irrational hormones.

What would Mom do?

Makenzie led her friend to the bed and pushed her to sit. She sank onto the quilt next to her, wrapping an arm around Drew's shoulders.

"It'll all work out," Makenzie said.

Drew sniffled for a silent minute. Makenzie was afraid she'd go into full meltdown, but Sarah yelled up the stairs.

"Drew? Makenzie?"

"Coming." Drew stood, dabbing at her eyes with a tissue.

Another uniformed officer waited with Officer Chandler at the bottom of the stairs. Makenzie struggled to carry Spirit in the pet suitcase without bumping her against the walls. *These steps are a nightmare.*

"There's some damage to the exterior of the window frame," the male officer said. "Not enough to compromise the integrity of the window, but your uncle should probably have a handyman look at it soon."

"Someone pried at the latch area with some sort of tool," Sarah said.

"That's terrible," Drew said.

"Why would someone try to get in here?" Makenzie asked. "I mean, it's just a lot of papers and stuff."

"Valuable antiques?" Officer Chandler asked, glancing around. "You'd be surprised the lengths to which people go to steal items of less value than old clocks. And I see some ceramic art pottery. Like the stuff from your factory, Makenzie."

The response wasn't really satisfactory, but unfortunately, probably true. Makenzie didn't understand the criminal mind.

That's probably a good thing. Until the book club is trying to solve a case. Then it could come in handy.

"You're right. Some of the Brieswell pottery is worth a lot," Makenzie said. "I noticed some nice early pieces on the fireplace mantle."

"Could someone have been after legal files?" Drew asked.

"We might never know," Sarah said. "Since they didn't get inside."

"Is it okay to have repairs made?" Drew asked. "Are you done examining the window?"

"I found prints and took photos," the male officer said. "But if the wannabe burglar wore gloves, the prints might belong to the last window cleaner or repair person Tobias hired."

Spirit meowed.

"I'd better get her home," Makenzie said. "Unless you want me to stick around, Drew?"

"I'm fine. I need to go home, too."

"I'll see you at the bookstore later," Makenzie said.

She waved goodbye to Sarah as she exited the cluttered Victorian-style house.

Drew's family was growing. When Makenzie first met the lawyer, she had lived in the old farmhouse with her son, Parker. Now her husband Joel was a frequent visitor, and the puppy Boomer was a new addition. Uncle Tobias could become a permanent resident. In a few months, a baby would be added to the mix.

Makenzie glanced at the cat carrier. Spirit poked her nose against the mesh.

"Is there going to be room in their house for you, kitty?"

* * *

When Drew reached the porch of the farmhouse she rented from her uncle, Joel stepped outside.

"Did you miss me?" Drew asked with a smile.

"We need to talk." Joel glanced over his shoulder, then steered Drew back down the stone steps and onto the sidewalk. "It's about Tobias."

Drew's uncle had only been living with them since yesterday evening. Not even twenty-four hours had passed. Were things falling apart already?

"The police found evidence someone attempted to pry open his office window," Drew said.

They strolled slowly along the sidewalk under the shade of leafy trees. This early, it was already warm. Sunday was going to be another hot, dry, late summer day.

"That's disturbing," Joel said.

"A burglar tried to enter his office in the middle of the night. That's terrifying. Is this what you wanted to talk about? Or is it about Parker?"

"This involves them both." Joel had a grim set to his jaw. "Tobias decided to clue me in on his big surprise birthday present for Parker."

"I've been wondering," Drew said. "He's been hinting about it for over a week."

"It is big," Joel said. "Really big. A horse."

"I had my suspicions." Drew stopped. "But I was hoping I was wrong."

A neighbor waved at them from his front porch, greeting them cheerfully. They waved back and continued walking.

"How can he give Parker a horse?" Drew asked. "Without discussing it with us first? That's a huge commitment."

"One we can't accept," Joel said. "We can't hope to move a horse anywhere near Boston. The costs would be prohibitive."

"You didn't want Parker to have a dog," Drew said. "But you changed your mind."

"That was because the condo doesn't allow animals," Joel said. "We'll be selling it soon, provided we can find a house that's a reasonable commuting distance from my office. A place with a yard. Boomer's not going to be a large dog, and basenjis aren't noisy. He'll be fine as long as he has some space to run around, in an area safe enough that Parker can take him for walks. But a horse? Even if we both work, it would be a stretch to afford a horse property anywhere near the city."

"You've decided," Drew said. She pressed her lips tightly together. She'd already made a weepy fool of herself in front of Makenzie. She didn't want to cry again. Or start yelling. "I expect a little more discussion. Joel, our family's future isn't your decision alone."

"Before, I agreed with you," Joel said. "I saw a positive change in our son. But after his attitude yesterday? And the fistfight at Makenzie's barbecue last night?"

"He's dealing with a lot," Drew said.

"And all this uncertainty isn't helping him. I'll admit, your Oklahoma experiment drew Parker out of his shell. And strengthened our marriage. We weathered a separation that dragged on longer than either of us expected. It's time to go home."

"I pulled Parker out of school mid-term this spring," Drew

said. "That was unfair to him. We told him he could attend school here fall semester. We have to let him finish."

Joel shook his head. "When Jim made that boys-will-be-boys crack, I wanted to take Parker back to Boston right then and there."

"I know," Drew said. "That seemed like such an antiquated attitude. We know the Esselberrys. Jim was probably just trying to de-escalate a situation. His kids are reasonably well-behaved."

"Better than Parker is right now," Joel muttered. "Well, we'd better head back. I want to shut down this talk of getting Parker a horse before it's too late."

"If Parker continues his interest in riding," Drew said, "maybe sometime in the future we could consider getting one. But now's not the time. I'm with you on this." As they approached the house, Drew felt herself tensing. Home should be a haven, not a battleground. "Maybe I should tell the ladies I can't make it to the meeting this morning."

"You need to go," Joel said. "Whenever you go to book club, you come home more relaxed."

"Girl time," Drew said. "It's important. We'll have a big brunch when I get back."

Drew imagined the calming effect a nice meal of bakery blueberry muffins, scrambled eggs, and turkey sausage would have on her family. Cooking would calm her nerves.

They walked up the steps. Parker burst out the door.

"I heard Dad and Uncle Tobias talking. He told me everything. I'm getting a horse!"

Chapter Eighteen

Makenzie gave the coffee cups a quick rinse and handed them one by one to Mrs. Weddell to load in the dishwasher. She nearly dropped a saucer. The supply of dishes in the church kitchen cupboards had been dwindling over the months, frequently due to Makenzie's butter-fingers.

This morning, she couldn't stop the gears in her brain from spinning, despite the sermon urging congregants to place their burdens on Jesus. She hoped Jesus could find a way to calm her from worries about her job at Brieswell Pottery, and the body in the hayloft.

Makenzie had signed up weeks ago for the kitchen cleanup crew. Just because her life was crazy was no reason to shirk her commitments to the church ladies. Most of the women were advancing in years. Makenzie was part of the small new guard stepping up to eventually become the next generation of church ladies. The thought made her smile.

She lifted the heavy coffee maker and dumped the remains down the drain. Fortunately, most of the coffee had been consumed. It was still far too heavy for either Mrs. Clarice Weddell or Mrs. Ava Hansen to manage.

Lukewarm coffee splashed into the sink. A tidal wave rushed up the front side of the sink and splashed out, dousing Makenzie.

"It's a good thing you're wearing an apron," Ava said. A smile spread across her plump cheeks, and amusement twinkled in her faded blue eyes. "It'd be a shame to ruin that pretty new dress."

"I lucked out," Makenzie said.

"There is no such thing as luck." Mrs. Weddell sniffed dismissively, looking down her narrow nose at the shorter woman. Although she attended Rose Creek Christian Church, she exhibited a strong streak of Calvinist predeterminism. Everything turned out the way it did by preordination. It was not an attitude Pastor Foster subscribed to, but some folks came to church with their own ideas.

Mrs. Weddell was careful to cover her tailored peach skirt and jacket with an apron. She frequently patted her stiff permed hair into place, even though not a hair had escaped the heavy hold of hairspray. In contrast, Mrs. Hansen had flyaway white curls and a colorful patchwork tunic over leggings.

Makenzie was still finding her signature look. One thing was certain, though. She refused to ever again cover her plus-sized curves under baggy, bland clothes. Today's look was a sleeveless, figure-hugging jersey dress in a summery flower print. Comfortable, yet cute.

When the kitchen met Mrs. Weddell's standards, she left. The woman trusted her minions to properly return the clean silverware to the drawers. Makenzie hadn't realized she'd been holding her breath.

"Maybe now we can relax." A mischievous grin creased Ava's wrinkles deeper. "I like to end my Sunday morning on a peaceful note."

Makenzie couldn't stop her giggle. "Well, it's peaceful now."

"Do you have time for a cup of tea?" Ava asked. "I hate to waste the last of the lemon wafers."

Makenzie suspected Ava was more concerned about returning to her empty apartment than tossing the store-bought cookies. She had been widowed six months ago.

"I have a little time." Makenzie filled a cup with water and placed it in the microwave. Soon, they were both seated at the small kitchen table with hot herb tea and lemon wafers.

"Forgive me for prying," Ava said, "but you seem a little off this morning."

"Oh, just a lot going on."

"Sometimes it helps to talk it out."

Makenzie thought she was doing Mrs. Hansen a favor by chatting over tea. Instead, it was the elderly woman who sought to comfort her.

"I don't want to burden you," Makenzie said. "It's all silly stuff, anyway."

"Nothing is silly if it's weighing on your mind." Ava bit into a cookie and chewed thoughtfully.

"You remember how I found a stray cat with a litter of kittens a couple of months ago?" Makenzie asked.

Ava nodded. "I couldn't take one because of my parakeets. Birds and cats. It didn't seem like a good idea."

"They were feral, actually," Makenzie continued. "But they've adapted to domestic life beautifully. We – my mom and I – managed to find them all homes. But that was only because she and I both adopted kittens." Makenzie pulled her phone out of her skirt pocket and showed Ava the newest photos of Pat Pat and Peaches. "But now I'm worried the mother cat might need to be placed elsewhere. I don't know yet. It bothers me the poor cat might have to be yanked out of what we thought was her forever home."

"The cat made the adjustment once," Ava said. "She'll be fine if she has to go to a new home. But you said you don't know whether that will happen or not. So why fret about it?"

"Okay. You're right. And worst-case scenario, I can take her, and let my mom keep Pat Pat with his sister."

"One problem solved. What else is bothering you?"

"It's that obvious?" Makenzie asked.

"You're wired tight, dear. Don't tell me you're having problems with Dustin? He seems like such a nice young man."

"No. Not at all. It's just that, well, no one knows for sure, but Brieswell might close down, or be downsized, or something. Those of us in the chemistry lab are worried our work might be outsourced."

"Have you told Dustin?" Ava asked.

"I don't want to burden him," Makenzie said. "Especially when I won't even learn what's going to happen until Tuesday."

"Is that fair to Dustin?" Ava asked.

"Fair?"

"If he truly loves you, he's bound to notice your tension. What if he thinks he's the cause of your upset?"

"I hadn't thought of it that way. But there's another thing. I'm afraid he'll feel obligated to be my knight in shining armor."

"Having watched Dustin growing up in this church, I don't think you want to rob him of the opportunity to be your knight."

"Not that I wouldn't mind being swept off my feet and carried into some happily-ever-after," Makenzie said, "but that's not the way things work now days."

"That's such a pity. But you're wrong."

"Oh?" Makenzie was surprised by how blunt the elderly woman was.

"Even in my day, the rescue was mutual," Ava said. "In a marriage, sometimes the husband saves the wife from travails, and other times the roles are reversed."

"We aren't married," Makenzie said. "We're not even engaged."

"Oh, you will be soon," Ava said. "I see all the signs."

Makenzie felt her cheeks heat with a blush, hoping Mrs. Hansen was right.

"I don't want Dustin to propose because I'm destitute," Makenzie said with a laugh. "If the lab closes, I don't know what kind of work I can find in Rose Creek."

"Talk to the boy," Ava said. "Dustin might have to rescue you this time around, but you'll have your turn."

Makenzie's cellphone alarm buzzed. "Time for me to go. Dustin and I are spending the afternoon at the Garcia ranch."

"The big horse event." Mrs. Hansen nodded. "I believe I'm ready to go home to my parakeets."

When she arrived at her small house, Spirit greeted

Makenzie with mews and purring. Well, if she had to, she would keep the mature cat. She would still be close to Pat Pat. Maybe when enough time had passed, the kittens could hang out with their mother without the danger of reverting to their baby relationship with her.

Telling Dustin she might be facing unemployment would be more difficult. Ava was right. She did need to share her fears. Soon.

But first, the book club was meeting to update the murder board.

*   *   *

Shanice settled into a wicker chair on the back deck of Rose Creek Reads. Water splashed over the waterwheel on the side of the brick bookstore. Rose Creek flowed past the lush green lawn, shaded by willow trees. Dragonflies and red-winged blackbirds played in the cattails growing thick along the bank.

She leaned back, making room for the large butterscotch tabby. Mitch launched himself onto her lap, then made himself comfortable.

Of the formerly cat-less book club, she was one of the members to have not succumbed to the temptation of cat ownership. Partly because she lived in an apartment. Besides, she could get her kitty needs met whenever she came to the bookstore.

"Hi Shanice." Emiko exited the back screen door and took a seat at the umbrella-shaded picnic table. She dressed for comfort and the summer heat in cut-off jeans and a baggy T-shirt declaring *Keep calm and trust me, I'm an engineer*. "I haven't talked to you since our little espionage mission."

"What did I miss out on?" Makenzie struggled through the screen door and onto the deck, her arms full. Emiko hopped up to help carry the tri-fold posterboard and a bulging tote bag.

"Old news," Emiko said, reclaiming her seat under the umbrella. "Shanice and my Saturday morning adventure. We already texted the group about it. Where's Agatha?"

If anyone needed a cat, it was Emiko. She was cat crazy. But she was a graduate student and engineering instructor at the university branch. Emiko had resisted taking one of Spirit's kittens, knowing she might move on to a Ph.D. program elsewhere in a couple of years.

The calico with the Elizabethan-style white fur ruff around her neck walked directly to Emiko. "Mew." Agatha allowed Emiko to lift her from the wooden planks and snuggle the cat to her face.

"Makenzie, Callie, and I talked about the case at the barbecue last night," Shanice told Emiko. "Rather than try to do this via texts, we wanted to update the murder board with the entire club, in person."

"We might not have much more to add this morning," Makenzie said, "but every clue helps complete the puzzle." She unfolded the murder board on a small wheeled cart to the side of the picnic table, then extracted sticky notes and markers from her tote bag. "I want to hear all the details about your espionage mission. Spill."

Shanice smiled. The last time the book club had taken on a mystery, she'd been hundreds of miles away, visiting her sisters in Chicago. Another death in Rose Creek was a tragedy. That was nothing to smile about. But she was glad she was in the thick of things this time, ready to apply her expertise to solving the problem.

"Wait for me." Drew pushed open the screen door to the bookstore's back deck. "Sorry I'm late." She looked around the picnic table. "Oh, I'm not last. Scratch that apology."

Drew settled onto a cushioned wicker chair. She looked tired. Shanice's sister Breona had been hyperemotional prior to her delivery of a healthy baby. Drew was thirty-four, just one year older than Breona, but she seemed to be more stressed out. The lawyer also had more going on, with her long-distance marriage and a son turning nine tomorrow.

"The gang's all here," Emiko said, looking toward the

screen door.

Emily backed through the door, holding it open with her backside for Callie. The bookstore owner carried a pitcher of iced tea and a plate of cookies, but Shanice was more interested in the cardboard tray of fancy coffee drinks in Callie's hands.

"We're ready to start our recap session," Makenzie told the newcomers. "Updating the board." She tapped a marker against the tri-fold board papered with colorful sticky notes, pictures, and newspaper clippings.

"That's a good idea," Emily said. "As each of us gathers information, it's easy to forget who knows what."

"Shanice and I were just starting to give Makenzie the details of our espionage mission," Emiko said.

"I'm ready," Makenzie said.

"I've already texted about Gemma, the new instructor at the university, and the veterinary school drug safe." Shanice plucked a coffee drink from the tray and picked a treat from Emily's plate of homemade cookies. "Gemma claims it doesn't contain quebrachine. She didn't mention xylazine."

"Ugh!" Emiko rolled her eyes. "Only because I didn't tell her about it."

"We decided to check the lab safe for the drugs Marcia told Callie about," Shanice said. "In case Gemma was trying to cover up her own involvement."

"We couldn't open the safe," Emiko said, her brown eyes glittering with excitement. She waved her half-eaten snickerdoodle in the air for emphasis, spilling crumbs on Agatha's fur. The cat didn't seem to notice. "We almost got caught. And then when we left, we ran into a vet school student who came in to feed the mice. Shanice bluffed our way out of trouble."

"Now we have what we think might be the safe code," Shanice said. "At the least, it's the code to enter the building. Security at the university could use some help," she said with a nod toward their resident IT expert, Callie. Even though Callie was semi-retired after making a fortune selling her security software, she kept up with industry trends.

"So you don't know what drugs are in the safe?" Makenzie asked, her marker poised over a sticky note.

"Not yet," Emiko said. "We're going back."

A return trip to the lab was definitely in Shanice's future if she wanted to prove Gemma's innocence or guilt.

"Gemma said she did an inventory," Shanice said, "and told us nothing's missing. The conversation felt . . . premature."

"Like a preemptive strike?" Callie asked.

Shanice nodded and sipped her latte, a sweet hazelnut concoction.

"The autopsy report would clear up a lot." Emily held out the plate of cookies, encouraging the ladies to take another. "Until we know the exact cause of death, we can't hope to connect the various dots our group has collected."

"Like whether Marcia overdosed on quebrachine?" Makenzie asked. She shrugged and gave a sheepish smile. "Dustin accidentally confirmed the overdose theory. But not the drug."

"Seems like a big red herring," Emiko said. "Courtesy of my big mouth. Gemma only knows what I told her. Right? Unless she was actually there in the hayloft?"

"But during lunch at the ranch," Shanice said, "Sam told us a quebrachine overdose is unlikely." Shanice studied the murder board, still thin on facts.

Drew had been quiet, sipping on a glass of iced tea. "Who exactly is this Gemma person who thinks Marcia overdosed?"

"An annoying new instructor at the university," Emiko said.

"Gemma Lopez," Shanice said. "She doesn't seem to know about the xylazine."

Drew nodded, causing her dark curls to swish across her shoulders. "According to Uncle Tobias, the autopsy tox results aren't in yet. It might take longer for the testing to be completed due to the holiday weekend."

Makenzie scribbled "Gemma" on a sticky note and affixed it under the suspect column.

"What's her motivation?" Callie asked.

"We're at the brainstorming stage," Makenzie said. "Everything goes on the board. We'll add motivation and concrete clues as we get them."

Shanice was glad someone else took a critical view of Gemma. She had feared her own reaction was due to petty jealousy of a potential rival for Sam's affections.

"Let's move on," Emily said. "That woman in the old barn was acting strangely. The groom?"

"Groom?" Makenzie asked. "Isn't that a man?"

Callie explained to the group the position of a groom on an Olympic equestrian team. Shanice thought she had learned all there was to know about horses by taking riding lessons and dating Sam, but attending the workshops had opened a whole new world to her. From miniature horses to kids' saddle ponies to half-million-dollar dressage horses, there was an animal and a sport for every budget.

"I thought it odd that a woman in service to an Olympic hopeful would dig around in someone else's tackle box," Emily said.

"Tack box," Callie corrected. "I agree, it was peculiar. But what would her motivation be for harming Marcia?"

"Team rivalry?" Emily asked. "You said she works for Sydney."

Shanice sat up straight, jostling Mitch. "What's she look like?"

"Blonde hair, but not my color," Callie said.

"More of a dirty blonde," Emily chimed in. "And curly. She's a white woman, perhaps five foot five tall, medium build, older than you gals. I'd estimate her age as mid-forties."

Impressive. The bookstore owner sounded like a detective. *It must be all those mystery novels she reads.*

"Sam and I ran into Sydney before coming to the barbecue," Shanice said. "Her groom was unsaddling Sir Maximus."

"I'll add her to the list," Makenzie said. "What's her name?"

"I don't know," Shanice said. "Sydney didn't introduce us.

She ignored the woman, but she was obviously the groom for Sir Maximus."

Makenzie wrote "Groom X" on a sticky note and added it to the suspect column.

"I'll have to look up her name," Callie said. "It'll be on the attendee list. In the meantime, I'd like to add another suspect, but it might be pretty shaky. I was approached yesterday afternoon by Ted from Fulson Minerals Acquisition. He was pressuring me about buying the ranch's mineral rights."

Drew set her glass of iced tea on the table. "That's the man who tricked Mr. Nibley into signing a contract."

"Yeah, he struck me as a real sleaze," Callie said.

"I'll add his name," Makenzie said. "Drew, do you think he's creepy enough to break into your uncle's office?"

Drew looked surprised, then thoughtful. "I don't want to jump to conclusions," she said, "but the burglar could be someone involved in a recent case. Unless, of course, it was a random thief hoping some antiques might be worth the risk."

"How is Spirit doing?" Emiko asked. "Oh, I mean your uncle."

"Uncle Tobias is living with us for now," Drew said. "He can't manage stairs yet."

"And Spirit is at my house," Makenzie said. "Until we can get this sorted out."

The murder board suspect list was lengthening. Groom X, Ted Fulson and Gemma Lopez were the newest additions, below a list of animal rights protestors that included Aster, Everly, and Josie. Marcia's husband, Alistair Fallows, remained, despite Callie arguing for his removal. Then there was an anonymous drug dealer, and Marcia herself via accidental overdose. Shanice didn't want to add to the clutter, but she had to mention her new information.

"Please add Sydney Byron," Shanice said.

"I agree," Callie said. "Sydney claims her horse was disqualified from competition last season because Marcia doped the horse. Not to make him calmer for competition, but to get him loaded in a horse trailer. The drug was still in his system when a random drug test caught it."

"That's big," Emiko said. "But that also means the RAOR people aren't lying. There is doping going on."

Data was being gathered for the equation. From past experience, Shanice knew something would break soon. The autopsy report would be released. Suspects would be added or eliminated based on the discovery of motivations, or the lack thereof. When enough factors were known, the problem would be solved.

"Ladies, I think we've done all we can for now," Emily said. "Feel free to continue your discussion, but my shop opens soon. I'll leave you to it."

Everyone had places to be. The meeting ended with no more revelations.

Chapter Nineteen

Shanice considered the list of suspects as she drove to the Double C Ranch. This morning, they had added more. Was there anything she could do to eliminate names? By uncovering evidence, obviously. Callie was in constant contact with the horse people. So was Shanice, but only indirectly by way of her relationship with Sam.

She and Emiko had access to the university. It was odd how Gemma knew about the quebrachine, but didn't seem to understand its effect on the human body, if Sam was right about it being unlikely to cause an overdose. Of course, Gemma was presumably an expert on veterinary medicine, not a human doctor.

As she turned into the long driveway, Shanice pretended to ignore the RAOR protestors while taking mental notes. There were only three near the entrance to the Double C. Aster wasn't among them. Josie, the girl who had handcuffed herself to the barn door, clutched a sign in her hands as she marched in tight circles. A gauzy tie-dyed skirt swirled around her ankles. She had removed the dog face paint, but Everly wore fresh face paint, making her look like a lion. Perhaps leaving her hair in disarray was an attempt to imitate a lion's mane. The third protestor was a young man who had been there on Thursday.

If a person committed murder or caused a death, would they linger around the scene of the crime? True crime shows mentioned that as a quirk of killers, but was it really a thing?

Enough of crime. Time to have fun.

Shanice had volunteered to be Linda's gofer, assisting her before she entered the arena for another training demo. The Equi X workshops rolled out like clockwork. These folks were professionals, certain to pick up new clients due to their participation in the event. Especially because the event was televised on an equestrian channel.

By early afternoon, she caught up with Sam after another amazing demo of his training techniques. A cynic might not believe the dramatic transformation in equine and rider had actually taken place during the hour-long class, if they didn't know Sam had just met the horse and its owner.

Fans crowded around Sam after the demo, peppering him with questions. He handed out business cards and signed autographs as he worked his way through the throng of horse owners seeking advice about equine behavior problems.

"There you are," he said to Shanice. "Let's hide out for a few minutes. I have cold beverages in my refrigerator."

"That sounds great."

Sam's fifth wheel was pleasantly cool after the growing heat of the late summer Oklahoma afternoon.

Shanice's fashion-conscious sisters would be horrified by her dusty boots and jeans, and the perspiration dampening her sleeveless cowgirl blouse. But Shanice was having the time of her life. Despite the snobbery of some of the elite equestrians, most horsey people were warm and welcoming.

"I need to wash up," Sam said.

"Me, too," Shanice said. "You take the bathroom this time. I'll use the kitchen sink."

She had been in the trailer enough times to know her way around. Clean kitchen towels were in a drawer to the left of the stove. Sam might be a bachelor cowboy, but he stocked clean, soft towels. The ones with pretty prints might have come from his mother or sister. Shanice hadn't met them yet, but framed photos of Sam's parents and two siblings sat on a small counter.

The kitchen island had a double sink. Shanice scrubbed her hands and splashed water on her face. She used a towel with a print of colorful vegetables to dry her arms and neck.

"That was refreshing," she said to herself. "Now for drinks."

For a guy fridge, Sam's was well-stocked with healthy options, in addition to a six-pack of specialty brew-pub beer with one bottle missing. The shelves were light on sandwich fixings and grab-and-go foods, and heavy on ingredients needing preparation, like meats, eggs, and vegetables.

Sam had varieties of bottled tea, lemonade, and a few soda pops. Shanice selected an Arnold Palmer, getting the best of both the tea and lemonade worlds. She began to close the door when a small storage container in the vegetable crisper drawer caught her eye.

She pulled out the clear plastic tub. Inside was a sandwich-sized baggie stamped with a print of horses' hooves. But the horse-themed bag wasn't what attracted her attention to the tub. It was the syringe and two bottles of quebrachine sealed inside.

*   *   *

"Excuse me. Do you work here?"

A man in the expensive attire of a hunter-jumper rider planted himself in front of Callie. A helmet dangled casually from the fingers of one hand while he brushed his hair back with the other. None of the local cowboys wore hair that perfectly styled, steel gray except for white highlights at his temples. His knee-high black leather boots cost more than Callie's favorite saddle horse.

Callie closed a stall door and grabbed the handles of a wheelbarrow full of manure. "You could say that."

"I have a complaint," the man said. "Please direct me to management."

"That depends on which management you want." Callie didn't wait. She pushed the wheelbarrow down the wide aisle between stalls. Her rubber boots were designed for cleaning stalls, not riding in horse shows. Faded jeans and a barrel racing

T-shirt must have made her look like a stable hand, not the multimillionaire co-owner of the Double C ranch. "There's two different outfits tryin' to keep this monkey show from runnin' off the rails."

"I was seeking someone on the Equi X staff," the man said. "But now I believe I'd like to speak to your employer."

Callie laughed. "Well, I suppose you could talk to Clint."

She waved a hand at her husband. He finished a conversation with another workshop participant and headed her way. Clint had dressed in Western attire. Expensive, though. Not plain old jeans and a shirt off the rack from the downtown outfitter.

"May I help you?"

The jumper responded to Clint's professional appearance and attitude. It wasn't fake with Clint. Tall and handsome, he naturally commanded attention. Callie just couldn't work up the energy to care about impressing people. Plus, she kind of liked being underestimated.

"Commander McClennan's water trough is contaminated with a dead fly," the man said. "This isn't the first time I've found objectionable contaminants in his water. He can't be expected to drink such filth."

"I'll make sure it's attended to," Clint said.

"See that you do." The man walked away, tapping his riding crop against one boot-covered calf.

"I don't know how you do it," Callie said. "People just seem to know you're in charge."

"For one thing," Clint said, "I don't dress like I pulled my outfit from a thrift store donation bin."

Callie placed her hands on her hips. "I'll have you know my clothes would be rejected by any self-respectin' thrift store."

Clint laughed and draped an arm over Callie's shoulders. "Come on. Leave cleaning water troughs for George or one of the stable hands. Let's go to the house and get a cold drink."

"George and the crew can't keep up with these people," Callie said. "They complain if their horses pass gas and someone's not right there to spray air freshener for the poor dears."

"We're fortunate we struggled for our wealth," Clint said. "We're grounded in a reality some of these people will never understand. And we're fortunate we can enjoy a few luxuries now. And we should." He glanced at Callie with one raised eyebrow.

"I have a wardrobe, you know," Callie said.

"That you rarely wear."

"You like me okay in jeans and t-shirts," Callie said. "Or have you just never told me it bothers you? Do you want me dressing up like these snooty women?"

"I want you to be happy and comfortable. But I also don't want anyone thinking they're better than you."

"Ha. Doesn't bother me," Callie said. "I know who I am."

But she did shower and change while Clint created a mocktail in the kitchen. Callie avoided anything that might negatively affect her efforts to conceive. Alcohol had been an easy thing to cut out of her life. Especially after Cousin George brought his alcohol-fueled problems to the ranch, before his recent reformation.

She stepped into the kitchen feeling refreshed. Winston trotted at her heels. "Better?" She asked Clint.

Callie spun in a circle while Clint watched with an appreciative smile. The above-the-knee shirt flared out. In blue-green and earth tones, the belted, sleeveless dress had a Southwest look that went well with her turquoise jewelry. But the cowgirl boots were a requirement, even though this pair she reserved for dressing up, not riding.

"Now you look like a woman of independent means."

"Okay," she said. "This is comfortable. Nice and cool."

Clint kissed Callie's cheek and handed her a strawberry-lime-ginger drink he had developed. Chunks of red berries were thick at the bottom, and a slice of lime perched on the rim of the glass. He set a mid-afternoon snack of cheese, crackers, and fruit on the table.

"Mmm. This is delicious."

"I've been thinking of ways to make cleaning the stalls easier," Clint said.

Callie grimaced. "Did you have to bring that up while I was takin' a sip?"

"Sorry," Clint said. "I have been preoccupied about increasing ranch efficiency."

"By hirin' more staff?" Callie asked.

"The logistics of hiring for events is challenging," Clint began, but Callie pounced.

"There aren't going to be more events," she said. "This has been a nightmare."

"Only because we agreed to host Equi X at the last minute," Clint said. "With better planning, the next event with operate more smoothly. More safely."

"None of these 'challenges' will present themselves," Callie said, "if we plain don't host anything like this ever again."

"I understand your negativity," Clint said. "It was a shock finding Marcia in the hayloft."

"And she wouldn't have been there if we weren't hostin' Equi X."

"True," Clint said. "But because she was, I feel responsible for the ranch not being a safe place."

"That's ridiculous," Callie said. "Someone killed Marcia Bentworth-Fallows. Or did somethin' that helped her die. There was nothin' you could do to prevent that."

"Homicide," Clint said. "Emily explained the distinction at lunch yesterday. But if we had surveillance cameras in more places, we might have been able to assist the police in learning what happened. Who caused her death. Or contributed to it."

"Or murdered her."

Chapter Twenty

Makenzie climbed up the metal steps of a portable bleacher. Callie had informed her it was the best location to watch the outdoor jumping workshop. The higher, the better. When two young men took a shortcut, hopping quickly down the seats instead of the stairs, they shook the entire bleacher. Makenzie felt a wave of vertigo.

"Over here." The Brieswell lab manager, Bob Pierpont, waved an arm vigorously. He and his wife were only halfway up the bleachers. Makenzie gladly abandoned Callie's recommendation for the mid-tier seat.

Lois Pierpont wore a broad-brimmed hat, tan capris slacks, and a loose-fitting cotton blouse. Bob's cargo shorts and cotton Western shirt were a male version of his wife's outfit, but his head was shaded by a worn straw cowboy hat.

"I'm excited to see horse jumping," Lois said. "The grandkids jump low fences at our place, but these people are elite in the sport."

"The obstacles here are much higher," Bob said.

Horses and riders entered the outdoor arena. Sydney rode Sir Maximus. Marcia's gray mare Moonstone was ridden by a young man. Alistair gave him last-minute instructions, then left the arena. The horses trotted around, avoiding the rails set up as jumping obstacles as they warmed up.

"I didn't realize you had a horse property," Makenzie said to Bob. "Until you told the lab group at breakfast yesterday morning."

"It's more of a gentleman farmer's place," Lois said. "We never intended to earn our living from farming or ranching, but we both love the seclusion."

"Elbow room," Bob said. "Our kids grew up on horses, well, at least since we moved to Rose Creek. Now the grandkids are horse lovers."

"I can't imagine moving away," Lois said. Concern pinched her features. "We've lived here for more than half our marriage."

"We've been together for thirty-three wonderful years." Bob reached for Lois's hand. "If Brieswell closes the lab, I won't find work close enough to the farm for a reasonable commute."

"That's terrible," Makenzie said. "I suppose I should look for a job with the university. That might require getting a Master's degree. Frankly, my heart's not in it."

"I hope they make an announcement soon," Lois said. "We've been on tenterhooks ever since Bob heard the rumor."

"I haven't even told my parents or my boyfriend," Makenzie said. "I didn't want to ruin their holiday." Although Dustin had been working more than vacationing this weekend. "Do you think they'll make an announcement on Tuesday?"

"I hope so," Bob said. "It's absolutely cruel to send everyone home for a long weekend carrying this burden."

"But the company hasn't given you any information," Lois said. "If not for the rumor mill, you might have been blindsided by whatever happens Tuesday."

"Isn't that worse?" Makenzie asked. "Learning you'd been laid off after enjoying time off? Maybe going on a vacation you can't afford now?"

"Whatever the outcome, some good may come of this," Lois said. "We've had a dream for the past few years. We keep putting it off, thinking the time isn't right. But then one day you're too old."

Makenzie remembered Bob mentioning something at Stockman's about a B&B, but she'd been so concerned about her own lack of alternate plans, she hadn't paid much attention.

Bob shook his head. "We don't have anything in place. It's

too soon."

"Some of the best things in life happen without advance planning," Lois said. "You tend to overthink things. But I'm a right-brain person. I teach art at the grade school."

"And I'm definitely left-brained," Bob said. "The job in the Brieswell chemistry lab has been a perfect fit for me. After retirement, we can pursue our new dream. But I need more time. I want a formula carved in stone before making a move."

"We've been talking about it for three years now, Bob." Lois looked at Makenzie. "A horse B&B. We can accommodate human and equine guests with a little renovation. We're close to a network of public trails."

"We'd need access across part of the Double C," Bob said. "I was hoping to ask Clint Garcia about that possibility, but he's been tied up."

"I can make an introduction," Makenzie said. "Maybe we should wait until after this crazy weekend is over. He and Callie agreed to host the Equi X event at the last minute. They're both left-brain people, Lois, so going with the flow has made both of them tense."

"We won't know about our jobs until Tuesday," Bob said. "I suppose there's no rush."

Unless management terminates us the minute we arrive at the factory.

"The workshop is starting." Lois pointed to the arena.

Makenzie was glad for the change of focus. As the horses lined up in a row facing the trainer, she tried to forget about her career being in peril. Bob and his wife had a dream outside of the Brieswell lab and school building walls. Makenzie had always assumed her position was secure. She hadn't imagined she might need to find work elsewhere. Or switch to a different career. Rather than being excited by new opportunities, Makenzie felt depressed.

Everyone faced changes, whether they were planned for or unexpected. Like the person in the center of the arena. Marcia had been the scheduled trainer to troubleshoot issues with jumping techniques. Her replacement was a middle-aged man with steel gray hair fading to white at his temples.

Cameras livestreamed the jumping workshop. This trainer had lucked out in obtaining a place on the agenda, possibly gaining publicity and new clients as a result.

Unless luck hadn't been involved, and he had made sure Marcia would be unable to attend.

*   *   *

"Are you ready?" Clint offered Callie his arm.

"Back into the fray," Callie said. "Ugh. I guess so."

After cooling off and dressing up, Callie was as ready as she was going to be. They headed for the patio door. Winston followed at Callie's heels.

"No, kitty. You can't come outdoors. It's not safe."

And not just from the predators. Owls and coyotes stayed away from crowds of people. Winston was in danger of getting stepped on by a human or horse rushing to a workshop. Callie nudged the fluffy white-and-pumpkin cat back with her dressy cowgirl boot and closed the door.

"I wonder if he thinks he can find Marcia?" Clint asked.

"Poor little guy. I need to remind Alistair I have the cat. I don't think he's interested. Maybe Winston reminds him of his wife too much."

"She passed away on Thursday," Clint said. "It's only Sunday. That's not enough time to process a catastrophic event. Alistair must still be in shock."

"I can't even imagine." Callie considered carefully her next words, because she wasn't sure how she felt about the possibility herself. "What if Alistair doesn't take Winston when he leaves?"

"Hmm." Clint stopped near the old barn. "Perhaps another family member would take the cat. A friend."

"If we can locate one," Callie said. "My friends already have cats, or reasons they can't have one. It might not be terrible to—"

159

A figure slipped between the horse trailers parked behind the old barn's paddocks. Callie grabbed Clint's arm.

"Was that Aster?"

All Callie had glimpsed was a flash of tie-dyed fabric that didn't fit in with the Western wear or fancy dressage outfits worn by most of the people on the ranch. More like late 1960s hippie clothes.

"Maybe," Clint said. "Because there goes George. Huh."

"Aster isn't a good influence, in my opinion," Callie said. "George has been workin' hard on the Equi X workshop, and then she goes and brings her gang of sign-wavin' loonies here."

"George is really turning his life around," Clint said. "With her help. Maybe they're having a private chat?"

"Ick. Between the horse trailers?" Callie asked with a grimace that probably undid her effort to look nice for her husband.

"Not that kind of chat," Clint said, laughing.

"What does RAOR think they're gonna accomplish? They're wastin' their time. These horse people get upset if a bug falls in their animal's drinking water."

"I agree. RAOR would be more effective protesting factory farm conditions. Let's see what George is doing."

"And hopefully we won't interrupt a chat," Callie added with a shudder.

She followed Clint, stepping as quietly as she could on the dirt and gravel in her dressy cowgirl boots.

"Let me go!" A woman who was not Aster struggled wildly in George's grip.

Is he assaulting her? Aster's not gonna like that, and I'm sure not gonna put up with it.

Clint raced up to George, grabbing his arm. But George wouldn't release the woman.

"What's goin' on?" Callie asked. "George, have you lost your mind? Let go of her!"

"Not on your life," George huffed. "Until she drops her firecrackers."

Now Callie noticed the girl's fists. They clutched around small red tubes strung together with fuses.

"What on earth?" Callie raced up to the woman and pried her fists open, not bothering to be gentle about it.

"Ouch!"

Firecrackers fell to the ground. Twenty or more had been in each of her hands. George began to loosen his hold on her arm.

"Wait," Callie said. "Don't let her go just yet. What are you up to?"

The woman still had traces of face paint at her neck and hairline. She was the dog-face girl who made local headlines by handcuffing herself to the barn door Thursday. Josie tugged against George's grip, then sighed heavily.

"Forcing horses to jump over obstacles is dangerous. I'm going to stop the abuse."

"By setting off firecrackers?" Clint asked.

"The horses would have run away from their captors," the woman said. "They could have escaped. But you stopped me. Now they'll risk broken legs and death."

"Do you know anything at all about horses?" Callie was shouting, and she only just managed to refrain from punching the woman. "Firecrackers? They'd go crazy! What are you? A complete idiot?"

Clint stepped aside and tapped on his cellphone.

"Josie, you're the one endangering animals," George said. "Did Everly or Aster know what you were planning to do?"

"Aster isn't any help," Josie said. "She acts like animal exploitation is okay, as long as she's the one doing it."

Callie couldn't see how milking goats and harvesting eggs was exploitation. But she was glad to hear Aster was losing favor with the lunatic fringe.

"Someone could have been hurt really bad," George said.

"The humans deserve pain," Josie said. "It's only fair after what they put the horses through."

"A good jumper loves the sport," Callie said. "If a horse hates jumping, or is scared of it, they can't be used for show jumping. Like any athlete, they need to be engaged in the sport or they'll never be any good at it."

"What about drugging them?" Josie asked, spittle flying from her lips. "Don't you dare tell me animals can't be coerced into doing unsafe things. Like racehorses running until their hearts burst."

Callie couldn't argue that animal abuse didn't happen out in the big wide world. But it wasn't happening here. Not on her watch. The only being allegedly hurt by drugs at the Double C was Marcia. A human.

Clint stepped back to them. "The police are on their way."

"Police!" Both George and Josie said the word at the same instant.

"I didn't mean for the police to become involved," George said. He was likely thinking of Aster's reaction to George helping arrest one of her buddies.

Josie wrenched her arm from his grip, but didn't attempt to run away.

"You planned to disrupt the workshop," Clint said, "by committing assault. This incident has to be reported to the police."

"That's ridiculous." Josie folded her arms across her chest.

"He's right," Callie said. "By deliberately setting off fireworks in an arena, you could have caused serious injury to riders, horses, and spectators. Do you really understand what happens to horses when they break a leg?"

"I just wanted to make a point," Josie said in a small voice. "No one was listening."

"I'm all for sending a message," Callie said. "If your group doesn't like horse events, you can protest peacefully, if you get a permit. But you went way over the edge."

Callie thought that was a thing if you were on public property. Requiring a permit to hold a demonstration. The Double C was private property. They should have the right to deny access to disruptive people. Unless holding the Equi X workshop had opened them up to public access somehow.

Maybe Drew could explain the legal issues to them. Another reason not to muddy the waters by opening up their ranch to regularly include public events.

While they waited for a police officer to arrive, Josie glanced around nervously, until her attention settled on the old barn. Was she staring at the hay loft door?

The crazies in the animal rights group didn't base their protest on reality as Callie knew it. They were unhinged. Were they so out of control, one of them murdered Marcia?

Chapter Twenty-One

Shanice leaned on the railing of the indoor arena, watching miniature horses pull tiny carts. They were less than three feet tall at the shoulder, while average horses were closer to five feet.

A team of white horses pulled a surrey. Four brown minis pulled a buckboard. In all, seven small carts and twenty horses performed under the encouragement of an instructor specializing in miniature horse training.

But Shanice's attention wasn't focused entirely on the arena floor. Her thoughts kept going to the two vials of quebrachine and the syringe in Sam's refrigerator. The labels had indicated they came from a veterinary medical supply company. Sam had acted surprised. Either he was innocent of placing the drug in his refrigerator, or he was a gifted actor. He claimed to keep veterinary supplies in his office, not his living space. And definitely not in his refrigerator.

Sam had encouraged her to enjoy the workshops while he waited for the police, which hadn't done anything to encourage her trust. Shanice wanted to hear him answer the questions the police would surely ask. Who had access to Sam's trailer? Was the drug really placed there without his knowledge? Or did the vials belong to him?

Maybe I should have insisted on staying there. After all, Shanice was the one to notice the baggie in the refrigerator drawer.

"Adorable, aren't they?"

Shanice jerked when a hand touched her shoulder.

"Oops. I didn't mean to startle you." Emily took a step back. "I thought I made so much noise in these boots, you surely heard me coming."

"Sorry, Emily." Shanice threw out her arms and welcomed a quick hug from the bookstore owner. "My mind was elsewhere." She considered telling Emily about her discovery, but the book club sleuths could wait until Shanice had more information. She returned her focus to the mini-horse teams. "Which one is your son's?"

"Mason is the fellow with the bushy beard, and the natural wood country wagon pulled by the four pintos."

The instructor, a plump woman with poofy Country music star hair, dressed in a fringed denim dress and bright red cowgirl boots, told the workshop participants to change direction. Most managed to turn around smoothly, but a couple made awkwardly large loops, almost running into other teams.

"Your son's team did well," Shanice said.

"They're wonderful in harness," Emily said. "Each horse has its own personality. They're generally very sweet and eager to please. But two of them have given Mason fits in the past when he tried to load them in a trailer."

This was the second time Shanice had heard about problems with convincing horses to enter trailers. Sydney claimed Marcia had drugged Sir Maximus to get him trailered, ruining his chance to compete for the rest of last year.

"Has Mason ever sedated his horses to get them loaded in a trailer?" Shanice asked.

Emily's smile melted. "Why, no. Not to my knowledge. My son is a big man, and they're so tiny, he jokes that if they give him too much trouble, he can pick them up and carry them into the trailer. Some time ago, he began using your Sam's techniques to convince them that trailers aren't scary."

Your Sam. Shanice liked the sound of Emily's words, but she wasn't convinced they were true. *Too soon to tell.*

"You're not asking about Mason specifically." Emily watched the small horses pulling carts in the arena while she spoke to Shanice. "This is about the case."

"At our meeting this morning, we discussed Marcia giving Sydney's horse a sedative to get him loaded into a trailer, and then a drug test catching him with the banned substance in his system before a big horse show." Shanice hesitated, then decided the bookstore owner could be trusted with any information. Emily might be able to set Shanice's worries at ease. "I just found quebrachine in Sam's trailer. He claims he doesn't know where it came from."

"That's not a sedative," Emily said. "As we learned in book club, it's a stimulant."

"But it may be used to awaken an animal that has been given a sedative. Like after surgery."

Emily watched the mini-horses, but it was clear the amateur detective gears in her mind were spinning. She turned to face Shanice. "Since it seems unlikely Marcia overdosed on quebrachine, did she have a sedative in her system instead? Was she asking Callie for the antidote? Did Marcia self-administer a sedative? Did someone force one, or both, drugs on her?"

"This is so frustrating," Shanice said.

"The police will learn the truth," Emily said. "There are pieces of data we don't have access to. That the police don't even have yet. Patience."

Easy for Emily to say. She wasn't dating a man who might be involved in a murder.

As the mini-horse workshop ended, Emily went to visit with her son. Shanice headed for the big white food tent. She needed a cool drink, and didn't want to impose on Callie or Sam.

Or maybe I'm afraid to see Sam. Afraid of the truth I might learn.

Chilled dispensers offered free water for refillable bottles. Shanice held hers under a spigot, then immediately took a drink.

I must be getting dehydrated. And hungry. It was a little early for dinner, but Shanice had started her day with the rising sun.

Food smells lured her further inside the tent. Shanice was so focused on an Italian food vendor, she didn't see Gemma.

"Hey, fellow Boomer Sooner." Gemma held a disposable plate of ravioli and salad in one hand, and a cup of something carbonated in the other. Boomer Sooner was the fight song for the University of Oklahoma. "I'm sitting over there." She tilted her head toward a table. "With that eye candy."

Shanice managed to suppress a groan. Timothy, the overly muscled physical education instructor, smiled and waved. He wore a snug, sleeveless t-shirt with the university logo and a battered straw cowboy hat. He pointed at the empty seat next to him.

If Shanice hadn't suddenly realized she was famished, she might have made excuses and exited the tent. There was no need to be a jerk to her annoying coworkers. And miss a meal. Besides, maybe she could pry some information out of Gemma.

After obtaining a plate of steaming hot spinach and ricotta ravioli and crisp green salad, she joined the two at a table.

"I didn't know you were coming to the Equi X workshop," she said to Timothy.

"I didn't even know about it, until Gemma told me." He cast an adoring glance her way.

Timothy had pursued Shanice for an entire semester before focusing on another unfortunate but more willing university employee. Now Gemma seemed fated to be in his sights. From the smile she returned his direction, maybe Timothy had finally found The One.

Looking at her plate, Shanice asked in as innocent a tone as she could, "What time did you two get here?"

"Right after my morning workout," Timothy said.

"Do you ever take a day off from the gym?" Shanice asked.

"Not even," Gemma said. "I went with him. I'm into bodybuilding." She flexed a modest bicep. "But I wanted to be here in time for the breakfast buffet. These horse people really know how to eat."

Breakfast. Sam had been grooming his horses, prepping for workshops, and presumably having breakfast himself. It might not have been difficult for Gemma to sneak into his trailer and plant the quebrachine.

Shanice glanced at a sign near the main entrance to the tent. Breakfast was served from six to nine. She hadn't found the drugs in Sam's refrigerator until after noon. Gemma had hours to find the right opportunity to frame Sam.

But why?

"Did you come on opening day?" Shanice asked.

"Thursday?" Gemma asked, shaking her head. "I was too busy tweaking my classes. Then Saturday morning, we had the homecoming committee. This is the first chance I had to spend the day at the ranch."

"Same here," Timothy said. "I like horses, but I don't get to ride very often. I need an extra-large horse."

Gemma smiled at him. "They have some horses here that are big enough to carry a sturdy guy like you. Maybe we can go for a trail ride sometime."

Shanice needed to steer the conversation back in a direction helpful for the investigation.

"Do you know anyone here? Other than us." Shanice waved a hand at herself, Gemma, and Timothy.

"I've met Dr. Grady, of course." Gemma bumped Shanice with her shoulder. "No thanks to you. And Emiko was here earlier."

"I missed her," Shanice said. She hadn't seen Drew, either, although Joel and Parker had been at the event for a few hours. Shanice hoped Drew was doing some self-care. She seemed truly stressed out lately.

"You and Emiko are buddies, right?" Gemma asked.

Shanice almost told Gemma they were in a book club together, but that might lead to having to invite Gemma into her sanctuary. The Rose Creek Reads book club was her territory, and Emiko, Drew, Callie, and Makenzie were her friends.

Am I really that selfish?

Shanice told herself she needed places to spend off-campus without running into coworkers. That was one disadvantage to life in a small town. *You have to make an effort to carve out privacy.* She disguised her delayed response behind needing to chew and swallow. The ravioli was excellent.

"Emiko and I have gotten to know each other," Shanice finally said.

"The engineer?" Timothy asked. "She totally blew me off when I asked if she wanted a tour of the barbecue huts in Rose Creek."

"Are you disappointed?" Gemma didn't give Timothy the chance to respond. "If Emiko went out with you, I might not be sitting here today."

"True." Timothy's face flushed red. "Anyway, I don't think Emiko likes Oklahoma food. But Gemma, you love barbecue. Just like me."

"Not everyone is a fan of barbecue," Gemma said. "Which is exactly why I think the homecoming committee should take a new direction."

"I still think the best approach," Shanice began, "is to propose the New York theme for later in the year. When weather might force us indoors anyway. The chuckwagon theme is tried and true."

"I'm voting for New York," Gemma said. "Although I'm certain my idea will be shot down by the cowboys on the committee." She eyed Shanice's Western attire with one raised eyebrow.

"It's not the idea," Shanice said. "It's the timing. If you're willing to compromise on when to have the New York-style homecoming party, I'll back you all the way."

Gemma smiled. "Really?"

"Yes."

The conversation was more relaxed after that. Shanice could almost like the go-getter. Gemma's energy just needed to be directed in non-destructive directions.

Emily frequently emphasized the need to collect all the available data. Until Shanice could gather more information, she decided to enjoy getting to know her new coworker. The woman might not be guilty of running an illicit drug ring. Or attempting to poach Shanice's boyfriend.

Chapter Twenty-Two

Drew's uncle took a pain medication and went to his room to take a nap soon after brunch. Joel and Parker planned a day at the ranch.

Drew welcomed a chance to rest after her visit with the book club that morning. Part of her out-of-control emotions were due to plain exhaustion. She was glad Uncle Tobias was the independent sort. Besides checking on him, making sure he was following doctor's orders, it was a quiet Sunday. Drew curled up on the screened back porch and caught up on reading the book club selection. Then she moved on to her own to-be-read pile.

Having Boomer around was actually a comfort during Uncle Tobias's long nap. Drew realized a person was never completely alone when they had a pet. Maybe Tobias did need Spirit. But not in his Victorian house, with that awful staircase.

Drew's thoughts strayed to the unresolved question of Tobias's planned birthday gift for Parker. She and Joel had tried to explain to their son that people didn't simply give horses as presents, like they'd give Lego sets or basketballs. Tobias insisted nothing was too much for his great-great-nephew. Before they got anything settled, it had been time for Joel and Parker to head to the ranch. The delay in addressing the issue was only going to make things more difficult.

At dinnertime, her husband and son returned from the Equi X workshop. They brought two boxed pizzas and a large salad from the Main Street restaurant.

"No cooking?" Drew asked as Joel set the square boxes on

the kitchen table. "I think I love you."

"I certainly hope so," Joel said with a grin. He kissed Drew's cheek. "The feeling is mutual, by the way."

Parker hugged Drew briefly, but his mind was on his puppy, who needed some backyard time. When they rushed outside, the screen door slapping closed behind boy and dog, Drew pulled Joel close.

"We need to talk to Uncle Tobias," Drew said in a low voice. "We have to tell him he can't give Parker a horse."

"I'm glad you're on board with me," Joel said. "It's going to be a tough talk. For both of them."

Shortly after Drew set out plates and a pitcher of lemonade, Uncle Tobias hobbled down the hall from the first-floor bedroom.

"Do I smell pizza?"

Joel leaned out the back door. "Dinnertime!"

Parker and Boomer hurried back inside. For a precious few minutes, there was calm in the house. Everyone managed to eat a little salad and a slice of pizza before Drew and Joel opened the topic that had been bothering her since earlier that morning.

"We need to talk about Parker's birthday present," Joel said.

"I haven't made the purchase yet," Uncle Tobias said.

"Thank goodness for that," Drew said.

"I didn't know which horse Parker wanted," Tobias said. "Give me credit for having a little common sense. Buying a horse isn't like buying a bicycle." He turned to the boy. "A real cowboy needs his own horse, but we do need your parents' approval. Let's hear them out."

"A horse is even more responsibility than a puppy," Joel said.

"Uncle Tobias, you can keep it for me," Parker said, turning to his great-great uncle. "If Mom and Dad say no."

"That's not the way this works," Joel said. "We had to make adjustments to invite Boomer into our lives. This isn't the right time to add a horse to the family."

Parker's emotional outburst she expected, the quivering lip

and teary eyes, but when Uncle Tobias teared up, she nearly caved.

"I promise I'll be good," Parker sniffled. "I'm sorry I acted bad about going to temple, and saying I didn't want the baby, but I didn't throw the mallet at the party. It slipped out of my hand. I wasn't trying to hit anyone. I do want a little brother or sister. And I want to play with my friends at temple, and go to yeshiva, and I love school here and Jill and Tommy and Bear. I want to keep Boomer."

Parker clutched the puppy in his lap. Boomer squirmed.

"Be gentle," Joel said. "No one's taking Boomer away from you."

When he relaxed his grip, Boomer hopped up to lick Parker's chin. The boy giggled despite the tears.

"The dog is part of the family now," Drew said. "No matter what. We've made a commitment. But we're not ready for a horse."

Tobias wiped a sleeve across his eyes.

"A commitment to what?" the old man asked.

"To Boomer," Drew said. "Once you take an animal into your household, you're responsible for them for the rest of their life. Boomer is staying."

"I'm not talking about the puppy," Uncle Tobias said.

"Uh, what do you mean?" Joel asked.

"What I have to say is an adult topic," Tobias said. "Let's move this discussion to the living room."

Joel shook his head, but not meaning no. It was more like he was weary of dealing with stubborn old men and children.

"Parker, take Boomer outside."

When Parker glanced her way, Drew nodded, struggling to paste a smile on her face. One emotional family member at a time. Her nice, relaxing day had collapsed.

After Parker left with the dog, she settled onto the sofa. "I can't handle the stress."

"I have a solution," Tobias said.

"To which problem?" Joel asked. "We can't seem to have

less than a dozen at a time."

Tobias raised his hands. "All of them."

Joel raised his eyebrows. "Well, that's good news. Have at it. How do we solve all our problems?"

Drew didn't like his sarcastic tone, but she held her tongue. For now.

"Make a decision." Tobias reached for his lemonade on the coffee table. He raised the glass to his lips, then looked inside with a disappointed expression. "I need a refill."

"Let me." Joel took the glass and stepped into the kitchen. "Just a decision?" he called. "For which problem?"

"They're all connected," Drew said. "Right, Uncle?"

He nodded, his thinning white hair waving in complete disarray. The cuffs of his long-sleeved Western shirt were rolled back at different lengths. His bolo tie was crooked. But Uncle Tobias's appearance was deceiving. He was extremely focused and organized.

"I give Parker the horse, requiring you to stay in Rose Creek. Or, you move back to Boston, and obviously you aren't going to ship an ordinary saddle horse all the way to the East Coast, so my gift to Parker is out of the question. You can choose to continue this madness of maintaining two households until your marriage crumbles under the chaos and the pressure. The horse becomes a meaningless side issue. What's really at stake is whether you move permanently to Rose Creek, or return to Boston, as a united family."

Joel brought a full glass of lemonade to Tobias. "Either Rose Creek, Boston, or chaos. But it's not as simple as that."

"Isn't it, though?" Tobias asked. "You found it easy enough to make a commitment to a dog."

"Because adopting Boomer didn't curtail the other options," Joel said. "We could stay here, or move to Boston, and the puppy goes with us."

"Ah." Tobias sipped his lemonade. "The dog was not really a decision point, then."

"I'll admit," Drew said, "I thought Boomer offered an

anchor. Something to keep us in Rose Creek. Then you," she directed at Joel, "fell in love with him, and decided we should sell our condo." She turned her attention to Uncle Tobias. "The building has a no-dogs rule. Really, it's no place for a little boy, either. But we haven't decided what to do when we sell the condo."

"We've talked about finding a place in the suburbs," Joel said. "A house or townhouse with a yard."

Drew was entrenched in her belief that Rose Creek was the best place for Parker. She was happier here, too. The silence stretched on uncomfortably long, until Joel spoke again.

"My firm is on the verge of offering one of the associates a junior partnership." His words were calm, although Drew knew he was anxious to learn whether he was selected. "I'm under consideration. Even if I don't get the promotion, my current position is secure. Although that means I'm stagnating. What would I do in Rose Creek? I can't work remotely."

"I took a demotion to do that," Drew said. Not as an argument. It was a statement of fact. Her firm allowed her to work remotely from home. Her status had gone from up-and-coming lawyer to more of a paralegal. It would have been crushing if she were still the career-focused workaholic she'd been up until this spring. Having three jobs might sound like she was solidly in workaholic territory, but the theater job was occasional, the Boston law firm less than twenty hours a week, and the caseload at Uncle Tobias's office was light.

"Some choice," Joel said in a discouraged tone. "Drag my family back to Boston, where my wife and son claim they'll be miserable, but where I have a solid career. Stay here, taking a leap of faith we can thrive on much less income. No offense, Uncle Tobias. Yours is the only viable law firm in the Rose Creek area, but there aren't enough cases coming in to keep two lawyers busy, much less the three of us."

"No offense taken." He sipped his lemonade.

Joel continued. "We can try to hold things together with a foot in both worlds. Career security, but separation."

"With a new baby," Drew said.

"There is another option," Tobias said.

"I welcome any new ideas," Joel said, without sarcasm this time.

Drew watched Tobias. What option could he have that they hadn't already discussed?

"Option four we don't know yet," Tobias said. "It's the unexpected opportunity thrown in your lap by the Higher Power." He pointed upward.

That wasn't helpful. But Joel smiled.

"You could be right. We're trapped in an either-or mindset."

"Country versus city," Drew said. "High-visibility career versus more modest aspirations. There are families living comfortable lives in Rose Creek. Selling our condo, and with our savings and retirement accounts, we'd be among the more financially well-off in the county."

"The Garcias brought their wealth with them," Joel said, nodding.

"You're assuming we'd take a big step down, Joel, but not everyone imported their wealth. Uncle Tobias's friend Dobry has oil money. And moving to Rose Creek doesn't mean the end of our careers."

"Oil barons need lawyers," Uncle Tobias said. "I chose to be a solo practitioner in a small, relatively non-litigious town. The work is out there."

"Your case involving Mr. Nibley has piqued my curiosity about mineral rights law," Joel said. "But changing my specialization mid-stream . . ." He seemed to consider Tobias's option for a moment. "None of this speculation addresses the issue of the horse. I'd like to get back to that topic."

"We agree on this, Uncle Tobias," Drew said. "Our family is not ready for horse ownership. Parker is welcome to continue lessons."

"Perhaps someone at the ranch has an extra horse?" Uncle Tobias said. "One that needs a boy's attention, without the requirement of purchasing the animal?"

"I'll call Clint, although I doubt he'll pick up," Joel said, tapping his fingers on his cellphone. Apparently, he did answer. Joel put his phone on speaker. "Hello, I have a question. Maybe several."

When Joel inquired about having the use of a horse without purchasing it, Clint directed him to Callie. She confirmed the possibility of leasing a horse. It was similar to leasing a car. Instead of taking chances your favorite saddle horse would be available when you took lessons or went on a trail ride, a person could lease one particular animal. The lease could be for any length of time. Parker could have his "own" horse through the end of the year. When Joel got off the phone, Uncle Tobias nodded.

"That is a reasonable alternative," Uncle Tobias said. "I'm afraid I made a mess of my gift-giving attempt. Perhaps it will ease the pain if we let Parker know right away that he can still have access to a horse."

"Let's not tell him yet," Drew said. "We need to confirm which horses are available, and which would be the best match for Parker. I don't want to disappoint him twice, if the lease option doesn't work out."

"I agree," Joel said. "We can string him along for one more day. Shall we bring him back in?"

Uncle Tobias held up one hand.

"First, I must apologize," he said.

"For what?" Drew asked.

"For being a meddlesome old man. You took me in out of the kindness of your hearts. And I've made a mess of things. As soon as the doctor gives her okay, I'll return to my own home. And my cat."

Joel met Drew's eyes. "Your uncle should live here permanently."

Tobias's eyes teared up again. Was he happy? Sad? Furious they were interfering in his life? As Drew thought of the narrow, steep staircase in Tobias's Victorian house, this sounded like a terrific option.

"But this is your home," Tobias said.

"It's your house," Drew said. "I'm only renting it from you."

"With a little remodeling," Joel said, "we can create a private apartment for you. Just add a locking interior door, make a private exterior entrance for you, and you'll have your own space."

"What happens if Drew and Parker return to Boston?" Tobias asked.

"We move your law office to the first floor of this house," Joel said. "Think of all the space. No more tripping over boxes."

"No more stairs," Drew said. "Everything you need is on the ground floor."

"But what about Spirit?" Uncle Tobias asked. "You wouldn't let me bring her here because of Boomer. She can't live alone in the Victorian."

"With your own apartment," Drew said, "Spirit can have her own space. But we should try introducing the animals to each other. They might get along."

"I'd feel better knowing a man is in the house," Joel said, "until we get this figured out. Drew and Parker need someone to keep an eye on them when I'm out of town."

The independent woman in Drew wanted to raise an objection, until Joel winked at her. She and Parker had managed fine living on their own for half a year. But it was an argument that might sway Uncle Tobias. He would never admit *he* needed to be watched over.

"Well." Tobias sighed. "It's a lot to think about."

"We don't have to make any decisions today," Joel said. "Let's bring Parker in and explain what's going on."

"But not about leasing a horse," Drew said. "Just to explain you might be moving in permanently with us."

Tobias's lips twisted to one side in a distressed expression. Then his hand dove into his rear jeans pocket, extracting his cellphone.

"Just a moment." Tobias waved his hand, holding the

device. "I'm getting a text. It's from my little birdie."

His code name for the woman whose nephew worked with Coroner Hiram Stanley.

Chapter Twenty-Three

Callie turned to straighten a halter and lead rope hanging from a hook beside a stall. She pretended not to be interested as Alistair led Moonstone down the wide aisle, stopping outside stall fifteen. The handsome young man who had been riding the horse in the workshops walked beside him.

"I don't know what's going to happen," Alistair said. "Obviously, it won't be business as usual. I'm not a trainer. That was Marcia's shtick. But I know the business, the horses, and the clients."

"I wish to remain a client."

When the gossips weren't merely being snarky, they were informative. Callie had learned Darion Fernandez was a shirt-tail relation of the Spanish royal family. He removed his helmet, revealing curly blond hair.

"Moonstone is ready for the Olympics. I feel it in my bones."

"And you'd like to be in the saddle when he takes a medal." Alistair sounded weary.

"Not for me," Darion said. "Marcia made me feel like I am part of your family. She would have wanted this. She would have approved."

Alistair slung an arm around the young man's shoulders and gave a quick squeeze. "You are family, Darion. You're the son I never had." He released Darion from the side hug. "You and Moonstone need to make it through qualifications first. I don't know how we'll manage without Marcia." Sadness was thick in his voice.

"We will carry on because we must." Darion clapped a hand on Alistair's shoulder, then began unsaddling Moonstone.

"I've got that." An older Black man stopped Darion. "This is what you pay me for."

Royalty, whether the real blood-related kind or the self-appointed money kind, didn't tend to their own horses. They hired grooms.

"Thank you, Tyrell." Darion patted Moonstone's neck, then walked down the aisle.

Alistair remained for a moment longer, asking Tyrell to take a close look at the horse's right rear leg and hoof.

"I might be imagining it, but it seemed as though Moonstone was favoring that foot."

"I'll do that, boss."

Alistair seemed satisfied, and went the direction Darion had gone. Probably to the big white tent for dinner. Callie's own stomach was demanding sustenance, but she wanted to finish checking just one more stall. George and his crew of stable hands were doing an excellent job, considering the demanding guests and the heavy workload. If they missed cleaning up a recently soiled stall, she'd pitch in to help, even though she was currently wearing a dress. The crew probably weren't even aware of their secret helper. Callie smiled to herself. Not many millionaires took joy in mucking out stalls.

A glance inside stall twelve showed immaculate straw bedding and a clean watering trough. She stepped back into the aisle. *Maybe one more stall.*

Tyrell moved smoothly around Moonstone in the wide aisle, cooing softly to the horse as he removed the saddle and bridle. Callie might not have noticed the man had one prosthetic leg if he hadn't been wearing cargo shorts.

Working for elite stables as a horse groomer could be a well-paying career. The groom was the first line of contact with the animals, often noticing health or emotional issues before anyone else.

Callie glanced into stall thirteen. She might as well clean the automatic waterer while she had the chance. When she finished, Callie stepped backward and almost onto the toes of Ted Fulson.

"Whoa. You startled me," Callie said.

"I was hoping for a minute of your time," Ted said. "Did you have the opportunity to talk to your husband about my proposal?"

Like I need Clint's permission?

"No, I did not." She had a few more words for the guy, now that she knew for certain he was the sleaze who swindled Mr. Nibley out of his mineral rights. But she held back. Callie didn't want to endanger Drew's case with the guy by letting him know the entire county was on to his deceptive business practices.

"In that case," Ted continued, "maybe we can find your hubby and have a sit-down over dinner."

"I am not interested. *We* are not interested. Now git out of my face."

Tyrell peeked under Moonstone's neck, glaring at Ted while addressing Callie. "Is this guy bothering you?"

"Ah," Ted said. "Mr. Smith. Did you remind Mr. Fallows about my offer?"

"No sir, I certainly did not." Tyrell stepped around the horse, then flicked a glance toward Callie. "This ghoul's been hounding Alistair since his wife's passing. Trying to buy the mineral rights to the horse farm."

"Really bad timing, Ted," Callie said. "If your offers are such a good deal, you wouldn't need to ram them down people's throats."

"I'm just trying to help Mr. Fallows." Ted shrugged. "He'll have expenses. Loss of income."

Callie folded her arms and made a point to look down at Ted. At nearly six feet, she was a couple of inches taller than the mineral rights buyer. Tyrell was even taller, and bulky with toned muscle.

"You might be used to tricking old farmers," she said to Ted, "but folks here this weekend have lawyers on retainer."

"And financial advisors," Tyrell said. "Heck, even I have one. I wouldn't sign a contract without asking my money guy. If you keep bothering Mr. Fallows, I'm gonna suggest he file a complaint with your employer."

"I think he's self-employed," Callie said.

"Then a restraining order," Tyrell said.

The horse groom's threat worked. But not before Ted pushed a Fulson Minerals Acquisition card at him. Tyrell frowned, and the card fluttered to the sawdust-covered aisle floor. Ted hustled off, glancing back over his shoulder once.

"I need to let our ranch foreman know that guy is not welcome here," Callie told Tyrell. "I apologize for him gettin' onto the ranch. Twice now that I know of."

"Not your fault," Tyrell said. "The vultures are circling, hoping a distraught widower is vulnerable to making a bad decision. A fool and his money."

"Are soon parted," Callie finished for him. "But Alistair's no fool. It seems to me his employees and clients hold him in high regard. And respected Marcia, too."

"God rest her soul," Tyrell said with genuine emotion. He picked up a brush and smoothed Moonstone's already glistening pearl-gray coat. "The two of them hired me after I graduated from a therapeutic riding program for veterans that was hosted on their farm." He tapped a fist to his prosthetic leg. "Lost my leg to a landmine. I had PTSD pretty bad after a tour in Afghanistan."

"Understandable," Callie said. "Thank you for your service."

Tyrell dipped his head in a quick nod. "Thanks, ma'am. When I couldn't serve as a Marine anymore, at least not in a combat capacity, I was pretty down. Horses saved my life. I've been with the Fallows ever since. Well, I'd better tend to Moonstone. See what's going on with his hoof."

As Callie left him, Tyrell began whistling a tune softly. Moonstone closed his eyes, clearly relaxing with the routine.

The groom had raised some thoughts for Callie. Marcia might have been seen by other people as having a difficult personality, but those closest to her were devoted. She headed for the tent, feeling the need to chat with Alistair.

He and Darion were walking out, disposable drink cups in their hands.

"Oh, hey Alistair." Callie was unsure how to lead into a discussion of murder suspects. She was certain the man blamed Callie for not acting quickly enough to save Marcia. *The cat.* "I wondered when you wanted Winston back?"

"I'm going to the trailer," Darion said.

"I'll be along in a few minutes," Alistair said.

Darion gave a wave and headed toward the pasture where the human trailers, RVs, and larger horse trailers were parked. Alistair turned to Callie.

"I owe you an apology," he said.

Darn right you do, Callie thought. But she just nodded, waiting for Alistair to continue.

"I had no right to blame you for Marcia's death," he said. "You did all you could do to help her. You even took in her silly cat." He paused, seeming to struggle to control his emotions. "I've heard about you and your friends."

"Oh?"

"Your private detective agency."

This might be good. Or bad.

"It's nothing like that," Callie said. "Just some women meetin' to talk about books and the local happenings."

"Happenings like murders?" Alistair asked, his ruddy complexion flushing deep red. "Marcia was not a drug addict. She was not suicidal. Many people found her difficult, but that's because she was driven. Mrs. Garcia, I need your help. To find out what really happened to my Marcia."

People began to file through the tent entrance. Heading to their homes, trailers, or local motels after a long day at the ranch.

"This isn't a good place to talk," Callie said. "How about we go up to the house?"

"I'd appreciate that," Alistair said.

Callie was certain Alistair had not murdered his wife, but she texted Clint to let him know she was taking the guy to their house. They took the back way to avoid being obviously "at home." Callie didn't need strangers trying to pop into her house.

When she opened the door to the mudroom, Winston trotted up to her. To Callie, not to Alistair. She lifted the cat.

"Here's your kitty," she said.

"Not mine," Alistair said. "Marcia's. She loved Winston so much." He reached to give Winston a pat on his fluffy head. "I'm terrified he'll escape again. May I ask, if it's not too much trouble, would you mind keeping him a little longer?"

The cat was growing on Callie. She didn't mind at all. "Sure. It's no problem. Can I refresh your drink?" she asked, opening the refrigerator.

"Do you have plain tea?" Alistair asked.

After pouring them both unsweetened iced tea and setting a plate of shortbread cookies on the table, Callie fetched a notepad and pen from the kitchen counter. Old school, but she didn't want to take the time to get a laptop. Alistair seemed in a mood to talk. She silenced her phone to avoid interruptions.

"Tell me more about Marcia. Could someone have wanted to eliminate her from the competition for a spot on the Olympic team?" Callie figured that was as high stakes as it got.

"Marcia wasn't planning to ride in the Olympics, but Moonstone is a strong contender. We both expected Darion would ride for us."

Winston stood at Callie's feet and mewed. She lifted him onto her lap.

"Like a jockey rides for the horse's owner," Callie said, to which Alistair nodded. Sometimes racehorses had multiple owners. Moonstone was probably unusual in that his owner had also been his trainer. "So Darion wouldn't have a reason—"

"Darion is like the child we never had," Alistair said sharply. Callie had heard him say the same thing in the barn when he didn't know anybody was listening. So it was probably true. "He's been sleeping in Moonstone's stall since Thursday to make sure no harm comes to the horse."

"Oh, wow," Callie said. "I didn't mean anything."

Alistair waved a hand. "You have to eliminate all the suspects. Like those animal rights crazies."

"They're on our radar," Callie said. "Although they shouldn't cause any more problems."

After the police arrived for the firecracker incident, she and Clint declined to press trespassing charges. But only because the group agreed to stay off the ranch property and not interfere with people entering or leaving the Equi X event. Even so, Callie wasn't removing any of them from the murder board suspect list yet.

"Did you ever find Marcia's cellphone?" Callie asked.

"No," Alistair said. "It vanished. Who knows? Maybe it's still in that hayloft somewhere. Although I called her number when the police . . . when I went to her . . . None of us could hear it ringing." Anguish twisted his ruddy face. "She was a wonderful woman. Why?"

Callie paused, waiting for Alistair to wipe his teary eyes with a paper napkin.

"I met Moonstone's groom," Callie continued. "Tyrell had nothin' but good things to say about you and Marcia." She wanted more information about the veteran's program. If Clint insisted on hosting more events at the ranch, Callie would be in favor of something that gave back to people. Especially veterans and first responders. But she'd ask later. Now was about Marcia. "You must treat your staff really well."

"Yes." Alistair frowned. "Another loyal employee. If you're looking for people who had intentions to harm my wife, I would look at Sydney Byron. She's been caterwauling about her horse being disqualified last year for failing a drug test."

"What was the drug?" Callie asked.

"Xylazine," Alistair said.

She had half-expected that to be the answer, but Callie still felt a jolt of shock.

"Sydney's horse, Sir Maximus, is a monster to trailer," Alistair said. "Xylazine is a sedative that is approved for use up to seven days before a performance. Marcia swears – swore – she did not administer the drug to Sir Maximus."

"Could someone else have drugged the horse?" Callie stroked a hand gently down Winston's fluffy white fur. He gazed up at her with what she imagined was an adoring look, his pumpkin-highlighted ears flicking back and forth between Callie and Alistair.

"Well, if they did, the person never stepped forward. Frankly, Sydney herself may have been the culprit. After Sir Maximus nearly trampled a stable hand prior to another event, Marcia threatened to drop him from our team if he couldn't be trailered safely."

"Hmm." Callie jotted notes. "Sydney sure tells a different story."

"Yes, she does." Alistair's phone pinged. He studied his phone screen. "Tyrell wants to discuss Moonstone's hoof." He returned his phone to his pocket. "Please keep me apprised of anything you learn about our case. I want to know the truth. And see the person responsible for Marcia's death punished."

"That's the goal of the book club," Callie said. "Find the truth."

"I'm grateful for any information you can provide," Alistair said. "Do I need to sign a contract? Give you a deposit?"

"I couldn't charge you if I wanted to," Callie said. "We're strictly amateurs."

She set Winston down. That cat had shown no interest in Alistair. Not that it acted afraid of him or anything like that. Winston had definitely been Marcia's cat.

As Alistair left, Callie considered the new clues. Marcia may not have drugged Sir Maximus, but Sydney believed she had, and still held a grudge despite the woman being dead. Alistair might not act completely grief-stricken in public, but he was grieving, Callie was certain.

And then there was Ted, pestering a newly widowed man to

make financial decisions. What was with that guy? Could he have committed a murder just to get a contract signed?

The more important issue right now was dinner. Callie had silenced her phone for her meeting with Alistair. She unmuted and began to message Clint. There was an unread text from Drew.

Chapter Twenty-Four

Makenzie set her phone down. This was how life would be, married to a police officer. Her attempt to arrange a dinner and movie date ended when he kept yawning on the phone.

Dustin sounded relieved when she released him from the obligation to go out.

"It's just you and me, Spirit." Makenzie sat beside the cat with the scarred face and torn ear.

The orange and white momma cat was affectionate and well-behaved, but Makenzie missed Pat Pat. Her hopes for a holiday weekend with Dustin had been dashed by the unfortunate death of Marcia in the hayloft. Makenzie struggled with the desire to have a good cry. Or bury her depression in a bowl of ice cream. The healthier alternative was clear. A bowl of popcorn and a Rom Com. A movie where the hero and heroine were guaranteed a happy ending.

"I don't need date clothes for an evening with you," she told Spirit. "No offense intended. You're always fabulous in your orange stripey coat."

"Meow." Spirit took a swipe at her own shoulder with her raspy tongue, as though making certain not a single golden hair was out of place.

Makenzie reached for her pajamas when her phone blew up with texts. She looked at the screen. There was an incoming text she'd ignored earlier while talking to Dustin.

Drew. Maybe she wants me to bring Spirit to her house.

The original text was not about cats.

"Looks like I'm going out after all," Makenzie told Spirit. "But not on a date."

Uncle Tobias was calling a meeting of the book club to discuss the autopsy results. The original four members of the book club were available. Or made themselves available, anxious for a break in the case. Emily was enjoying time with her son and grandkids, while Emiko was putting in a lot of hours digging into the new semester.

"I'm dressing for comfort."

After changing into leggings and a loose-fitting tunic, Makenzie packed her murder board and supplies.

Drew opened the front door to her home when Makenzie arrived and led her to the kitchen. Callie stood at the small table.

"Help yourself to leftover pizza," Drew told Makenzie. "Salad in the refrigerator."

Callie popped a slice of veggie pizza into the microwave. "I missed out on dinner."

"I was going to eat popcorn for dinner," Makenzie said.

"Clint dropped me off," Callie said. "He and Joel took Parker and the older Esselberry kids to the movies."

"Shanice is on her way." Drew glanced at a clock on the kitchen wall. "We have two hours for case talk, before my son returns."

Tobias limped down a short hallway. "Makenzie, I assume you brought your famous tri-fold board. May I help you set up?"

"Uncle, can I reheat you a slice?" Drew asked. "We can eat in the dining room. We hardly ever use it."

"There was a profound loss of appetite during dinner," Tobias said. "Thus, the plentiful leftovers. Yes, Drew. I would very much like more pizza, and salad if any remains."

The dining room furniture was vintage, if not antique. A long oak table provided the perfect base for the murder board, which Makenzie and Tobias arranged quickly. Shanice arrived just as everyone settled into the old farmhouse's formal dining room.

"Two meetings in one day," she said. "This must be

important."

"Pizza?" Drew asked.

"Thanks, but I ate dinner at the ranch," Shanice said. "I'll get myself lemonade."

Two pitchers, one of iced tea and one of lemonade, sat on a tray in the center of the table. People drank from mismatched glasses. Drew had told Makenzie she enjoyed decorating in a farmhouse chic style, resulting in the warm, rustic appearance of her home. Once everyone was seated, some eating and some not, Drew stood.

"Uncle Tobias has a development, but first, does anyone want to add to the board before he shares with us?"

Callie didn't wait. "This morning, George stopped the dog-faced girl from lighting firecrackers and tossing them in the arena," she said. "While there were horses and riders there. Remember her? She handcuffed herself to the new barn's door on Thursday."

While she told the alarming story of Cousin George catching the woman nearly in the act, Makenzie added to the existing sticky note with a black marker for suspect Josie Blackston. Attempt to disrupt jumping workshop. Weapon – firecrackers. Police intervention – no arrest.

"Does Josie have a motivation to kill Marcia?" Makenzie asked.

"She's a fanatic," Callie said. "Josie wasn't thinkin' about the consequences of her actions. She was gonna do whatever it took to stop people from ridin' horses. That's just crazy. I met Moonstone's groom. He's a veteran, and he told me horses saved his life."

"Does he go on the suspect list?" Makenzie asked, her pen poised over another sticky note.

"No," Callie said. "Definitely not. Here's the thing. Marcia's husband and employees were really devoted to her. I overheard things that convinced me none of them wanted her dead. Not Alistair, her husband. Not Moonstone's groom, Tyrell, or the rider, a young Spanish kid named Darion Fernandez. But

Alistair did tell me who he suspects. He felt pretty strong about it, actually."

"Okay," Makenzie said. "Who is it?"

"Already on the board," Callie said. "Sydney Byron. Alistair told me she's his top suspect, and he does believe Marcia was murdered. He also believes that if Sir Maximus was drugged, Sydney did it herself."

Makenzie added a star beside her name.

"She's a vicious gossip," Shanice said. "But a killer?"

"Remember I told you about Emily and me catching Sydney's groom digging around in somebody else's tack box in the old barn?" Callie asked. "Everything about Sydney strikes me as sketchy. Even the people working for her."

"Like Groom X? Already on the board?" Makenzie asked.

"I looked her up," Callie said. "Her name's Trisha Pinkton. Been working for Sydney for the past decade."

"Add her name to the Groom X note," Drew said. "We're brainstorming, right? There are no wrong ideas or incorrect suspects at this point. So, does anyone else have additions?"

"Unfortunately, yes," Shanice said. "I found quebrachine in Sam's refrigerator."

Makenzie waited for more details while everyone exclaimed with various defenses of Sam. He was certainly a well-liked guy.

Shanice told the group her story, with equal parts facts and venting. She expressed concern that Sam hadn't seemed to want her around while he reported the mysterious appearance of drugs to the police, even though she'd been the one to discover the quebrachine in the crisper. Unless he'd been the one to place it there. Did he really call Chief Holloway? Had Sam sent her away so he could dispose of, or alter, the evidence before talking to the police?

Makenzie felt for her friend, and her anxiety over Sam's guilt or innocence. They seemed like such a compatible couple, it would be a shame if Sam turned out to be a stone-cold killer. Then Shanice continued with her follow-up investigation of

Gemma in the event food tent.

"Gemma and Timothy came to the ranch early enough to have been able to plant the quebrachine in Sam's trailer," Shanice said.

"Motivation?" Makenzie asked, peeling a new sticky note off the pad.

Shanice shrugged. "Trying to deflect suspicion from herself? She's in the veterinary medicine school. She has access to animal drugs."

"Does she have a connection to Marcia?" Drew asked.

Makenzie hadn't started pinning string between suspects and the victim yet.

"Unknown," Shanice said, sounding a little disappointed. "Unless she's selling drugs? I have to admit, Gemma doesn't seem like the type."

Tobias had been silent during the murder board update. Now he stood, pressing his palms against the oak table to steady himself.

"If you are all finished?" he asked.

"We came tonight to hear your news," Callie said. "I'm on pins and needles."

"I heard the results of Marcia's autopsy," he said. "Her death has nothing to do with quebrachine, also known as yohimbine. It is not present by any brand name or means of consumption. Marcia died from an overdose of xylazine, an animal sedative. And it does not appear it was self-administered."

"That explains homicide as the cause of death," Makenzie said. "Another person was involved?"

"Unfortunately," Tobias continued, "the injection was very likely given against Marcia's wishes. There were signs on her body of a struggle."

Callie looked ill.

"Are you okay?" Shanice placed a hand on the tall cowgirl's shoulder.

"That's just sickening," Callie said in a weak voice. "If I'd heard Winston just a few minutes sooner—"

"No!" Drew shouted, startling everyone. "You stop that, Callie. The responsibility for Marcia's death falls squarely on the shoulders of a murderer." She jabbed a finger in the direction of the tri-fold poster. "Maybe a name on Makenzie's board."

"Why did Marcia say the names of two drugs?" Makenzie asked. "And think about this: she used the real names, not street slang like 'tranq.' It seems like that's the language she'd use if she'd been a drug addict. If xylazine was what the killer injected her with, why mention quebrachine?"

"It's used to bring animals out of sedation," Shanice said. "Marcia wasn't a doctor or a veterinarian, but she'd spent her life around horses. Maybe the killer jabbed her with the sedative, and she thought a shot of quebrachine might counteract it."

"Marcia received a dose typically given to a horse," Uncle Tobias said. "A full-sized horse, not one of the mini varieties. There was nothing you could do, Callie. Even if you'd been there sooner, or if you'd understood what she was asking. There was no coming back for her."

Tobias sat. Callie looked stunned. Shanice draped one arm around Callie's shoulders while tears ran down the cowgirl's pale cheeks. Makenzie hoped her friend recovered from the shock and misplaced sense of guilt soon.

"What is the official time of death?" Shanice asked.

"Twelve thirteen," Tobias said. "But the question critical to solving this is when Marcia was injected with the sedative. And the coroner estimates it occurred within an hour prior to her death. Probably sooner."

"So some time after eleven in the morning," Makenzie said. "Closer to eleven fifteen. And when did Alistair say Marcia went missing? Or the cat? Or both?"

Makenzie added the information to the top of her murder board. Not just a homicide. A murder with a defined timeline.

"Alistair started searching for Marcia before the opening barbecue," Callie said.

"And he said Winston went missing around eleven," Shanice said. "I ran into Alistair as the barbecue lunch was getting ready to start."

"What do we do now?" Drew asked. "Solve the murder, obviously, but how? What are our next steps?"

"Eliminate suspects," Tobias said. "Although the Rose Creek police are perfectly capable of solving this mystery, I have noticed your book club is equally capable of lending an occasional hand in the form of insights."

"One place we can start is checking the veterinary school drug safe," Shanice said. "Emiko and I snuck into the lab once, but this time I need to get into that safe. I'm going back."

A spy mission? Makenzie could think of no better way of freeing up Dustin's time than assisting him and the rest of the police with solving the crime. Especially doing something they couldn't. *A quasi-legal break-in. Maybe totally illegal.* Makenzie decided not to confirm it with Drew and Tobias. Her mind was made up.

"You are not going without me."

Chapter Twenty-Five

Shanice still wasn't certain she was doing the right thing. Getting caught sneaking around the veterinary school on a Sunday night could risk her career. Was she craving excitement? Time with her chemist friend? Was her goal really to find Marcia's killer?

Before she could talk herself out of it, she picked up Makenzie and drove toward the university.

"We have to clear up Gemma's involvement one way or another," Shanice said, "or I'll never be able to work around her."

"No kidding," Makenzie said. "Who wants to have a killer for a coworker?"

"Although I seriously doubt she's a murderer," Shanice said. "Still, if she's peddling animal drugs to human addicts, that's as bad."

Shanice pulled into the dark parking lot behind the veterinary college annex. Her red Mazda Miata wasn't exactly discreet. Parking under the leafy branches of a tall elm, she gripped the steering wheel, then glanced at her passenger.

"Are you sure you want to do this?" Shanice asked.

"Now that we're here, it seems a lot riskier." Makenzie giggled nervously. "But how much trouble can we get in? It's a vet school, not the FBI headquarters."

"We're not breaking in," Shanice said. "I have the code."

Not officially. She and Emiko had done their clumsy spy work Saturday morning. The numbers she had obtained by watching a grad student punch the code onto the keypad weren't something to which she was technically entitled.

"Last chance to bail out." Shanice placed a hand on her door handle.

"If this helps clear Sam," Makenzie said, "I'm in. Let's roll."

Shanice opened her door. The interior overhead light flashed on. They hopped out and slammed the two doors in unison, shattering the quiet night.

"We're not very good at this," Makenzie whispered.

"Come on," Shanice said. "Let's get this over with."

"Before we get busted."

Shanice and Makenzie had debated dressing in all black, but decided that would definitely look suspicious if they ran into anyone late at night at the university. Normal summery street clothes would fit in on campus, and sneakers would enable a fast escape.

Shanice led Makenzie to the side door of the veterinary college annex. They tried to walk with an "I belong here" attitude. A math Associate Professor and a woman who had never attended college here. Entering the vet school Sunday night.

They were on a mission. There might be animal sedatives in the drug safe that could prove a connection to Marcia's death. Especially if the inventory list showed a discrepancy between what was supposed to be in the safe, and what she and Makenzie found tonight.

If Gemma was a viable suspect in Marcia's murder, what was her motivation? Had she been involved in a drug deal gone wrong when Marcia accidentally overdosed?

Makenzie held her phone flashlight over the door keypad while Shanice tapped in 8-6-7-2-5-2-2. The lock clicked. Shanice pulled the door open, and they were in.

Their sneakers padded down the hall, squeaking occasionally on the polished linoleum floor. Ambient light from instruments provided enough of a glow that Makenzie clicked off her flashlight app.

The lab was unlocked. Shanice tapped Makenzie's arm and pointed to a glove dispenser. Makenzie nodded. They both pulled on blue nitrile gloves. Shanice tiptoed through the lab, even though the building was silent. She pulled open the cabinet door Emiko had discovered. The clear glass of the drug safe door emitted a bright glow.

Shanice tapped the code onto the keypad. The lock clicked. She tugged the door open.

"Here's the list," she whispered to Makenzie, handing her the safe's inventory. "I'll do a physical search."

Shanice tried to remove the vials and plastic bottles carefully, so she could return them to their correct locations. Now that they knew Marcia had definitely overdosed on the animal sedative xylazine, against her will, their mission seemed even more urgent.

The drugs had various brand names. Both Shanice and Makenzie compared names on labels to the two drugs using their phones.

"I don't see quebrachine on the inventory list," Makenzie whispered. "Or yohimbe, yohimbine. Nothing. But there are several sedatives. Including, oh look, one of the brand names for xylazine. One bottle."

"Ah," Shanice said. "Got it." She held the vial in her gloved hand. "Just one. The top looks sealed. Unopened."

"What now?" Makenzie asked. "Do we take it to the police?"

"Let's take photos," Shanice said. "The bottle and the list. As for how to report our sleuthing to Chief Holloway, I haven't thought that far ahead. We're not supposed to be here."

"Shh." Makenzie held a finger across her lips. "I hear something."

Whoever was walking in the hallway was not trying to disguise their steps. Makenzie tiptoed to the door and peeked out.

"Security guard," she whispered.

Shanice scrambled to put the drugs back in the safe, trying

not to drop them in her haste. Makenzie handed her the inventory notebook. She tucked it inside and closed the safe with a click just as the wobbly light of a moving flashlight shone in the hallway. Makenzie scooted across the floor and under a counter. Shanice duck-walked under a stainless-steel table.

The light became stronger. Shoes clipped louder on the floor as the guard approached the lab.

Had she made the wrong choice? And endangered the reputation of her friend Makenzie? But their excursion had proved there was a source for the drug that killed Marcia right here.

And Gemma had access to it.

The flashlight fanned across the floor of the lab. The sound of the guard's shoes tapping paused. Shanice held her breath.

The light flashed across Makenzie's hiding place. Maybe black clothing would have been the better choice. The white background of her floral print tunic seemed to glow briefly. The light moved on. The footsteps resumed. Shanice exhaled.

*   *   *

Callie stood behind the closed French doors to her bedroom's balcony early Monday morning. Not to savor the air conditioning before heading out into the heat of the day. No, she kept the doors closed and peeked through the sheer curtains to avoid being seen.

Privacy. It was a luxury she hadn't been able to indulge in since agreeing to host the workshop, other than taking refuge in her and Clint's giant house. But the point of having a large piece of property was to be able to wander around outdoors without seeing other humans.

Today was the final day of the Equi X event. Every guest would be gone by Tuesday at the latest. Callie thought she just might survive with her sanity intact. All she wanted was to have her peaceful ranch back.

The bedroom door nosed open. Clint must not have latched

it fully closed when he left after showering and dressing.

"Mew?" Winston stuck his head through the opening, then pushed the rest of the way through.

"Come on in."

Callie lifted the fluffy white cat. He was all fur, no substance. He nuzzled his flat nose into her neck and purred.

Callie's cellphone pinged. Morning reports from the Rose Creek Reads book club. Callie smiled. She sat on a chair in the sitting area of the expansive bedroom. Winston settled onto her lap in a tight ball.

Shanice and Makenzie were excited about their foray into the veterinary lab at the university. Texts came in a jumble, each announced with a ping that caused Winston to flick his pumpkin-colored ears.

The safe contained one vial of the drug xylazine. The same drug that had been discovered during a blood test given to Sir Maximus. The same drug listed in the autopsy report as the cause of Marcia's death.

Shanice reported that nothing was missing from the drug safe, and the xylazine appeared unopened.

After a two-month delay in beginning a relationship with the horse doctor, Shanice had finally seemed to find happiness. As the just-shy-of-six-foot cupid in cowgirl boots, Callie felt responsible if the match was doomed. But she and Clint had known Sam way longer than they'd known Shanice. Sam was one of the good guys. She tapped her own message.

Sam didn't have xylazine in his fridge. He's innocent of any wrongdoing. I'm positive.

Shanice answered. *I hope you're right.*

Callie continued tapping her own notes. She reminded the book club about Sir Maximus being improperly sedated prior to an important competition, while Alistair claimed Sydney was the one who drugged her own horse. He really had it in for Sydney, but why would she kill Marcia if she caused her own horse to be disqualified? Neither Sydney nor Alistair had access to the university vet lab, but being heavily involved in the equine world, they probably could have obtained the drug elsewhere.

Callie continued, texting that she was upset that Ted Fulson hovered like a vulture, grasping for the Fallows' horse farm mineral rights. Maybe Fulson eliminated Marcia, thinking Alistair would be more agreeable to selling the rights with his wife gone. Ted should move up a couple of notches on the suspect list.

Drew are you there? Makenzie texted.

Prepping for birthday party.

As if there wasn't enough going on, Parker was turning nine today. Callie had promised to attend, and hoped to drag Clint away from the workshop for a couple of hours. They were gifting the boy with a tote full of horse grooming gear, plus a gift certificate for more classes with Linda. Hopefully, the horse lease would work out, and the boy could feel like Flash, the pinto Parker rode during lessons, was his own horse, even if it was only for the length of a contract.

Drew texted her agreement that Ted was a sleazy businessman. They had hoped to get Mr. Nibley's contract cancelled on a technicality, but so far they hadn't found a loophole to release the old farmer from a bad deal.

Could Ted be a murderer? Drew saw no reason to remove him from the list, but there were still questions about the RAOR group. Especially after the firecracker incident.

Emiko texted her discouragement that last night's mission had neither confirmed nor eliminated Gemma as a suspect. *Is there anything else we can do to narrow our list?*

Pinpointing who was where and when would help, Drew texted.

Marcia went searching for Winston around eleven on Thursday morning. Her time of death was confirmed as twelve thirteen.

Shanice reminded the group about her dinner with Gemma and Timothy at the ranch last night. Both claimed they hadn't attended Equi X until early Sunday.

I'll keep an eye out for RAOR people, Callie texted. *Ted's been banned from the ranch, so I shouldn't see him today. I need to get this cat off my lap and get ready for another busy day.*

After a flurry of texts from the ladies asking about Winston's well-being, they all signed off. With Clint's comments about her clothing choices the previous day in mind, Callie dressed in an above-the-knee denim skirt and a pretty Western-style blouse. She grabbed a quick breakfast and a cup of coffee Clint had thoughtfully left warming in the kitchen. She checked Winston's food and water and gave him a pat.

"I envy you gettin' to hide out here all day. But I'd rather be able to go outdoors. At least I'm too big for the owls to carry off." She stepped out of the kitchen door to take the back way to the barn. "Time to face the crazy."

Outside the old barn, the location of Marcia's murder, Aster raked a pile of straw into a mound. She abandoned the hippie skirt for cut-off denim overalls over a tie-dyed t-shirt. Her round eyeglasses were shaded with clip-on sunglass lenses of a different size and shape. Aster lifted the rake loaded with manure and straw, scooping it into a wheelbarrow with gloved hands.

Speaking of crazy.

"What are you doing here?" Callie asked.

"Helping George finish his chores." Aster wiped the back of a gardening glove across her forehead, mopping up sweat. "We want to go to Pastor Foster's Labor Day picnic this afternoon. No alcohol. Lots of games and music."

It still boggled Callie's mind how George had gone from a lazy drunk to a church-going upstanding citizen in just a few months. She hoped it lasted a lifetime.

"That sounds like more fun than bein' here," Callie said sincerely.

"You should come," Aster said. "I was always turned off to the Bible thumpers, but I really like Pastor Foster's message. For a fundamentalist, he's cool."

"I need to stick around here," Callie said. "Maybe you can help me out on one thing."

"Gladly."

"Are your friends with the animal warpaint gonna attempt a return appearance?"

"The RAOR zealots," Aster said, leaning on the rake. "Not after the firecracker incident."

"I'm really grateful George stopped that gal before someone," Callie said, then paused, "or some horse, got hurt."

"They promised to stay outside the front gate," Aster said. "I believe they will. The encounter with the police really scared Josie. They mean well, but their leader, Everly, the one with the cat paint, she's so rigid."

"Meaning?" Callie asked.

"We sort of had a falling out. Everly is a strict vegan. Me, Rosemary, and Silas are lacto-ovo vegetarians."

"Remind me again what that means?" Callie asked.

"On the Red Cedar Meadow farm, we raise and consume dairy products and eggs. But no meat. Everly doesn't eat any animal products at all, including honey."

"Right," Callie said. "In your opinion, would a vegetarian be capable of killing a human?"

Aster wrinkled her nose, causing her glasses to rise up. "I know where you're going with this." She pointed into the old barn. "The woman who died in there. But we were all outside. First at the front gate, and then at the new barn when Josie cuffed herself to the door."

"The girl with the dog face paint," Callie said. Aster nodded. "Did you have an eye on everyone all the time?"

"Well, all you have to do is check your security cameras, right?"

Callie sighed. Life was going to be interesting if this girl ended up as part of the family. That certainly seemed to be where she and George were headed. Marriage. Pastor Foster might put the fun in fundamentalist, but he wouldn't condone shacking up in his congregation.

"The police aren't tellin' us much," Callie said. "I'm just tryin' to get a sense of what happened when."

"I can tell you this," Aster said. "RAOR arrived at the ranch at ten. We were all at the gate until noon. Shanice and Sam saw us coming up the driveway. Josie handcuffing herself to the barn door is well documented in the press."

The welcome barbecue had started on Thursday around noon. Tobias said the autopsy listed Marcia's time of death as twelve thirteen. The fatal injection was estimated to have been given to her within an hour prior. Between eleven and twelve or so? It was easy enough to turn Clint loose on the security footage to confirm where the animal rights folks were from their arrival to the discovery of Marcia's body. There wasn't a camera aimed at the old barn, but finding people on the other cameras at the right times might at least confirm their innocence. Making progress on the case would be nice.

"First Everly gives me grief for eating cheese and eggs," Aster said. "Then Josie nearly succeeds in hurting the animals she claims she's trying to help. I thought their hearts were in the right place. That's why I wanted to support them. But I'm done with those people. If one of them is involved in that woman's death," she tilted her head toward the open doors of the barn, "then let me know what I can do to help catch them. But I'm guessing your spy cameras will account for them being at the gates or at the new barn the entire time."

Callie raised her hands in surrender. "Okay. We'll get it straightened out. I'm tryin' to get people off the suspect list. Narrow it down to the actual killer so we can solve this case."

"So it's murder?" Aster asked, her bristly attitude melting into concern. And a little fear.

Callie still didn't know whether to trust Aster with inside information. She didn't want to get Tobias's "little birdie" in trouble.

"We'll know for sure soon. Until then, please keep what I said on the down-low. And thanks for your info."

Aster drew her fingers across her mouth, indicating her lips were zipped. Then she turned back to her task, scraping the rake over the ground and gathering another mound of soiled straw.

"Hey," Callie said, "for the record, I never seriously thought you would hurt anyone."

Aster looked up, smiling. "Thanks for having faith in me."

"Anybody that can straighten out George must be a little bit of an angel."

The words had slipped out of Callie's mouth without thought. It must have been the right thing to say, because Aster dropped the rake and grabbed Callie in a hug.

I sure hope I'm right about checking her off the suspect list.
But not the rest of that RAOR group.

Chapter Twenty-Six

The holiday weekend was flying by. Tomorrow, Shanice had to return to business as usual. That wasn't going to be easy, considering all the unanswered questions. About Marcia's death. Sam's potential involvement. And whether her new colleague Gemma was dealing in animal drugs. To a human clientele.

Just one more day to spend at the Double C ranch, immersed in the world of horses. Shanice wished she could take Tuesday off to recover. Until earlier this year, teaching math had been the most significant component of her formula for personal satisfaction. The Rose Creek Reads book club had changed the trajectory of her personal life. But a homicide investigation definitely couldn't be allowed to interfere with her career. No more taking risks. Last night could have ended her idyllic life teaching math at the Rose Creek branch of the university.

Although it had been exciting.

"Good mornin', Shanice." Callie waved from the new barn doorway.

Shanice walked up to the Texas cowgirl. The IT genius had abandoned her usual worn jeans and nerdy t-shirts for a skirt and blouse. Still with cowgirl boots, but that was the fashion at all the workshops involving Western-style riding.

"Are you going to Parker's birthday party?" Shanice asked.

"Yeah. That's hours from now. Lots of work to do in the meantime."

"I hope you're not mucking out stalls in that cute outfit," Shanice said.

Callie glanced down at herself. "Clint asked me to try lookin' like the owner of the place, not the hired help." She laughed. "Hopefully I can resist the temptation to shovel manure, and wear this get-up to the party later."

"I got Parker a gift that's partially for Boomer," Shanice said. "A sweatshirt with a picture of a basenji dog for Parker, and a neck scarf for Boomer with a matching design and color."

"That sounds perfect," Callie said. "You did great in the workshop Saturday."

"It was a blast," Shanice said. "I'm not ready for the responsibility of horse ownership, but I'm definitely taking more lessons."

"Sam has two horses," Callie said with an innocent look. "Just sayin'."

Shanice crossed her arms in front of her. "Realistically, I'm not able to count on having access to his horses." She paused. "I'm not able to count on anything. My usual luck in romance."

"You might have your doubts," Callie said, "but I don't. I wouldn't have tried to get you two together if I thought Sam was a deceitful person. He's a straight arrow. I'm certain."

"I wish Marcia's death could be cleared up," Shanice said. "It cast a shadow over everything." She glanced up at the cloudless sky. "Despite another hot day in the forecast."

"Nope. No rain clouds," Callie said. "I'm glad for that, at least. Rain would make a mess of the ranch, with all the extra foot and hoof traffic."

Shanice glanced at her cellphone. "I'd better go. I'm meeting Sam at his trailer before the events get started."

Instead of feeling happy anticipation, Shanice dreaded seeing Sam. Would he tell her whether the police had learned anything about the quebrachine in his refrigerator drawer? Shanice wanted desperately to believe Callie's assessment of Sam's good character, but she had been burned before. Her judgment had been so wrong in her previous relationship with her cheating fiancé, Shanice didn't trust her own heart. *Please let Callie be right.*

When she tapped on the door, Sam opened it immediately.

"Come on in." He waved a hand, inviting her up the steps.

Shanice sat on the little sofa. Sam offered her a drink, and she accepted a bottled lemonade.

"So," Sam began, "let's get the elephant in the room out of the way." He handed her a copy of a police report. "Chief Holloway wants to talk to you, too, when you have time. I'll give you a moment to look it over."

He sat in a cushioned chair and thumbed through an equine magazine.

Shanice stared at the papers in her hand. She wanted to thrust them back and tell Sam she trusted him without needing evidence of his innocence. But that would be a lie.

Sam's statement in the report was that Shanice had discovered an animal prescription drug in his refrigerator. He had not placed it there. Sam had a separate, locked refrigerator and cabinet in a small area of the trailer he used as an office. He never kept drugs, ointments, sprays, or anything used in his veterinary practice anywhere near his human food and drink.

That makes sense. The university veterinary lab kept tight control of its animal drugs. Well, if you considered an easy-to-guess key code tight control.

When this is all over, I'll ask Callie to talk to campus security about their keypad coding.

Shanice read the report carefully, searching for any red flags, and finding none. The police noted that trailer door locks were notoriously vulnerable. She lowered the papers.

"Why?" she asked. "Why break in and plant quebrachine in your refrigerator?"

"To deflect guilt away from a killer and onto me?" Sam asked.

"That makes no sense." Shanice debated for a moment, then plunged ahead. "I learned last night that the quebrachine overdose rumor is untrue."

Sam nodded. "Okay. As I said, it's unlikely to cause a fatal overdose, but not impossible. Does that mean the autopsy report has been released?"

"Yes. It's official." Shanice felt like she was being interviewed when her intention had been to grill Sam until she was confident of his innocence. Or guilt. "Marcia was injected with a dose of xylazine typical of what a full-sized horse receives." She studied Sam. "Probably unwillingly."

His deep brown cheeks paled to a lighter shade as the blood seemed to drain from his face. "Why?"

Shanice shook her head. "Callie said Marcia's family and employees speak of her with affection and loyalty."

"People often do when someone has recently passed," Sam said.

"This sounds genuine. Marcia did have rivals. Other trainers. People who were competing against her clients and horses for a slot on the Olympic team."

"Then why did someone plant the quebrachine in *my* trailer?" Sam asked. "I don't compete in dressage and hunter-jumper events. Sure, I work with horses in any specialty, but I'm a Western rider. What threat am I to anyone?"

Sam was distressed. Not in a guilty, I've-been-caught way. Shanice was certain he was upset and baffled at being drawn into Marcia's murder case.

"Let's consider the scenarios," Shanice said, channeling her inner sleuth. "Sydney says Marcia injected Sir Maximus with xylazine, causing his disqualification from competition last year. Alistair thinks Sydney drugged her own horse. The animal rights group accused the entire equine world of abusing horses. And, just to make things interesting, there's a pushy guy trying to buy up mineral rights, who could have wanted Marcia out of the way to make a deal with Alistair."

"Whew. Well, I'm glad I'm not the only suspect." Sam leaned forward in his chair. "I still don't understand planting drugs in my trailer. The killer just randomly decided I was a good subject to take the blame?"

"Sam, this is uncomfortable, but there is one way to clear your name. Of murder, anyway."

Sam raised one dark eyebrow. "There are other potential charges?"

"There is xylazine in the university veterinary school," Shanice said, hoping Sam wouldn't ask how she knew. "Makenzie learned humans add it to other drugs, with horrible consequences. Could someone be selling drugs?"

"That ended up killing Marcia Bentworth-Fallows," Sam said. "Meaning there could actually be someone going about their business as though they hadn't killed Marcia just days ago. Unless they fled immediately? There have been hundreds of people here and gone this weekend."

"And more leaving this afternoon," Shanice said. "Back to my proposal about a way to clear your name. We learned the time of death."

"On the autopsy report."

"I'm uncomfortable asking, but can we review what we did Thursday afternoon?" Sam was silent, so Shanice continued. "Everyone in the book club was tasked with nailing down the timeline."

"I see. As I recall, we found Callie in the old barn."

"Before that," Shanice said. "And the exact time is important."

Sam leaned forward and placed his elbows on his jean-clad knees.

"We were in the new barn, rearranging horses," Sam said. "We moved Ulysses and Andromeda from their stalls to paddocks." Sam's beautiful Appaloosa horses.

"I think I took a picture." Shanice scrolled through her phone. "Okay, I snapped a photo of Andromeda at exactly 10:42." She turned her screen to face Sam. The black mare with a white blanket of polka dots on her hindquarters posed for the camera like a cover girl. "And I met up with you right afterward."

"Ah. Marcia must have died close to that time."

Shanice didn't want to give anything away yet. "So right after I took this photo, Alistair and Sydney had their argument over stall assignments."

"Yes." Sam pointed at the photo. "See, the stall number seven, that's where Andromeda was before we moved them to a paddock to make room for Sir Maximus and Ladybird. Afterward, you and I cleaned up in my trailer."

"Before heading to the tent where the welcome barbecue was being staged." Shanice turned to her phone again, scrolling and tapping to open the Equi X event schedule. "Which began at noon."

"I was all set for a plateful of gourmet barbecue," Sam said, "but we saw Clint at the entrance. Callie had gone hunting for Marcia's cat. Now both the cat and Marcia were missing, and Callie hadn't responded to a text Clint sent."

That was exactly the way Shanice remembered the encounter.

"We volunteered to go to the house to see if Callie was there," Shanice said. "That couldn't have been much past noon."

"On the way to the house, we had an unpleasant meeting with the RAOR people," Sam said. "Then we saw the ambulance drive up to the old barn."

Callie's 911 call and the arrival of the EMTs were public record.

Sam and Shanice had been together the entire time from 11:00 to 12:13, the range the coroner established for the fatal injection. But what if that estimate was off by a few minutes? Where was Sam before 10:42? She checked the schedule.

"It's not on the official program," Sam said, as if reading her mind. "I had a private session with a small group for forty-five minutes before I met you in the new barn. It started at 10:00. I have witnesses."

He opened his business social media site and showed Shanice photos that participants had posted from his Thursday morning class. Thanks to the modern obsession with instantaneous look-at-me posts, the times confirmed Sam's location during the critical timeframe.

"I'm sorry, Sam. Of course, I don't believe you killed

Marcia. We're trying to narrow the field of suspects in order to identify the killer."

"You have a list?" Sam asked.

If Shanice didn't trust Sam by now, she should run from his trailer and never go back. She'd only known him for a little over three months, but Clint and Callie vouched for him, and they'd known him for three years.

Maybe I can trust my heart after all.

Shanice opened her cellphone notes and showed Sam the list.

"Interesting. I suppose the spouse is always the first suspect, but Alistair and Marcia seemed devoted to each other."

"Callie agrees with you," Shanice said. "She wants to cross him off the list, but until we have solid evidence—"

"Alibis," Sam said.

"Right."

"Is my alibi good enough?" Sam asked. His smile was tinged with a bit of awkwardness.

"Yes. When the club meets again to discuss our findings, I will insist your name is removed from Makenzie's murder board."

Sam laughed long and hard. Shanice was beginning to feel seriously insulted by the time he finally stopped.

"The police have used information our club gathered to solve crimes," Shanice said with an icy air.

"I meant no disrespect," Sam said with a smile. "The image that conjured in my mind was of your friends crowded around a wall covered with photos, newspaper clippings, and pushpins attached to red strings."

"It's not like that at all," Shanice said. "Makenzie's board is portable, for one thing."

Sam's phone chimed with an alarm. He glanced at his screen. "I need to prepare for my next workshop. Marcia's sudden absence opened slots for other trainers. My schedule became very busy as a result."

"Could someone have coveted being in the limelight

enough to attempt getting her out of the way?" Shanice asked.

"It is a competitive business," Sam said. "I hate to think mere business would be enough to motivate a person to harm another human."

He stood and reached a hand to Shanice. She grasped his hand and let him pull her to her feet.

"Are we good?" he asked.

"Being completely honest," she said, "I won't feel right about anything until Marcia's murder is solved. As for you, Callie is your most vocal defender. I trust her opinion. You tolerated an awkward conversation during which I basically accused you of a heinous crime. And your reaction was to laugh at me. So, yes. We're good."

Sam grinned and shook his head. Then his expression turned serious. "I hope the police figure this out soon."

"They will," Shanice said.

With a little help from the book club.

Chapter Twenty-Seven

"Good morning," Joel said softly.

Drew opened her eyes to sunlight filtering through the curtains. "What time is it?"

"Early. If you want to sleep in, I can take Parker to the ranch."

Joel was already dressed in jeans and a short-sleeved cotton Western shirt. His wavy black hair looked a little wild, not slicked back for business. He looked good as a cowboy. Drew rolled onto her side and glanced at the clock on the bedside table. *It is early.*

"No, I want to go. We were both there for the opening parade. I need to be there for the closing parade."

"It doesn't start until noon," Joel said. "You can sleep in. I'll come back for you."

"I want to go," Drew said. "If only to present a united front." She sighed and shook her head.

"Too many changes in his young life," Joel said. "We need to pick one of Tobias's options and get things on an even keel."

"Now one of the options includes my uncle." Drew swung her legs off the bed. "How can we consider remodeling the house to accommodate him, and then move back to Boston?"

"One decision is out of my hands." Joel looked at himself in the antique dresser's big mirror, combing his hair back from his forehead with his fingers. "I received an email hinting the junior partner position will be decided sooner than I expected."

Drew bit her lower lip. More money, more responsibility,

more hours. If Joel received the promotion to junior partner, their lives would return to the frenetic big city pace. The continued commuting from Boston to Rose Creek would be untenable.

Does it make me a bad person if I pray for my husband's failure?

She kept silent as she pushed her feet into slippers and pulled on her bathrobe.

"I can't believe this holiday weekend is almost over," Joel said. "The more we dig into the Nibley case, the more interesting mineral rights litigation becomes."

At the beginning of the summer, Joel had hoped Drew and Tobias would wrap up the Nibley case quickly so she and Parker could return to Boston. Instead, they had reached a compromise. Parker would attend school in Rose Creek for the fall semester.

Pushing the decision off for another few months. After that? Nothing was going to be resolved this morning. *Change of topic.*

"What do you think of Callie's theory that Ted Fulson killed Marcia to get easier access to her horse farm's mineral rights? It's not working, by the way. Alistair despises Mr. Fulson."

"I'm beginning to share his opinion," Joel said. "I wouldn't be surprised if he was the burglar trying to break into Tobias's office."

"What would be the point of that?" Drew asked. She grasped the edge of the dresser for support as a thought struck her. "He might have intended to harm Uncle Tobias. Kill him?"

"I doubt it was anything that dire," Joel said. "If Fulson eliminated the opposing law team, Mr. Nibley's family could simply hire another firm. No, I'd guess he was nosing around to see what information you and Tobias have gathered. What potential witnesses you were interviewing. Murder? That's a stretch."

"People kill over money every day," Drew said.

"And Uncle Tobias's cat tried to warn him. Like a watch-cat. He loves that scroungy alley cat."

"Feral cat," Drew said. "Spirit is a country girl. I'd like to try bringing her here, to test whether she and the puppy can coexist."

"I'd be more worried about Boomer than Spirit," Joel said with a laugh. "That cat looks like she's been in a few fights."

Spirit had been a filthy, bony mess when she demanded Makenzie help her. By the time Drew met the cat, she had been bathed by veterinarian Donni Ashton. Spirit's white belly and legs glistened, and her orange tabby topside and tail shone like burnished copper. But cleanliness and nutrition couldn't erase the cat's scarred nose and torn ear.

"You could be right," Drew said. "Boomer would probably be the loser if they had a disagreement. I need to get breakfast started."

"Let's go to Stockman's this morning," Joel said. "It's Parker's birthday. He's wallowing in angst over not getting a horse today."

"And everyone's managed to keep it a secret that we're going to lease Flash from Linda," Drew said. "Okay. Give me a few minutes. Rose Creek fashion might be casual, but I need to wear something more substantial than a bathrobe to go to the café."

Transporting Uncle Tobias was tricky. He was wobbly from pain medication and the painful bruises. Joel found a parking space right in front, on cobblestone-paved Main Street. Inside The Stockman's Café, the stools at the long lunch counter were filled with diners. Square tables had been squeezed in between the counter and the red vinyl booths. Almost every seat was taken.

"I've got one free booth," Sandy, the waitress, said.

"We'd like a table," Drew told her. "It might be painful for my uncle to slide into a booth."

"If you hang on a minute," Sandy said, "I can separate those two tables."

Drew followed the direction of Sandy's head nod. Mr. Putnam Nibley sat with another man. There had been more diners, apparently, as the busboy cleared dishes and coffee cups. Putnam looked up, and waved them over.

"We'll sit with Mr. Nibley, if that's okay."

"Perfect," Sandy said. "Be with you in a minute. We're hopping today!"

The busboy hastily swiped the table clean with a damp towel. Joel helped Tobias ease onto a chrome and red vinyl chair. Parker claimed a chair close to his uncle and began a careful study of the menu's breakfast selections.

"Nice to see you in a social setting, Putnam." Tobias extended a hand across the table. They clasped hands briefly.

"And you," Mr. Nibley said. "Although I'm not certain how social this meeting is, seeing as how you brought the entire legal team."

Tobias laughed. He looked at the man seated next to Putnam. "You must be one of the sons?"

"Carter." The fifty-something-year-old had the look of an office worker. His sandy brown hair was neatly styled. He dressed business casual, in khakis and a polo shirt. "We've spoken on the phone. I had extra time off with the Labor Day holiday, and decided to visit Dad. Check out the farm."

"It's always good to put a face with a name. This is my family." Uncle Tobias made introductions, after which Parker stuck his nose in a Western Horseman magazine.

"You just missed meeting my brother and his family," Carter said. "They're driving home today. We really enjoyed visiting the farm."

Putnam clasped a hand to his son's shoulder. "The boys had forgotten what a nice spread we have."

"If we can extricate Dad from this contract with Fulson Minerals, we're determined to keep the farm in the family."

"And me in charge," Nibley said, "if I refrain from signing contracts without their go-ahead."

"We'd like to place the farm in a trust," Carter said. "To avoid future issues."

"That would be beneficial for avoiding family conflicts down the road," Joel said.

Drew nodded her agreement. *Much better than trying to*

declare Putnam incompetent.

"I assume your firm can draw up that paperwork for us?" Carter asked.

"Certainly," Tobias said. "With the assistance of my partners."

Interesting. Uncle Tobias had never referred to Drew and Joel as partners before. He had expressed the desire for them to take over his law firm in the unlikely event he retired. So far, Drew had been operating as a quasi-employee. The arrangement definitely needed to shift from informal to official.

Sandy took their orders, and their food arrived quickly. Putnam and Carter lingered over coffee and pie.

"Can I have pie?" Parker asked, his eyes fixed on the plates of peach and apple wedges.

Pie for breakfast. Why not?

"It's your birthday," Joel said. "You can have whatever you want."

"But first," Drew added, "make an attempt to finish some of your eggs and pancakes."

Drew hoped Parker wasn't disappointed that his birthday breakfast had been dominated by business. So far, he seemed absorbed by food and his horse magazine.

"How is that cat working out for you?" Putnam asked Tobias.

"Spirit is a wonderful companion," Tobias said. "I'm surprised you didn't take her indoors years ago."

"I have a cat. Boots. And the two pups. I can't take in every stray that gets dumped on the farm."

"She may have saved my life," Tobias said.

"Really?" Carter asked.

Tobias nodded. "I nearly had a break-in Friday night. Spirit was having none of that, and raised a ruckus. Woke me up, and scared off the burglar."

"Did they get anything?" Carter asked.

"Didn't even make it inside," Tobias said.

It had been Drew's idea that the book club should pin down

the location of their suspects during Marcia's murder. She doubted she'd get any information, but she needed to try.

"I'm not making an accusation," Drew said, "but I do wonder whether Ted Fulson might have attempted to break into the law office."

"I'd believe anything of that jerk." Carter folded his arms across his chest. "He came out to the farm on Thursday. Surprised him to no end that I was there."

"That's completely out of line," Tobias said. "We're disputing the validity of the contract in court. He shouldn't have approached your farm."

"That's what I told him," Carter said. "Using less polite wording."

"A restraining order may be our next order of business," Tobias said.

"What did Fulson want?" Joel asked.

"He was hoping to catch me alone," Putnam said. "I'm certain of it. I made a mistake signing that contract. I'll never do that again. Not without consulting the expert." He patted Carter's arm.

Back in early summer, Putnam had seemed frail, mentally and physically. Whatever bad patch the elderly man had been going through, he seemed to have recovered his energy and sharpness over the summer. Perhaps he benefited from receiving more attention from his children. It was unfortunate that Ted Fulson had swooped in while Putnam was vulnerable.

"My guess is Fulson was going to try bullying Dad to stop fighting the contract," Carter said. "The guy is a crook."

"And maybe dangerous." Drew was even more convinced that Fulson was capable of killing Marcia, seeing her as an obstacle to getting the Fallows Horse Farm mineral rights. "Thursday, you said?" Both Nibleys nodded. "What time was this?"

"I arrived late Wednesday night," Carter said. "My brother didn't show up until Friday afternoon. I slept in pretty late, then I was helping Dad mow and clean up the front yard when Fulson rolled up. What time did I get up, Dad? Do you remember?"

Putnam shook his head. "Before noon, but past midmorning is all I recall."

"I was talking to my brother," Carter said. "That's in my call history." He tapped on his cellphone. "He called at 10:53. I hung up when Fulson arrived. Let's see. The call was nineteen minutes long. So Fulson arrived at 11:12."

"How long was Fulson at your farm?" Joel asked.

"Not long," Carter said. "I tried to hold my temper. I didn't want to endanger our case against him with verbal threats or by getting physical. But I did tell him to leave."

"Quite firmly." Putnam chuckled at the memory. "We'd better leave, son. People are lining up waiting for our table."

Drew glanced around. Stockman's was popular, but this weekend had drawn a capacity crowd. Parker had cleaned his plate, including his apple pie.

"We'd better go, too," Drew said.

Now she had a bit of data to add to the murder board. Drew wasn't certain how helpful it was in implicating Fulson. Or eliminating him as a suspect.

"Hey gang," Tobias said. "I'm afraid I'm going to have to bow out of the ranch activities. My leg is giving me trouble. I don't want to be on pain medicine while trying to negotiate excitable horses."

The side trip to the house to drop him off started a new drama. Parker couldn't bear the thought of leaving Boomer at home.

"I can keep your pup entertained," Uncle Tobias said.

"He'll be fine staying on the back porch," Drew said.

"Clint did say it's good to socialize puppies to crowds," Joel said.

"Please?" Parker bounced up and down on the toes of his cowboy boots.

Knowing Uncle Tobias would likely be tempted to turn the puppy loose in the house, Drew gave in.

"Okay, but I'm not carrying him if he gets tired."

While Parker readied Boomer, fetching his travel dishes, bottled water, leash, and harness, Drew tapped on her phone.

"What are you doing?" Joel asked.

"Checking to see how long it takes to drive from the Nibley farm to the Garcia ranch," she said softly. "Marcia was injected with the overdose sometime within an hour of her death at 12:13. Did Fulson have time to murder her after his visit to the Nibley farm?"

"And? How long is the trip?"

"It depends on how fast Fulson drove on the country backroads," Drew said. "It's not the distance so much as the curves and intersections. Fifteen minutes, according to my map app. If we suppose he did the deed before going to Nibley's farm, and he arrived there at 11:12, he didn't have time to inject Marcia with the drug, get from the old barn to his car, and then drive to Nibley's. That's an estimate, but the coroner said the fatal injection was given in the window between 11:13-ish to Marcia's death at 12:13."

"That does seem improbable," Joel said. "But if he left Nibley's at 11:15, let's say 11:20 at the latest, drove straight to the Double C, parked, found Marcia . . ." Joel's voice trailed off as he seemed to do the calculations.

"It's possible," Drew said. "Fulson could have made it within the timeline of 11:00 to 12:13. But it's tight. I'll let the book club know. Makenzie will want the information for her murder board."

Drew felt a little disappointed. Ted Fulson's movements didn't prove he was guilty. But they didn't provide solid evidence that he was innocent, either.

The book club still had a mystery to solve.

Chapter Twenty-Eight

Despite surviving the clandestine operation in the university veterinary lab undetected, Makenzie was still walking on eggshells the next morning.

She almost jumped out of her skin when Dustin's name came up on her cellphone. He didn't like Makenzie digging into Rose Creek mysteries, but he didn't try to stop her, either. She felt a little guilty about her obsession. Dustin wasn't trying to control her. He was worried about her safety.

And she just happened to be adding notes about their breaking and entering expedition at the college to her murder board at that very moment.

"H-hello?" She cleared her throat. "Hello, Dustin."

"Are you okay?"

"I was reading," Makenzie said, which was true. She was reading notes on her board.

"Are you busy?" he asked.

Makenzie set down her marker and sticky notes. "I always have time for you."

"Here's the thing . . ."

Makenzie cringed. Whenever Dustin used that phrase, something big was coming. Maybe good. Maybe not.

"Uh," Dustin continued, "my family decided on a cruise this December, instead of going to Disneyworld."

Dustin had mentioned the annual pilgrimage to the Disney park, and, in an offhand way, invited Makenzie. She didn't consider it a formal invitation.

"That's nice."

"I hope you don't mind," Dustin said. "You told me once that you haven't been to any of the Disney parks, so I thought you might be upset. I think the cruise will be okay."

Time to get to the point.

"Dustin, am I invited on the cruise? We haven't really made firm plans."

"Oh, well, yeah," he said. "I thought that was understood."

Makenzie wrestled with mixed feelings. Happiness that Dustin didn't seem aware she and Shanice had broken into the university lab, and frustration that he had made an assumption about their holiday plans.

Christmas was a huge event in the Selkirk household. It was only September first, but Mom was already making plans.

Mom. She would not be okay with her only child being absent on the biggest holiday of the year.

"When is this?" Makenzie asked. "Well, obviously December, but the dates? I'll need to let my boss know . . ." She stumbled on the words. Makenzie might not have a job by December. Ava had counseled her in the church kitchen to share her fears about a possible lay-off with Dustin. But now didn't feel like the right time. "Do I need to make reservations? Are your parents okay with this?"

"My sister Leah always makes the plans," Dustin said. "I'll get the details from her, but I think it's December twentieth through the twenty-seventh. Thereabouts. She mainly wants to know how many rooms she needs to reserve. Or cabins, I guess they call them on a ship."

"Before I make a commitment," Makenzie said, "I need to talk to my parents. They might be disappointed if I don't spend Christmas with them."

Devastated is more like it. Although they would be happy she and Dustin were building a stronger relationship.

"Of course," Dustin said. "That is a kind of stressful time of year. Crime doesn't take a holiday. But at least if I'm on a ship, Chief Holloway can't call me in to assist." He paused. "Like he cancelled our date by calling me in about Ms. Bentworth-Fallows, and then last night I faded out on you. I'm sorry about that. I hope we can reschedule goin' out for dinner."

Spirit wrapped herself around Makenzie's legs. She reached down and scratched the cat's golden head.

"Of course," Makenzie said. "I understand your job requires you to drop everything when you're needed."

My eyes are wide open about the demands of police work. Rose Creek was relatively peaceful. Makenzie believed crime was worse in big cities, where the police officer's job was more dangerous. *I have to stay in Rose Creek. No matter what happens with my job.*

"Have you heard anything about the case?" Makenzie asked, glancing at her murder board.

"Even if I knew, I couldn't tell you," Dustin said. "Hey, I'm going out to the ranch this afternoon. Not on police business. I want to see those miniature horses. Can I pick you up?"

"That would be nice," Makenzie said. "I'm planning to watch the closing parade. Parker is riding again, and then his birthday is at Drew's house afterward."

"I wish I could go to the party," Dustin said. "I'll send my present with you."

Spirit meowed loudly.

"Is that Pat Pat?" Dustin asked.

"No, I'm still babysitting Spirit."

"Will she be going back to Tobias?" Dustin asked. "Or is she a permanent resident?"

"Tobias might move in with Drew's family permanently. If not, he'll return to his own house. Either way, Tobias wants Spirit back."

"That's good news," Dustin said. "I'd hate to see you turn into a crazy cat lady."

He laughed, but Makenzie didn't think it was funny. Maybe because it hit too close to home. Until Dustin finally revealed his feelings for her this spring, Makenzie feared she might forever remain single, and living in her parents' converted garage mini-house.

Take away her job in the chemistry lab at Brieswell, add a couple cats, and Makenzie would be happy to adopt that lifestyle.

No. I have Dustin. And only one cat.

"I'll pick you up in an hour," Dustin said.

"I'll be ready."

* * *

Callie snagged seats high on the bleachers at the outdoor arena for Sam's final training workshop. He would demonstrate the proper techniques for training a horse to load in a trailer. Callie had texted the book club she was going to be at the event.

Shanice showed up first. Callie waved, catching the mathematician's attention. Shanice waved back and hurried over.

Even though she wore jeans and boots, Shanice managed to make it look fashionable with a blouse that looked more like it came from an import store than a Western outfitter.

"I really like your new look," Shanice said.

Callie glanced down at herself. The cowgirl boots were dressy, the denim skirt new, and the blouse a snappy coral with fringe and an embroidered yoke. Callie was stepping up her wardrobe choices. Making an effort to keep Clint happy, not to compete with the rich and famous equestrian set. Plus, dressing up really did make her feel nice.

"Thanks," she said. "I like your look."

"East meets west." Shanice glanced around. They were early. The bleachers were still pretty empty. But she lowered her voice anyway and leaned closer to Callie. "I just saw Sam. He showed me the police report he filed about finding the quebrachine in his refrigerator."

"I hope that set your mind at ease," Callie said.

"About Sam's innocence, but not about the lack of security living in a fifth wheel affords. Unless you have a custom lock installed, they're easy to break into. The only thing saving people who live in them is that most places they camp are relatively low crime."

"Clint's about to have a conniption about ranch safety," Callie said. "I told you about Sydney's groom diggin' around in someone else's tack box."

"Trisha," Shanice said.

"Right. Then Sam's trailer getting broken into?" Callie paused. "Marcia's murder. My solution is to never host another event. Too many strangers."

"I have to admit," Shanice said, "I enjoy the ranch more without a crowd."

Callie was glad Shanice was on her side. The ranch should be a peaceful haven, not a circus.

Several rows below their perch on the metal bleachers, Callie watched Sydney climb onto a seat in the center. Someone had tried to save a prime seat by placing a padded folding bleacher seat on the hard metal, but Sydney slid it to the side.

"Speaking of circus," Shanice whispered. She nodded toward dark-haired Sydney and the middle-aged woman she seemed to hang out with a lot.

"Yep, I could smell them coming," Callie answered quietly.

She guessed it was the older woman who smelled like a perfume bottle. The flowery scent rose in the summer air, causing Callie to wrinkle her nose. The women's voices rose, too. They spoke loudly, as though there wasn't another person around.

"I should have hired Dr. Grady last year," Sydney said, "when Sir Maximus became so put off on trailering. With the proper handling, I'm certain he would have been perfectly well behaved."

"Dr. Grady does seem to have the magic touch," the older woman said.

Callie whispered to Shanice, "I heard Sydney's horse is a monster to trailer."

"My hired girl Trisha has worked tirelessly with Sir

Maximus," Sydney said, "but he just loathes being loaded."

Talk about cringey, calling a woman over a decade older than yourself "girl."

"Perhaps the application of a buggy whip would help," Sydney's friend said. "To the horse, not your groom." She snickered.

"It's too bad the good doctor doesn't leave those Western types and work exclusively for our crowd," Sydney said.

From the look on Shanice's face as she silently mouthed the words "our crowd," Sydney's attitude was rubbing her the wrong way, too.

"True," the older woman said. "He could obtain a position working for the Olympic team."

"That whole mess with Sir Maximus being disqualified due to a certain someone's incompetence could have been avoided," Sydney said.

"Are you absolutely certain Marcia was responsible for drugging your horse?"

"Of course," Sydney said. "We hired a professional transportation service to ensure the safety of our horses. They're completely reliable. They would not sedate a horse without written permission from the owner. Marcia's job was to ensure the delivery of Sir Maximus from her stables to the trailer. The drugging had to happen while he was in her care."

"It's not too late to sue her estate," the older woman said with a disdainful sniff. "Anyone presenting themselves as a proficient handler of valuable equines who fails in their duties should be run out of business."

"Marcia Bentworth-Fallows is permanently out of business," Sydney said.

Both women erupted in extremely unattractive cackles.

Callie and Shanice exchanged a look. Shanice mouthed one word. "Guilty." Callie responded silently with, "Which one?"

The bleachers filled, despite the morning heat. Then a truck pulled a horse trailer into the arena. When it was parked, Sam entered the arena on foot. Four humans followed, leading four beautiful horses. Trisha Pinkton, the woman caught rummaging in a tack box in the old barn, had Sir Maximus on a short lead rope.

Sam had a way with horses, but Callie didn't believe it was magic. He had spent years learning how a horse's mind worked. Their emotions and instincts. Maybe some natural intuition was involved, but Callie believed Sam's talent was due mainly to hard work.

Even so, Sir Maximus challenged Sam's skill. The big copper horse balked at the trailer. Maybe he'd had some bad experiences trailering. Any attempt to strongarm the big gelding was bound to fail. Sam calmed the horse, eventually leading a willing animal inside the trailer.

When the crowd applauded, Sir Maximus spooked and backed out before Sam could close the gate. Instead of slamming it shut on his wide hindquarters, Sam let the horse back down the ramp. It looked like Sam was talking to Sir Maximus. The horse's ears flicked toward Sam.

The audience held their collective breath when Sam led the horse back to the trailer. Sam relaxed his hold on the lead rope. The horse made a couple of false starts. Sam did nothing to push the horse to a decision. After a pause, Sir Maximus walked purposefully up the trailer ramp and inside.

No one applauded this time, seeming to sense how delicate the horse's temper was concerning entering a narrow metal box, against all natural instinct. He did it, and Sam didn't close the gate. After a full minute, Sam coaxed the horse back down the ramp. Now the audience clapped.

Callie had seen Sam in action many times. It never ceased to impress her how patient he was with horses. No wonder the Japanese racehorse owner had brought Sam to his stables at great expense.

As the trailering workshop concluded, she snuck a glimpse of Shanice's face. Callie was certain that look wasn't just admiration for Sam's horse training skills.

The extra-tall cupid must have finally done good.

Chapter Twenty-Nine

Joel held Boomer in his lap. At first, Drew had been convinced that bringing the basenji puppy to the crowded ranch was a mistake. *So far, so good.*

"There's Callie." Drew waved when she saw her friend enter the bleacher area of the huge indoor arena. "Up here!"

Callie climbed to the seat they had saved for her.

"How's your uncle doing?" the cowgirl asked.

"Healing is a slow process for a man his age," Drew said. "He's been taking a lot of naps. That's unusual for a high-energy guy like Tobias."

"He wanted to be here," Joel said, leaning forward on the bleacher seat to look around Drew at Callie. "The fact that he decided to stay home must mean he's still in serious pain."

Callie reached a hand to Boomer. The puppy sniffed her fingers politely, but didn't lick.

"Nice pup," Callie said. She rubbed the top of his head.

Drew felt a swell of pride in the silly creature. *Such a little gentleman.*

"He seems to be handling this crowd well," Joel said.

"We couldn't leave him at home," Drew explained. "If my uncle heard whining on the back porch, he wouldn't be able to resist letting Boomer into the house. The last thing he needs is to trip over a puppy."

"I wish your uncle could be here," Callie said. "He really likes having a cowboy nephew, and Parker's a good rider. He caught on fast."

"It's starting," Joel said.

Drew raised her phone, deciding on the best angle and zoom to capture the event for her uncle and family back in the Boston area. The closing ceremony mirrored the opening, culminating in a parade.

"There's the kids," Callie said. "Entering the arena now."

Drew pressed record. She couldn't help smiling as Parker rode in on his lesson horse, and soon-to-be-leased horse, Flash. The chestnut and white pinto, with Western saddle and bridle, exuded an Old West look. A year ago, she never would have imagined her son falling in love with horses. Parker kept his horse in line with the other kids' and kept his flag upright.

After seeing the Olympic-quality jumpers and dressage horses this weekend, Drew wondered where Parker's interest in horses would lead. She wanted to encourage her son's chosen athletic pursuit. If only their lives weren't in limbo.

The weekend had been busy. There was one more big event. At Parker's birthday party, she and Joel would tell their son about the horse lease. Parker could ride Flash anytime during the lease period, not just for lessons. Drew eagerly anticipated springing the surprise on their son.

In between the parade and the party, she hoped she had time to put her feet up. The bleachers were hard, and the day had been hot.

As the last horse and rider exited the arena, Callie wiped a hand across her brow dramatically.

"Whew! We survived Equi X!" She began the climb down the bleachers, but turned and waved. "I'll see you at the party."

Drew must have looked as tired as she felt. Joel leaned close.

"Are you okay?" he asked. "Your uncle and I can manage the party if you're too tired."

"I've got nearly half my pregnancy to go," Drew said. "I can't believe how tired I am already."

"Too much activity the past three days," Joel said. "Although we should see a doctor, just to make sure everything's okay."

He shifted Boomer to his left arm as he offered Drew his free hand. They climbed down the bleachers slowly. Before reaching the bottom seats, Dustin and Makenzie hopped up to assist.

"I feel ridiculous," Drew said.

"Don't," Makenzie said. "It's never a bad thing to accept a helping hand."

"Parker looked like a natural," Dustin said. "I'm on duty tonight, so I'll have to miss the party, but Makenzie's bringing my gift."

"Our son's going to be so spoiled," Drew said. "You didn't have to give him anything."

"My sister's kids are halfway across the country," Dustin said. "I've gotta have somebody close by to spoil."

"We need to find Parker and get the birthday boy presentable," Joel said.

Drew and her husband parted ways with Makenzie and the deputy. They strolled down the aisle past horses and riders. The plan was for the kids to dismount and unsaddle in an outdoor corral. Linda and the ranch hands would handle returning the horses to a pasture.

"I'm glad I brought a hat." Drew placed a floppy sunhat on her dark curly hair.

"Now I know why cowboys wore hats." Joel tapped the brim of his newly purchased straw hat. Straw might sound cheap, but the nicely constructed cowboy hat with a braided hatband had been expensive.

They found a spot on the corral railing next to Hannah and Jim to watch the kids. Baby Clayton squirmed in the sling wrapped across Hannah's chest, while toddler Suzie attempted to escape her stroller.

"We need to get home for a nap before we head to your place." Jim re-buckled the straps holding Suzie in the stroller.

"I'm exhausted. It's been worth it, though," Hannah said. "The kids all had a blast."

"The outside of a horse is good for the inside of a man," Jim said. "The source of those wise words is muddled, but it's a good message all the same."

"It has definitely been good for Parker," Joel said. He scanned the corral. "Speaking of whom . . ."

Parker's colorful pinto stood out in a crowd. But Flash wasn't in the corral.

"I don't see Parker," Drew said. "Or Flash."

Joel craned his neck, searching. "Maybe he went to the restroom. Or took Flash to the pasture himself."

"Even though no other kids are leaving the corral with their horses?"

They waited a few uncomfortable minutes as the rest of the children handed their horses to ranch hands. The Esselberry kids exited the corral, wound up tight and chattering with big grins on their flushed faces.

"Where's Parker?" Drew asked.

Bear, the Esselberry's sturdy twelve-year-old, looked around as though just realizing his absence. "Parker was just here a minute ago."

Both baby Clayton and Susie chose that moment to begin howling.

"That's the kid expiration siren," Jim said. He didn't wait, hustling his family away.

"Parker will turn up," Hannah said with a wave. "He won't miss his own party. We'll see you soon."

Despite Hannah's reassurance, Drew felt panic rising in her chest, sending her heart into staccato beats. She followed Joel inside the corral, waving her hand at the riding instructor.

"Linda," Drew said, "where is Parker?"

She glanced around. "He was right here. His horse was one of the first taken to the pasture." Her tanned face went pale. "He has to be around here somewhere."

After checking the restroom then the new barn, Drew called Hannah.

"Hi, Hannah," Drew said. "By any chance did Parker catch

231

a ride with you?"

"No, we're all in the car right now," Hannah said. "Almost home."

Tears sprang to Drew's eyes. "We're still at the ranch. We can't find Parker. He just disappeared."

"After he drops us off," Hannah said, "I'll send Jim back to help. Parker has to be there."

Drew wasn't as certain. The ranch was crawling with strangers.

"Parker knows better than to leave with someone he doesn't know," Drew said, more to convince herself than to explain to Hannah.

"He was upset about not getting a horse for his birthday," Hannah said. "Maybe he ran off to have some alone time to work out his disappointment?"

"What are you saying? That Parker ran away?"

*   *   *

Dustin's cellphone pinged. He studied the screen while Makenzie walked beside him to the makeshift pasture parking lot.

"Work?" she asked when he returned the phone to his pocket.

"Nope. Family," he said. "Before I head to the station, I need to let my sister know for sure if you're coming on the cruise."

Makenzie wouldn't know until Tuesday whether she still had a job. She had a healthy savings account, but that was earmarked for a down payment on a house, and for emergencies. Vacation was not an emergency.

"Can she wait until tomorrow?" Makenzie asked.

"Leah's got a line on a deal, but she needs to pounce on it right away." Dustin stopped beside his truck. "If you're thinking it'll be too expensive, the ticket includes food and entertainment. Do you mind bunking with one of my cousins? It's lots cheaper to share a cabin, and my folks are sticklers about their unmarried kids not—"

Makenzie placed her fingers against Dustin's lips to halt the flood of words.

"I have to tell you something," she said. "And it's hard."

A blush rose up Dustin's freckled cheeks. "W-what's wrong?"

"Nothing's wrong. With us. I should have told you earlier. There's a rumor at Brieswell that they might close the lab. Maybe the entire factory. I could lose my job."

Dustin stared at Makenzie for several awkward seconds. Then he smiled and held out his arms. "Is that all? That's what's had you all wound up?"

"This is serious!" Makenzie placed her fists on her hips. "I've never lost a job before."

She tried to scowl, but Dustin was so handsome, she couldn't resist allowing him to fold her into a hug.

"Babe, we're in this together," he whispered in her ear.

"I should have told you as soon as I heard," Makenzie said. "But I wanted to wait until I knew for certain. You know how rumors are."

"I'm not interested in you because you have a job." Dustin held her at arm's length. "Although it's pretty cool telling people my girlfriend is a scientist."

He tells people about me?

"Dustin, the problem is, there aren't many opportunities in Rose Creek for chemists. If I lose my job at the lab, I'd have to consider a career change." In an unsteady voice, she added, "Or moving away."

Dustin pulled her back into the hug. "I love you. We'll figure it out together."

Makenzie melted into the comfort of his arms and mumbled, "I love you, too," into his shoulder.

"So you're going on the cruise," Dustin said. "My sister is the queen of the bargain hunters. It won't cost as much as you'd think. And if you do get laid off, we'll figure out how to cover your share. Right?"

"Right." Makenzie might have to follow the advice she'd just given Drew. Accept a helping hand. "But my parents. I haven't told them."

"They should go with us," Dustin said. "It'll be a great time for our folks to—"

Her phone buzzed just when Dustin's cell rang.

"It's Drew," she said. A call, not a group text to book club.

"Work," Dustin said.

"Hi Drew—"

"Are you still with Deputy Sage?" Drew sounded frantic.

"He's right here. I think the station just called him."

"Thank God. Makenzie, I'm so scared. Parker is missing."

<h1 style="text-align:center">Chapter Thirty</h1>

After the closing ceremony and parade, people streamed out of the arena. Life at the ranch might finally return to normal. With one exception: an unsolved murder mystery. Shanice watched people flow past her, observing faces. Watching for what? Obvious guilt? The killer might have already escaped days ago.

Or they could still be here.

A woman tapped on her shoulder. "Excuse me, do you work here?"

"No, but I'm a local rider," Shanice said, trying not to appear as startled as she felt. "May I help you?"

"I can't find my halter. Maybe it got mixed up with the ranch's tack?"

"Let's see."

"I'm Carmen Argos." She held out a hand. The woman's dark olive skin and thick black hair hinted at Greek ancestry.

"I'm Shanice Hailey. I take lessons here, so I know my way around the ranch."

Shanice led the woman to the new barn's spacious tack room. It was messy from visitors using the room, and locals not taking the time to stow their equipment properly.

Maybe I should volunteer to help Callie and Clint straighten things up. But not this afternoon. Parker's party began in a couple of hours.

Carmen rummaged through halters and bridles hung from pegs on one wall.

"It's my favorite," she said. "I'm packing to leave. I really would like to find it."

"What color is the halter? Leather or nylon?"

"Purple nylon with a beaded nose strap my mother handmade."

Distinctive enough that it should jump right out at them, if the halter was in the tack room. Shanice didn't see anything like it. They chatted about riding preferences. Carmen was a competitive trail rider, something Shanice hadn't heard of before. The distance events sounded intriguing.

"Would it be okay if I looked in these boxes?" Carmen asked. "Not that I think anyone stole it, but the halter could have been stowed in someone's box by mistake."

"I'm here to vouch for you," Shanice said. "Go ahead."

Two tack boxes were open, the lids leaning against the tack room wall. Carmen tugged on two drawers on a heavy-duty plastic box molded to appear like wood. Another tack box looked like an old leather-covered trunk repurposed to carry horse gear. Carmen lifted the lid on the third, a basic storage tote with removable trays. She dug around gently.

"Nothing." She sighed.

"Might as well check the last one," Shanice said.

"That's a fancy box."

Carmen seemed intimidated by the wood and brass fixtures. A logo for Fallows Horse Farm was imprinted on the lid.

"Odd." Shanice ran her fingers over the polished wood. "I wouldn't have thought the big-name trainers and teams would stow their gear in here with us ordinary equestrians."

Shanice unlatched the lid. *Not locked.* She lifted. It rose smoothly on hydraulic hinges.

"Whoa," Carmen said. "That's some nice stuff."

Shanice pulled out a drawer. "Here's your halter."

"Huh." Carmen snatched up the bling-laden halter. "I would complain to someone, but it had to be a mistake. And the horses are already loaded. I'm heading home. Thanks for your help!"

Although it seemed unrelated to Marcia's death, finding the halter in the Fallows' tack box was peculiar. Even more so, finding the tack box mingled among the lower economic classes of horses and riders. The book club might want more information from Carmen.

The police might even be interested.

"I'd like to hear more about your trail riding," Shanice said, trying to sound casual, but feeling awkward.

"I'm already running late. Let's exchange numbers."

In a flurry of tapping, they soon had each other's contact information. Carmen rushed out with a wave, the precious purple halter clutched in her hand.

"A Fallows' tack box," Shanice said to herself. "Who put it here?"

She glanced around, then gently pushed the door to the tack room closed. During the previous case the book club pursued, Shanice had been out of town, missing most of the action. This time, she had inserted herself into the middle of the equation. Sneaking and spying was becoming too much the norm in her life.

What's wrong with me?

Shanice felt an undeniable thrill of excitement as she examined the contents of the wood and brass tack box. Nineteenth-century steam ship passengers didn't have trunks as elaborate. Drawers, shelves, a folding rack to hang clothing, and even a mirror.

Shanice eased a small drawer open, tugging on the brass knob.

First aid. Rolls of leg wrap. Salve for muscle aches. She wasn't sure whether it was for the human or the horse. Antibiotic salve. Medicine.

Shanice pulled a small plastic tub from the drawer. She pried the lid off. Syringes and prescription bottles. Pulling one out, she turned the label to face her.

Quebrachine.

She sat heavily on the floor.

Pulling out her cellphone, Shanice snapped photos of the tub, the drawer, and the tack box. Did this warrant a call to the police? Was the drug so common that it was normal for it to randomly appear in tack boxes and refrigerators?

The door latch rattled. Shanice tossed the quebrachine back into the drawer. As she frantically slammed drawers and doors closed, she noticed a small box of the distinctive plastic baggies she'd seen in one other place. Sam's refrigerator drawer. Horse hooves danced across the clear plastic.

With a flash of anger, she slammed the drawer shut. She didn't have time to close the tack box lid. Jumping to her feet, she turned to straighten a bridle on the peg rack.

"Oh, there it is." Alistair stepped into the room.

The space suddenly seemed entirely too small.

"Hi," Shanice said. "Is that yours?" Just to confirm the tack box – and its contents – belonged to him. Even though it was clearly labeled with the Fallows Horse Farm name and logo.

"We keep our gear on the trailer," Alistair said. "I don't know how it ended up here. I was this close to reporting it stolen." He held his index finger and thumb a fraction of an inch apart.

"That's a rather large container to lose track of," Shanice said.

"Hmm." He crouched before the tack box, opened drawers, and shuffled through equipment. "Nothing seems to be missing. But Moonstone's groom will know for certain." Alistair stood. "Perhaps he'll know how it got in here. I need to send Tyrell around to fetch this. Everyone's busy packing up to head home."

Some guests and workshop participants were already on the road. Callie refused to believe Alistair was responsible for Marcia's death. Shanice now had proof that Alistair had one of the drugs Marcia told Callie about with her dying breath. Once Alistair rolled out of town, Shanice would lose the chance to clear Sam of suspicion.

"Kind of strange." As Shanice edged her way closer to the door, she punched Makenzie's number into her cellphone. She hoped her friend would pick up, hear her call, and send her deputy boyfriend to the rescue. "Seeing you inside the Double C tack room, Alistair."

"This entire weekend has been strange," Alistair said, keeping his attention on fastening and locking the tack box. "Horrific, actually. Me being in the ranch tack room is the most minor of aberrations."

"Having quebrachine in your tack box is not. Marcia knew it was an antidote for xylazine."

Alistair turned to face Shanice, but his hazel eyes didn't meet hers. He waved a hand at the tack box.

"Which is not in here," he said carefully, "because xylazine must be administered by a veterinarian. By prescription."

"It's not impossible for people to get their hands on any sort of drugs, unfortunately." Shanice placed one hand on the door handle, ready to flee if things got dicey. "Xylazine may be a controlled drug, but you have quebrachine. In there." Shanice jabbed a finger at the tack box, her heart racing.

"You've got some nerve." Alistair stood. He wasn't a small man. And he was angry.

"You're the one with nerve," Shanice said. "You set it up to make Dr. Sam Grady appear guilty. Sam would never hurt an animal, and certainly not a human being."

Alistair was silent for a moment. "Human?" His pale forehead crinkled.

"Someone planted quebrachine in Sam's trailer to make it look like he killed your wife. The drug and needle were inside a sandwich baggie with a horse hoof print. Just like the ones you have."

"Ah."

"Well?" Shanice rested her free hand on her hip and lifted her chin. "Explain yourself."

Alistair sat heavily on his tack box. "I'll have to admit, I behaved badly."

Shanice hoped Makenzie was hearing the conversation. Alistair Fallows was preparing to confess to murder.

"Everyone believed that Byron woman's story that her horse was disqualified from competition last year because

Marcia dosed him with xylazine to get him loaded in a trailer. It was a complete lie. I had to do something to take the attention off my late wife."

"Why would Sydney lie about that?" Shanice asked. She remembered his earlier claim. "Do you have any proof Sydney drugged Sir Maximus?"

"I don't know the answer to that," Alistair said. "And I don't care. I was hearing all over again Marcia's reputation being besmirched by that spoiled, ungrateful woman. If Marcia hadn't gone above and beyond working with Sydney, and taken chances with her own safety working with that dangerous animal, Sydney wouldn't have the ghost of a chance of going to the Olympics. Why would a trainer of Marcia's caliber risk her reputation by breaking drugging rules?"

Shanice remembered Sam's words. *A trainer's reputation is their most important possession.*

"You're as bad as Sydney," Shanice said. "Worse. You planted one of the drugs Marcia named with her dying breath in Sam's trailer. Now Sam is a suspect in Marcia's death."

"That seems a bit of a stretch." Alistair raised one red eyebrow. "Murder? If I was attempting to frame Dr. Grady for Marcia's murder, I would have planted xylazine. Which I have no access to."

Shanice frowned. Alistair had a point. She shook her head. "So your intention was to make it look like Dr. Grady was doping horses? Because quebrachine counteracts xylazine, right?"

Alistair closed his eyes and exhaled noisily. "I was infuriated at the spectacle of the equine community gathering over Marcia like a flock of vultures. Tearing at the meat of televised training workshops. What mattered most to me was ensuring the memory of my wife remained untainted by their false accusations."

"By making a false accusation of your own?" Shanice could see genuine pain in Alistair's eyes, but her own pain was real, too. If she had truly believed Sam was guilty, she might have destroyed their relationship. "You lied. And Sam suffered." *I suffered.*

Alistair sighed. "It was a heat-of-the-moment decision, clouded by grief. I didn't think it through, and my actions obviously didn't have the effect I'd hoped for. I will make my apologies to Dr. Grady before I leave."

"We need to talk to the police—"

The tack room door flew open, nearly knocking Shanice to the floor.

"Have you seen Parker Brauner?" Deputy Sage asked. He wasn't in uniform, still wearing cowboy-style street clothes.

"Yes, not long ago," Shanice said. "During the closing parade."

"What's this all about?" Alistair asked. "Who is this Parker whatever?"

"We've got a real emergency on our hands," Dustin said.

"Mr. Fallows?" Shanice asked. "We can clear this up later, right?"

"Okay," he said with a frown. "I'll talk to the police as soon as it is convenient. What's this emergency?"

"Come on. We need all the help we can get," Dustin said. "Parker's gone missing."

Chapter Thirty-One

Drew was absolutely shattered, but grateful to see her friends entering the corral.

"Okay, everyone," Dustin said. "Gather 'round. First off, Mr. and Mrs. Brauner, we're no doubt overreacting. It's only because there are people we don't know on the ranch that we're acting so quickly."

Drew tried unsuccessfully to stifle a sob. Callie and Shanice surrounded her, arms around her shoulders. Drew wanted to release the panic she felt in a good cry, but that wouldn't help Parker.

"I'm okay," she whispered, but grasped Shanice's and Callie's hands.

"We need to divide up into teams and do a systematic search," Dustin said.

He organized the crowd into two-person teams. Then he doled out assignments for which areas each team would search. Dustin was dressed like a cowboy, but he had on his police officer attitude. His shyness vanished as he gave instructions. His professionalism gave Drew some comfort as the book club, ranch hands, and workshop staff exchanged phone numbers. When Dustin's phone buzzed, everyone stared at him expectantly.

He lowered his phone. "Chief Holloway is at the ranch gate. It's shut. No one can leave now. Since Parker was verified to be here less than twenty minutes ago, it's unlikely he left that way."

But it wasn't impossible he'd been taken away through the

front gate before it was closed.

Every child abduction Drew had ever heard of, in real life or fiction, raced through her mind. She clutched her friends' hands tighter.

Clint was in his house, viewing the ranch security cameras with a police officer. They would know exactly who drove through the gates during the minutes between Parker going missing, and Chief Holloway closing the gate.

"Flash was returned to the pasture," Linda said. "Parker didn't ride anywhere."

Joel held Boomer's leash as he returned his cell to his shirt pocket. "Tobias will call if Parker shows up at home." He faced Drew. "Hannah is at our house, with your uncle."

Hannah was the calm, efficient mother of five children. Drew could relax on that front, anyway, knowing she would manage the guests until—

Until this situation is resolved, one way or the other.

As though sensing her rising panic, Shanice squeezed her shoulder and whispered, "It's going to be okay."

After a few more words from the Deputy, the corral emptied as people went on their assigned searches.

"We'll find him," Makenzie said. "You have Rose Creek's finest on the job."

Callie waved at Shanice. "Come on, partner. I have some ideas where to look. I've got my own favorite hidey holes for when I'm upset about somethin'."

The tall cowgirl led Shanice out of the corral.

"If that kid ran away," Joel said through gritted teeth, "my decision is made. We're returning to Boston."

"If someone took him—" Drew began, but couldn't finish.

"Parker's too smart to leave with someone he doesn't know," Makenzie said with a weak smile. "My guess is, he's doing some boy stuff somewhere on the ranch and forgot about the time."

"With a birthday party to attend?" Joel asked.

"A party where he thinks he's not getting a horse,"

Makenzie said. At Joel's harsh look, she added, "We'd better get busy. I'll go with you two, if that's okay?"

Joel nodded. "We need someone with a calmer head on our search team."

"I can't even keep track of one little boy," Drew said. "How am I going to raise a baby, too?"

*   *   *

Shanice had complimented Callie earlier on the denim skirt and fringed coral cowgirl blouse, but her clothing choices were a hindrance now.

I'm glad I wore jeans.

"One of the few times I dress up," the cowgirl mumbled. "Unfortunately, most of the places a boy might hide are not easily accessible in a skirt."

There were already two teams of searchers inside the old barn. Shanice felt nauseous at the thought of people digging around the hayloft where Marcia had died.

"Let's head around back," Callie said. "There's a trail up the hill."

Shanice followed Callie around the old barn. She glanced up at the pulley over a hay loading door. The barn butted up to the bottom of the hill.

"If Parker's avoiding people," Shanice said, "and he was hiding in the hayloft, it's not much of a leap from the hay door to the ground."

"My thoughts, too," Callie said. "From here, the only way to escape bein' found is up."

Escape what? A birthday party? Was Parker in danger? Fleeing a murderer?

"We've got this." Shanice led the way up a dusty, narrow path, brushing aside branches of undergrowth and low scrub oak trees. The trail zigzagged across the hill, climbing steadily. Finally, it opened up to an outcropping of rocks. "I can see how this would be a nice spot to get away from it all. You can see most of the ranch."

In addition to the rocks, a circle of scrub oaks shielded a person from view. Tall pines provided shade. A private space where you wouldn't be seen, but you could watch activity below.

In the pasture used for parking RVs and huge horse trailers and vans, Shanice saw four people trying to load a horse in a trailer. *Is that Sam?* She shaded her eyes, but there were too many leafy branches obstructing the view. *Maybe.* He hadn't answered his cellphone when she called to tell him about Parker going missing.

Glancing around the rocky hilltop, Shanice didn't see a boy. Or much in the way of hiding places.

"Is there somewhere up here you hang out?" Shanice asked.

"This is it," Callie said.

"So if Parker were here, we'd know."

"Yep. No Parker," Callie said.

"The old barn is right below us." Shanice stared down the hill at the green galvanized steel roof.

People swarmed around the two barns and outbuildings. Shanice heard voices. Shouts. But nothing indicating Parker had been found.

"Yep. We put new siding and a new roof on it. The building should last another fifty years."

Callie kept her eyes on the dusty, gravelly ground. She parted branches, and pushed her bare arms against tall bunched grasses. Shanice realized with a shudder her friend was searching for clues. A boy-sized cowboy boot. Articles of clothing. A body.

She couldn't watch. Shanice scanned across the brushy hillside. "Is that another trail? From this hill down to that pasture?"

Callie tore herself away from her grim hunt to look where Shanice pointed. "Game trail. Most likely from white-tailed deer."

"It looks well used," Shanice said. "Not that I know much about the habits of wild animals." Growing up in Chicago hadn't afforded many opportunities to learn woodlore.

"Deer trample down a path of least resistance in the forest." Callie went back to scanning the hilltop. "Other smaller animals use their trails. Raccoons or possums. Scavenging on the ranch, then using the deer trails to get home to their dens."

"What are you looking for?" Shanice finally asked.

"I dunno. But it looks like I'm not the only one to hang out up here recently."

Now Shanice noticed the bits of candy wrappers. A crumpled soda can.

Callie stooped to look under a thicket of low-growing scrub oak. The trees were nowhere near the size of regular oaks. They were more like bushes, not much taller than Callie. Their branches brushed the ground, providing cover for birds, animals, and maybe boys.

"No beer cans or alcohol bottles," Callie said.

"Keeping an eye on Clint's cousin?" Shanice asked.

"George is doin' great right now, but I'm not gonna ignore any signals he's fallin' back into his old ways. This is just ordinary trash, though. I'll clean up later. We have a kid to find." Callie stood, began to turn, but frowned. "Hang on." Callie picked up a dry stick and poked under leafy branches. "What?" She dropped to her bare knees.

"Not a raccoon, I hope," Shanice said.

"More interestin' than a trash panda," Callie said. "Is that what I think it is?"

She stood, brushing the dirt and debris off her bare knees, then parted the branches. Shanice crouched to peer past the green leaves. A small vial and a syringe peeked out from a hasty covering of dried leaves.

And a cellphone.

"My only question is," Shanice said, not even attempting to cover her exasperation, "where on your ranch *won't* we find animal medications?"

"Which one is it?" Callie asked, tugging the branches farther apart. "I don't want to touch anything in case the police need fingerprints."

Shanice leaned closer. She was sadly familiar with quebrachine vials, after seeing them in Sam's refrigerator and Alistair's tack box.

"It's definitely not quebrachine." She squinted at the label. "Xylazine."

Shanice extracted herself from the scrub oaks, brushing leaves from her tiered ponytail.

"Holy cow," Callie said. "Either a junkie has been hidin' up here," she began.

Shanice finished for her. "Or you just discovered the murder weapon."

* * *

Boomer wriggled in Joel's arms. The poor puppy didn't understand what was going on. He just wanted down to play.

"You should take him home," Joel said, lifting the dog toward Drew. "There are plenty of people here searching."

Drew shook her head. "I'm staying." Sitting at home, she'd only work herself into an ulcer or a nervous breakdown. "Tobias and Hannah both said they'd call if Parker shows up."

And neither has called.

"Your puppy should be okay out here," Makenzie said. "You've got a leash."

"He'll get covered with cockleburs and stickers," Joel said.

The basenji was an African hunting dog, originating in the savannah and rain forest. An Oklahoma pasture shouldn't be too much for the puppy to handle.

"He'll be fine," Drew said.

Joel held the puppy close to his chest. "I've got him. He's calm now."

Drew had been afraid Boomer might get stepped on among the crowds, but her trio had peeled off on their own search. The old and new barns were being dissected by teams of searchers familiar with the nooks and crannies where a boy might hide.

Others were hunting the pastures on horseback. Drew, Joel, and Makenzie walked through the cow pasture where the RVs and trailers had parked.

Her heart sank when she saw how many were gone already. Joel had to be thinking the same thing. Parker could be miles away by now.

"It's our job to check every trailer," he said. "We can't worry about those who have already left. Clint and the police will track them down."

"We'll walk a grid," Makenzie said. "Look for anything that might be a clue. Especially if you see something belonging to Parker."

The chemist had overcome much of the shyness she had shown when Drew first met her in April. Now she took charge with confidence. Drew was grateful, but the thought of Parker losing personal items in the pasture terrified her.

"Hey," Makenzie said. "There's Sam."

"You keep searching," Drew said. "I'll let him know what's going on."

The famous horse-whisperer seemed to be at the center of a controversy. The three people surrounding him spoke at once with raised voices. Two clung to lead ropes as a large chestnut horse backed away from the trailer, dragging them. The animal's nostrils flared, and the whites of his eyes showed.

"Just give him a good smack on the butt with the rope." The woman had to be Trisha Pinkton. Callie and Emily had described the woman with sun-tortured skin and messy blonde hair. They caught her rummaging through a tack box in the old barn. She was clinging to a lead rope. The horse shied away from her. "That always works."

"You've managed to undo in ten minutes what this horse and I accomplished in the arena just hours ago," Sam said in a scolding tone. He unclipped the lead rope Trisha held, then took the other from a young man whose soiled clothing was soaked through with sweat. "The longer you harass Sir Maximus, the longer it'll take to get him calm. You can either back off and learn, or leave the area."

"That's my horse, Dr. Grady," Sydney said. "I'll decide what happens to him."

Sam raised both hands in surrender. One held the lead rope still attached to Sir Maximus's halter. Loosely, Drew noticed. The horse wasn't trying to escape Sam.

Although Drew found the huge horse intimidating, she raced up to the group anyway. She waved her hands to get their attention, causing the animal to snort and show the whites of its eyes.

"Have you seen my son?" Drew asked. All eyes turned to her. *Good.* "He's about this tall." She held her hand a little below her shoulder. "Lean. With hair like mine." She touched her dark, curls.

"We're busy," Sydney said. "Keep out of the way."

Of all the suspects in the killing of Marcia, this woman seemed the most likely, emotionally anyway. She was cold-hearted.

"We're talking about a human child," Sam said. "Trailering your horse can wait." He turned his attention to Drew. "What's going on?"

Through tears and with a shaky voice, Drew explained quickly. "Parker rode in the closing parade. The kids unsaddled in an outdoor corral. Then he vanished."

"Oh, that boy," Sydney said.

Chapter Thirty-Two

"You've seen him?" Drew asked.

"He carried a saddle from the barn back to the trailer for me. Nice kid. Very helpful."

"Where did he go after that?" Drew asked.

Sydney shrugged. "I gave him a dollar. He went away." And she was done. "Dr. Grady, I was supposed to leave half an hour ago."

Drew clenched her hands into fists. "My son is more important than your crazy horse!"

Sydney smirked. "Have a look around. But my guess is he went back to the barn. The kid is obsessed with horses."

And you're not?

"I'm searching your trailer." Drew wasn't asking permission.

As Drew stepped up the ramp and into the large horse trailer, she understood the horse's reluctance to be loaded. It was dim inside. She detected a slight diesel odor above the smell of hay.

"Parker?"

The horse people outside were making too much of a racket, arguing over who was responsible for getting Sir Maximus in the trailer. A generator roared somewhere near, powering the interior lights and air conditioning.

These horses travel in style.

She texted Joel.

Parker seen by Sydney. I'm searching her horse trailer.

In a flash, Makenzie and Joel joined her inside the trailer, ignoring the objections of Sydney and her two employees. Drew relayed what Sydney had claimed, not holding back her opinion of a woman who put her own concerns above those of parents trying to find a missing boy.

There weren't many hiding places in the trailer, for a live boy or a body. Four stalls for horses were at a slight diagonal. Each stall had a window. The interior was cool. For being a vehicle used to transport animals, it was amazingly clean. But the interior felt dark after the bright summer sun outside, despite the lighting.

Joel lowered Boomer to the trailer floor.

"You're a hunting dog," Joel told him. "Hunt! Find Parker."

The puppy seemed delighted with the horsey smells and strange new objects. He returned to a spot furthest forward time and again, sniffing and pawing at the wall.

"He's going to scratch the paint," Makenzie said.

"I don't care if he claws a hole through it," Drew said. "But I can't see any hiding places in here."

Joel tugged the puppy's leash, pulling him away from the wall. Boomer explored the rest of the interior. After humans and dog had explored every inch of the trailer, they exited through a smaller human-sized door. Joel picked up Boomer, cradling him in his arms, but the puppy wiggled and squirmed. His curly tail jiggled wildly, and he scrabbled to be let down.

"Now what?" Makenzie asked.

Joel set Boomer on the ground.

"Something has his attention," Joel said.

Outside again, Drew could see another compartment extended in front of the horse stall part of the trailer, with a portion sitting directly over the bed of an enormous truck. Not the large pickup trucks Callie and Clint used on their ranch. This one looked like a cross between a diesel farm truck and a semi.

"There's more to this?" Drew asked.

"That has to be living quarters," Makenzie said. "Horses ride in the back. People live in the space in the front, like a combination RV and horse trailer."

Joel and Drew exchanged a look.

Drew raced the dozen feet to a door. It seemed so obvious now. A human area occupied one-fourth of the trailer. She tugged on the handle, then pounded on the door.

"Parker! Are you in there?"

Boomer leapt out of Joel's arms and stood on his hind legs, pawing at the door.

The generator shut off. Drew's ears echoed with the sudden absence of the noisy motor. She heard voices congratulating Sam for loading the contrary horse. Boomer erupted in a yodel-howling Drew had rarely heard. He clawed at the door. Joel wrenched at the handle, even though Drew had just tried it herself.

"Locked," he said.

"Hey!" Trisha trotted up. "That's private."

"We're searching for my son," Joel said. "Open the door."

Sydney exited the horse part of the trailer and approached the group. Drew grabbed her arm.

"Parker's puppy alerted us," Drew said. "We need to check inside. Unlock the door."

"That's the staff living quarters," Sydney said. "No one rides in there when the trailer is being transported." She turned to Trisha. "You locked up hours ago, right?"

"Not hours," Trisha said. "But it was a while ago."

"I don't care if it was last week." Joel picked up Boomer. "Open that door."

"Why are you so upset?" Sydney asked. "Kids get misplaced all the time. He's probably taking a nap in a hayloft."

Hayloft. Did the woman realize what she'd said? Or was she intentionally mocking them, suggesting Parker wound up where Marcia had been murdered?

Drew felt dizzy. She grasped Makenzie's arm.

"What's wrong with her?" Sydney asked. "I swear, you people are so dramatic."

"Listen, you pampered twit," Makenzie snapped. "You have to know a woman was murdered in the hayloft of the old barn just days ago. Everyone's been talking about it. Of course, Parker's parents are worried. There might be a murderer on the ranch."

"If the killer hasn't already escaped," Joel said. "With my son."

"That's the craziest thing I've heard all week," Sydney said. "What does Marcia's death have to do with a missing kid?"

The standoff with Sydney might have escalated to requiring police intervention, but a pounding on the inside of the door ended the dispute.

"Dad?" came the muffled cry.

Sydney rolled her eyes, but motioned to Trisha. "You have the key? Open it up."

Trisha's face went pale as she used a key fob to unlock the trailer door. It swung open swiftly as Parker tumbled out.

"What are you doing in there?" was Sydney's question.

Not "are you okay" or "what happened?"

"Parker!" Drew pulled her son into a smothering hug. "What on earth! Everyone is searching for you. We've been so worried."

Drew let the tears stream down her face. Joel joined the hug.

"Boomer!" Parker cried. He broke free from his parents to reach for his puppy. Boomer wiggled and licked Parker's cheeks.

"He found you," Joel said. "No thanks to these people. Makenzie, call the police."

"Already on it." The chemist had her phone pressed to her ear.

"Now tell us what happened," Joel said to Parker.

"I carried a saddle from the stable to here," Parker said. "I was helping Ms. Byron. She said she couldn't carry it herself. Then I had to go to the bathroom, but it's a long way to the barn, so some guy let me in."

A shiver of horror ran up Drew's spine. Before she could launch into uncomfortable questioning, Parker pointed.

"Him."

"Hey, little man." The twenty-something cowboy with dirty

jeans and a battered baseball cap waved. "You get business taken care of?"

Joel pounced. Sydney joined the questioning, causing genuine terror to appear on the cowboy's face. It began in a jumbled mess, but the story quickly boiled down to a simple matter.

Parker needed to "go." Sydney's traveling ranch hand and all-around gofer told Parker it was okay to use the trailer "just this one time." Parker was using the restroom when Trisha closed up the trailer in preparation for traveling to the next horse event.

"So it must've all been a mix-up," the cowboy said. "No harm. No foul."

Drew was satisfied there had been no deliberate intention to trap Parker. She phoned Hannah and Uncle Tobias to give them the good news and let them know they were on their way home. But then Deputy Sage arrived. The entire story had to be gone through a second time. Several searchers came to the trailer to see what had caused all the hullabaloo, and then to hug Parker, Drew, and Joel.

Dustin quickly questioned Drew's family. He told them they could go, and began talking to the ranch hand and Sydney.

Drew was sick with relief at finding Parker, but she couldn't help hesitating a moment when she heard Deputy Sage's question.

"Where's that other gal?" he asked. "I need to talk to her, too, seeing as how she's the one who locked Parker in the trailer."

Sydney glanced around. "Trisha? She can't be far. We're leaving as soon as you're done harassing us."

*　　*　　*

There was all kinds of commotion down in the cow pasture, where a few horse trailers and RVs remained. Callie watched people swarming toward the group that had finally gotten Sir

Maximus trailered. Even from this distance, she had easily recognized the big chestnut gelding.

She pressed her phone tight to her ear as she tried to make sense of the scene below. The police dispatcher, Gracie, finally got Callie connected to Chief Holloway. Callie quickly told him about their discovery of xylazine, a syringe, and a cellphone on the hilltop behind the old barn.

"We'll gather the evidence," Chief Holloway said. "I want to see it in situ, you know, leave it where you found it. But we're stretched a little thin at the moment."

"We can keep an eye on it," Callie said. "Until one of your officers can get here. Do you have any news about Parker?"

"Nothing yet." He ended the call with a click.

"Huh. That was abrupt."

Shanice's phone rang loudly.

"It's Makenzie!" Shanice said, putting her phone on speaker.

"Hey girls." Her voice was upbeat through the cellphone speaker. "So here's the good news. We found Parker! Or actually, Boomer found him. He was accidentally locked in a horse trailer. Or a people trailer. Kind of a combination thing. He's fine. If Boomer hadn't tracked him, Parker might not have been found until Sydney reached her destination. We're heading to Drew's house for the party now."

"The party is still on?" Callie asked.

"Absolutely," Makenzie said. "Although Drew is a basket case."

"I can't wait to hear all the details," Shanice said.

"We really have somethin' to celebrate now," Callie said with a smile. "Add to that, me and Shanice might have found the syringe and drug used to murder Marcia."

"We'll be late," Shanice said. "Callie and I plan to guard the evidence until the police get here. I found quebrachine in Sam's trailer and in Alistair's tack box, but those didn't have anything to do with Marcia's murder. We might have found Marcia's cellphone, too. Hidden in the bushes."

"It's within spittin' distance of the old barn," Callie said. "Emily noticed how the hay door opens onto the base of the hill. The killer could have escaped that way, then stashed the murder weapon up here."

The branches of scrub oaks crowding the trail rustled. Callie glanced down the hill. She had texted Clint before calling the police. Now that Parker had been found, maybe he decided to join her and Shanice.

"Don't wait for us to cut the cake," Shanice was telling Makenzie.

Callie watched the trail, anticipating seeing Clint. The person climbing the hillside paused. Callie almost called out and waved her hand, but she hesitated. The hiker was in stealth mode. Chief Holloway knew Callie and Shanice were on the hill. Any officers would have announced themselves. Or at least made more noise than this character.

Then the person came within sight. Instead of Clint's cowboy hat or his thick black hair, she glimpsed a messy, dirty-blonde mop.

Trisha? Sydney's horse groom? She'd been down in the cow pasture with Sir Maximus just moments ago. Callie grabbed Shanice's arm and held a finger to her lips. She pulled Shanice behind the rocks.

"What—" Shanice whispered.

Callie shook her head and pointed.

Trisha Pinkton practically tiptoed, but it was impossible not to make sound walking in cowgirl boots on the dusty, gravel-strewn trail. She brushed through the narrow gap in a cluster of scrub oak at the top of the hill.

Callie whipped out her phone and clicked through the options to call Gracie's cellphone. Praying the dispatcher picked up, and understood what was happening, Callie silenced her audio and started a video call.

"Who's up here?" Trisha whispered hoarsely. "I can hear you moving around."

She stood still as a statue, her head swiveling as she scanned the hilltop. Callie felt the woman's eyes brush right past her and Shanice's hiding place.

"Okay," Trisha muttered to herself. "Get it and go."

Trisha walked straight to the spot where Callie had discovered the drug and syringe. She groped around, then pulled her arm out from between the low branches. "Got ya."

Callie hoped her phone had caught Trisha in the act of retrieving evidence in Marcia's murder case. And that Gracie understood what was happening.

Where was Clint? Where were the police?

Chapter Thirty-Three

Shanice had been part of the book club during their amateur sleuthing in two other cases, but this was the first time she was face-to-face with the killer. Well, not quite. She could see Trisha's face, but hopefully Trisha couldn't see her.

Callie kept her cellphone aimed at the female groom as the woman thrashed around in the bushes until her hand landed on the cellphone. She grunted with satisfaction. Shanice hoped Makenzie was still on the other end of her call. With few words being spoken, none of the rustling and breathing offered a clue to what was going on.

But Shanice could see the pieces of data slide neatly into the formula in her head. The solution still didn't make any sense, though.

Trisha murdered Marcia.

Why? She wasn't the owner of Sir Maximus. Trisha wasn't even the rider. Months ago, Sydney might have had motivation to kill when the hurt of the disqualification was still fresh. Why now? Unless Sydney ordered Trisha to do her dirty work in an act of delayed revenge. Or had Sydney killed Marcia, then sent Trisha to retrieve the evidence?

A warm breeze rustled the leaves. The late afternoon sun slanted through branches in shafts of golden light.

Bright sun glinted off Callie's cellphone screen.

"Hey." Trisha glared toward the reflected light. She threw a hand over her eyes for a brief moment. "Hold it right there."

Shanice grabbed Callie's arm and pulled her out of their

hiding place. Abandoning any attempt at secrecy, they crashed through the underbrush and headed downhill. Branches scratched Shanice's arms and slapped across her face.

"Makenzie, send help!" Shanice yelled at the phone in her hand, hoping the message came through. "Trisha's after us!" She shoved the phone in her jeans pocket.

All the technology and connectivity in the world couldn't get the police to them fast enough. Besides, they were running away from the old barn. Into, what? Shanice couldn't see far through the tangle of leaves and tree trunks. They might pop out of the woods onto a well-populated scene or into an empty field. Or more woods.

"Why did you kill Marcia?" Callie yelled over her shoulder.

"She brought it on herself," Trisha said. "That witch was going to blame me for Sir Maximus being disqualified." Trisha huffed as she raced through the woods.

"Because it was you." Based on newly acquired data, Shanice was certain she was right. "Marcia figured out what really happened."

"Marcia's the guilty one!" Trisha shrieked. "She was going to cut us from the team just because Sir Maximus wouldn't load in the trailer like a good little boy."

Shanice had witnessed Sam coaxing the horse into a trailer during his workshop. It had required patience. Something Trisha obviously didn't have.

"Why'd you take Marcia's cellphone?" Callie yelled over her shoulder. "To keep her from calling 911?"

"She claimed someone sent her photos of me injecting Sir Maximus," Trisha said. "No one could tell a thing from those pictures, but I needed that phone. If your meddling little gang had stayed out of it, I could have taken care of everything just fine. You didn't even give me time to get rid of that ridiculous cat."

"You were gonna murder Winston, too?" Callie asked.

Shanice didn't think killing animals was considered murder. Although maybe it should be.

Trisha was closing in on them. Maybe rage caused her to push past the obstacles slowing down Shanice and Callie. She glanced at her friend.

"Split up," she said.

Trisha paused as the two women veered away from each other. Shanice waved her arms wildly, hoping to attract Trisha's attention away from Callie.

"You injected Sir Maximus with xylazine when he wouldn't load before that competition last fall." Shanice ducked behind the trunk of a tall pine. Trisha hadn't taken the bait. She chose to follow Callie. "It was your responsibility to get him in that trailer," Shanice continued. "Then you murdered Marcia. Using the same drug."

"That's what she deserved," Trisha said. "You bet I let her know, too. The same drug she was trying to end my career over."

"How did you get ahold of xylazine?" Callie asked.

"It's easy when the mobile vet service leaves their van unlocked," Trisha said.

There was one piece missing from the formula to solve the murder mystery – logic.

"No one deserves to be murdered," Callie said.

"Easy for you to say, little miss richie rich," Trisha said with a sneer. "How much do you think a groom gets paid? Not much! And I was going to lose my pathetic paycheck, my career, because Marcia was incompetent. It was her crew's job to load Sir Maximus into the trailer. They couldn't do it."

"Then why not kill them?" Shanice asked. "One of them might have taken those photos."

Callie yelped. Shanice peeked around the tree to see her trip and crash to the ground. Trisha was on her in an instant, landing on her back as she raised the hypodermic needle in her fist.

"No!" Shanice scrambled over rocks and brush. She grabbed a thick fallen branch and swung it.

The branch snapped with a loud crack as it connected with Trish's arm. The needle went flying. Trisha didn't even appear stunned. She snatched a rock and flung it at Shanice. It whizzed past Shanice's left ear, barely missing her.

Trisha grabbed for another rock in the underbrush. Shanice rushed at her, knocking her off Callie as the cowgirl rolled to her side. Trisha sprawled onto the ground.

"Hold it right there!"

Officer Sarah Chandler scrambled across the rugged hillside, coming up the same trail Trisha had used. Trisha groped through the fallen leaves and pine needles for the syringe, but came up empty. She struggled to her feet and bolted down the hill. Shanice considered briefly chasing after Trisha, but decided some things were better left to the professionals. Amateur sleuths had to know their limits.

"Are you okay?" Sarah asked Callie.

"She didn't get me," Callie said as she stood. She brushed her hands down her clothes. "Thanks to Shanice. But you'll be askin' Trisha if she's okay once I get my hands on her." Callie started to jog down the hill.

Sarah grabbed Callie's arm, pulling her to a halt. "Don't you dare. Leave this to me." She released Callie and plowed through the thick growth in pursuit of Trisha.

"Callie!" Clint pushed his way through the brush, following roughly the same path Sarah had taken. When he saw Callie, he broke into a sprint.

"Shanice!"

She turned. Sam raced up the hill from a different direction, coming from the cow pasture where RVs had been parked all weekend. He pulled Shanice into a smothering hug. She didn't mind. She hung on as though her life depended on being wrapped in his arms.

"When Makenzie told us what was going on," Sam said, "I was so afraid I'd lose you."

Sam planted a kiss on her lips. Shanice was pretty sure the feeling making her go weak in the knees wasn't all from her life-or-death chase through the woods.

Callie was having her own moment with her husband.

"Are you injured?" Clint asked her.

"Maybe a little banged up," Callie said. "But nothin' too serious." She looked at her blouse and skirt, soiled and torn. "Guess I'll have to clean up and change for the party."

"Me, too," Shanice said.

"The police will want to speak to us first," Clint said.

"I learned how that quebrachine ended up in your refrigerator," Shanice said, looking up at Sam. "I need to let Chief Holloway know who planted that evidence. But it has nothing to do with the murder. First, though, we have to find that syringe."

"That'll be like findin' a needle in a haystack," Callie said. "Almost literally."

Sam hugged Shanice tightly, then released her from his embrace. "Let's get busy, then."

* * *

Once she recovered from the initial shock of losing, then finding their son, Drew tried to focus on the birthday party.

During the first panic of realizing their son was missing, when they feared he'd run away, Joel had stated that level of misbehavior required their immediate return to Boston. His attitude softened when they learned Parker's captivity was unintentional. That didn't mean Joel would suddenly give up his career to move to Rose Creek.

The hot summer day cooled enough to make the party in Drew's backyard comfortable. Half the town had shown up at the house to offer help searching for Parker, and when he was found, they stayed for the party. Kids played games on the lawn. Men stood around the grill discussing outdoor cooking techniques. Joel was laughing with Jim and Hannah over a story about Bear disappearing, and the silly misunderstanding that nearly initiated a search party.

Boomer was the hero of today's story, as Parker told it. Jim and Hannah expounded on the virtues of basenji dogs in general, and Boomer specifically.

The earlier panic and accompanying adrenaline washed away, leaving Drew feeling weak with relief. And exhausted. She was debating whether she could make her excuses and leave the party when Parker tugged at her hand.

"Mom. We need to talk." He glanced over his shoulder at Uncle Tobias, who sat on a canvas camp chair. Boomer nested in the old man's lap, finally worn out from the long day. Tobias urged Parker on with a wave of one hand. Parker returned his attention to Drew. "I need to tell you something."

"What is it?" Drew asked.

Parker had already apologized for helping Sydney without telling his parents or his riding instructor, Linda. Drew suspected Sydney had commandeered her son without a thought that he might be needed elsewhere. That he would be missed. The woman was reprehensible.

She let Parker lead her to a quiet spot, unoccupied by partygoers. They sat on a low stone wall defining a flowerbed that needed weeding.

"The other day, when I heard you and Dad talking," Parker said, "and I thought we were moving back to Boston, I acted like a little kid. That was dumb, and I've been a jerk. I do want a baby sister or brother."

"Yes, Parker. You told us that. And I'm glad. I think you'll be great at the job. Who wouldn't want a cowboy for a big brother?"

That earned a smile from Parker. "We," he glanced toward Tobias, "uh, I need to ask next time before making an assumption."

Uncle Tobias had obviously had a talk with Parker and primed him with adult terminology.

"We all make mistakes," Drew said. "Your father and I are trying to make a big decision."

"I know. I want to stay in Rose Creek. Dad said Boomer goes with us wherever we live, especially after he saved me. But there's more than Boomer. It's my friends. Jill and Tommy and Bear. The temple and my friends there. I even like school here better." Tears filled his eyes. "And the ranch. Mr. and Mrs. Garcia. Miss Linda. Flash." He paused. "And Uncle Tobias. He'll hate Boston."

Drew pulled him into a hug. He had just turned nine. Too young to act so grown up. But Drew was proud of the changes in her son.

"We'll figure it out, Parker. As a family."

Callie, Clint, Makenzie, Shanice, and Sam walked around the house into the backyard.

"Everyone's here now. It's time to cut the cake," Drew told Parker.

Jim shook a small bell and motioned for people to draw near. The clusters of people scattered around the lawn assembled at a folding table covered with wrapped presents. Hannah took charge, even while carrying sleeping baby Clayton in a sling across her chest.

Joel, Jim, and the Esselberry kids distributed cake with dollops of rapidly melting vanilla ice cream to guests. Parker tore into wrapping paper and gift bags with wild abandon.

The small building block sets, paperback books, a chess set, a soccer ball, and other gifts were modest in price, but Parker was delighted with everything. Especially the horse-themed gifts, and ones that included Boomer.

Parker was excited to receive a Western saddle and bridle from Joel and Drew. Linda had helped them select the proper fit for both boy and horse at the Western outfitter in Rose Creek.

Parker saved the gift bag from Uncle Tobias for last. He pulled sheets of blue tissue paper from the bag. Inside was an envelope and a wrapped rectangle. Drew thought she detected an air of bracing himself for the worst. Parker unwrapped the paper, revealing a framed photo.

"It's a picture," he turned it to face the guests. "Me riding Flash." He swallowed, then walked to Tobias's seat and hugged him. "Thank you for the picture."

"There's something else in the envelope," Tobias said. "Something important."

Parker returned to the table and opened the envelope, peering inside. He pulled out a sheet of paper. "What's this?"

"Your contract," Tobias said. "I know you wanted your own horse. I couldn't buy Flash for you, but I did arrange a lease."

"What's that?" Parker asked.

"Flash is your horse for the rest of the year," Tobias said. "No one else gets to ride him. He's all yours, until the end of December."

When Parker burst into tears, Drew hoped it wasn't out of disappointment. Then he fell onto Uncle Tobias, giving him a ferocious hug that nearly toppled the old man, chair, dog, and all, onto the grass.

"Thank you! Thank you! Thank you!"

"Okay, okay," Tobias said, laughing. "You can thank me by taking good care of Flash and keeping your grades up."

The party had started late, due to extenuating circumstances. Right after the cake and presents, people began saying their goodbyes and making their exits from the backyard. Uncle Tobias and a chattering Parker went inside to, hopefully, settle down to bed.

As the party wound down, Callie, Makenzie, and Shanice gathered around Drew, pulling canvas chairs into a circle.

"There's so much to talk about," Callie said. "But it's late."

"The main thing I need to know," Drew said, "is that Trisha is locked up."

"Definitely," Makenzie said. "She couldn't outrun Officer Chandler. Trisha's cooling her heels in a cell as we speak."

"I want all the details," Shanice said, stifling a yawn, "but if I'm tired, Drew, you must be exhausted."

"Let's meet at Rose Creek Reads to close out the case," Makenzie said. "When is everyone available?"

After a check of phone calendars, they set the date for Friday afternoon.

"After work," Makenzie said, "if I still have a job."

"What are you talking about?" Drew asked. "You love your job."

Makenzie told the group briefly about the closure and layoff rumors. After a group hug, the women parted ways.

With the crowd gone, fireflies took over the yard. Drew watched the blinking lights, finally relaxing after an incredibly stressful day. She felt tears roll down her cheeks, but did nothing to wipe them away.

"I got the boys tucked into bed," Joel said. "The young one and the old one. Hey, are you okay?" Joel brushed a hand across Drew's damp cheek.

"Tears of joy," Drew said. "Or relief?"

"It'll take days to decompress from this weekend," Joel said. "Maybe I shouldn't head back to Boston tomorrow. They can spare me for another day or two."

"We'll be okay," Drew said.

"After seeing the entire town come together to search for our son," Joel said, "I know you're safe here. Despite the occasional murder. I hope we can make a mutually satisfying decision about our future soon. This commute is wearing me out."

Drew reached for Joel's hand.

"We survived today," she said. "We'll let tomorrow handle itself."

Chapter Thirty-Four

Friday afternoon, Makenzie packed Spirit in the cat carrier.

"Hopefully, this is your last trip."

Spirit pressed her scarred nose to the mesh door. "Meow."

"Not that I haven't enjoyed your company," Makenzie said. "You've been a great houseguest. I'm anxious to move your son back in with me."

"Meow."

Drew was ready to attempt integrating the cat into their household. When Makenzie arrived, Tobias was waiting on the front porch. Parker had Boomer on a leash. The puppy looked curious, but sat politely.

"Let's just scoot Spirit directly into your room," Drew told her uncle. "We'll follow Hannah's instructions for introducing Spirit to Boomer slowly."

Makenzie toted the cat carrier to Tobias's room. She stayed long enough to watch the happy reunion. Spirit was definitely Tobias's cat, snuggling into his arms and purring loudly.

"Well, I can see I'm not needed here," she said with a laugh. "Drew, do you want a ride to the meeting?"

"I'd love one. The boys can look out for each other."

Soon, they were on the short drive to Rose Creek Reads.

"Your parents talked to me and Joel about starting a business," Drew said. "I hope we weren't too harsh. They seemed overwhelmed by what we told them."

"I'm glad you were honest," Makenzie said. "They're postponing the idea of opening a barbecue hut, for now. I was afraid the three of us would become unemployed at the same time."

"I read the article about the pottery factory online," Drew said. "Brieswell is refocusing?"

"They made it sound prettier than it is," Makenzie said. "Shifting emphasis from commercial to art pottery is smart, I agree. But for now, it means a slight downsizing. Mostly through attrition. There are plenty of older workers on the verge of retirement."

"But your job?" Drew asked. "The lab?"

"We're almost there," Makenzie said. "I'll save the news to share with everyone at once."

Makenzie wasn't sure whether it was good news or not.

Water splashing from a tributary on its way to Rose Creek turned the water wheel on the side of the building, as it had done for over a hundred years. Makenzie appreciated the stability of the brick structure. Like a well-balanced chemical formula, it had stood the test of time. Yet the building hadn't been used to grind grain into flour for decades. Its purpose had changed.

The inevitability of change. Some of the changes in Makenzie's life had been positive. Others, she wasn't entirely comfortable with. But finding a group of friends had turned out better than she'd hoped. A support group. Confidants. Shoulders to cry on and to offer a shoulder to.

The bookstore cats, Mitch and Agatha, greeted them at the door of Rose Creek Reads. Callie, Shanice, and Emiko were waiting on the back deck, seated on wicker chairs in the shade of a striped patio umbrella. After a long weekend dressing up, Callie was casual in jeans, boots, and a Southwest print t-shirt.

Emily brought a tray of iced tea and sugar cookies.

"You've been quiet, Makenzie," Shanice said. "Your texts haven't exactly been informative this week. I've tried to be patient, but I really need to know what's going on."

"First things first." Makenzie placed her murder board on the small table close to the larger round picnic table. When she dropped a clear plastic sheet over the board on which she'd printed SOLVED, the book club applauded.

"A job well done," Emily said. "Everyone contributed invaluable assistance with this case."

As they reviewed their search for clues, Shanice relived her participation in the spy mission at the university. Twice. Digging through the drug safe, and suspecting Gemma, had led the book club to a dead end.

"I wanted her to be guilty," Shanice said. "I might have let my initial impression of Gemma be influenced by the university receptionist's opinion of her. Venetia was opposed to Gemma's idea for a new homecoming theme. Then Gemma called Sam hunky, and I thought she was chasing after him romantically. But it turns out she's dating Timothy."

"You're old nemesis?" Callie asked. "The bodybuilder?"

"Oh, he gave up asking me out weeks ago," Shanice said with a laugh. "Soon after Gemma's arrival. I'm glad for the entire female population of Rose Creek that he's focused on somebody who actually thinks he's hot."

"Well, Timothy is hot physically," Callie said. "Just not where it counts." She tapped a finger to the side of her head. "How are you and Dr. Grady doing?"

Makenzie was certain she detected a blush on Shanice's dark cheeks.

"We're good," was all she said. But her smile spoke volumes. "My sister Breona, her husband, and their new baby are coming for a visit. They say it's to check out Rose Creek. I've built it up as a great place to raise children, but I suspect they're on a spy mission for my family. Checking out Sam to see whether he's worthy of my attention."

While the ladies laughed about Shanice's overprotective siblings, Makenzie watched Callie's face. All these babies, and she and Clint had yet to have one of their own. Callie seemed to be coping well, but it had to sting to watch friends adding to their families.

"What about homecoming?" Emiko asked. "Have you managed to keep the opposing committee factions from declaring war on each other?"

"The first party will be our traditional Western theme," Shanice said. "The barbecue on the university lawn. After that, we convinced the committee that change is good. The winter homecoming will be the New York theme Gemma proposed."

"That could be fun," Emiko said. "A chance to dress up."

"I have to admit," Callie said, "dressin' up can be fun. In the right situation. I was sure sorry to be in a skirt while Trisha was chasin' us across the hilltop. I coulda saved us all a lot of time if Emily and I'd figured out what Trisha was up to in the old barn, where she didn't belong."

"It seemed innocent at the time." Emily topped off glasses of iced tea from a sweating pitcher. "With hindsight, I'm guessing she went back to make sure she didn't leave any clues behind in the barn."

"We did add Trisha to the board as a suspect," Makenzie said. "She wasn't completely off our radar."

"To think," Drew said, "that woman, a murderer, was so close to my son."

Emily placed a hand on Drew's shoulder and gave a gentle squeeze. Drew placed her hand over Emily's.

"If you hadn't raised a fuss about Parker being in the trailer," Emily said, "Trisha might not have panicked and gone up the hill to get rid of the evidence."

"Marcia's final words, naming the two animal drugs?" Drew asked. "Are we certain now what she wanted?"

"Marcia had to be asking for quebrachine as an antidote," Callie said. "Hopin' it would counteract the xylazine injection Trisha forced on her. But the coroner said it wouldn't have saved her. Trisha gave Marcia a dose that could sedate Sir Maximus. That's helping me feel less guilty about not being able to save her."

The book club ladies assured Callie she wasn't responsible for Marcia's death. Makenzie was certain only time would erase that from Callie's thoughts.

"What about Winston?" Emiko asked. "Did he go home

with Alistair?"

"In a moment of weakness," Callie said, "I offered to adopt that fluff ball."

The ladies congratulated Callie on her entrance into the cat companion club, but Makenzie frowned.

"It makes me mad that Alistair didn't get into any trouble for trying to frame Sam. And he even dumps responsibility for his dead wife's cat onto Callie. Ugh!"

"Winston wasn't dumped on me," Callie said. "I gotta admit, I fell in love with the goofy kitty. I wanted to keep him."

"Sam decided not to press charges for Alistair breaking into his fifth wheel," Shanice said. "He did talk to the police, and apologized to Sam. I might not have been as forgiving, but Sam believed Alistair was only trying to protect Marcia's reputation."

"That's a lame excuse," Makenzie said. "But the cat? Maybe Winston is too painful a reminder that Marcia's gone."

"Isn't it weird that there's always a cat involved in our cases?" Emiko asked. "I'm glad they all have happy endings. For the cats, anyway."

"It's clearly a team effort," Emily said. "Humans and felines."

"I contributed the least to this case," Makenzie said, "I was so preoccupied with my own worries about my job."

"You're the cornerstone of every investigation," Emily said. "And you bravely went inside the lab the second time. You helped clear up red herrings muddying the case."

"You and your awesome murder board," Emiko said. "We couldn't keep track of all the clues and suspects without you."

"What about your news?" Drew asked Makenzie. "Your job? The factory?"

Makenzie looked at Callie and shrugged. "Is it okay to tell them?"

"I don't see why not," the tall cowgirl said. "Clint got on a tear about upgrading the Double C for guests. I don't want anything like Equi X happenin' at our ranch ever again. Maybe a veterans' program, helping guys and gals with PTSD through horse therapy. But no more crazy big events. Then Makenzie told me about her boss Bob's dream of running a horse B&B."

"And needing access to a trail running across the Garcia ranch," Makenzie said.

"Clint's gonna help Bob and Lois create a business plan," Callie said. "Bob's ready to make a career change. We get calls all the time about short-term horse boarding. Asking about parkin' an RV in our pasture. Now we'll be able to refer them to Bob and Lois."

"How does that help Makenzie?" Emily asked.

"Are you going to work for your manager at the horse B&B?" Emiko asked.

"No." Makenzie took a deep breath. "It's not for certain, but I have a good chance of taking Bob's job as lab manager. Something I couldn't have considered six months ago. Book club helped me believe in myself." She dabbed at a sudden tear. "You've all made such a difference in my life."

After another round of hugs, Drew tapped a spoon against her tea glass.

"I have an announcement. When Joel returned to Boston on Tuesday, he was called into a meeting. He didn't receive the offer for junior partnership."

Makenzie held her breath. The other ladies looked the way she felt. Was this good news or bad?

"He's going to look into relocating," Drew added. "To Rose Creek."

The book club erupted in cheers and congratulations.

"What about Mr. Nibley's case?" Emiko asked.

"Did you guys nail that slimeball Ted Fulson to the wall?" Callie asked.

"The police matched his fingerprints to those on Uncle Tobias's windowsill," Drew said. "Fulson agreed to tear up Mr. Nibley's mineral rights contract when Tobias offered to not press charges for causing his fall."

"One last announcement," Makenzie said.

"There's more?" Emily asked.

Makenzie nodded. "I'm going on a Christmas cruise with Dustin and his family."

"That seems a long ways away," Callie said. "It's barely September."

"You have to get your reservations early," Makenzie said, "if you want a good deal. Dustin's sister is handling all that. The best part is that my parents are going with us."

The book club ladies agreed that it was a very good sign for Makenzie and Dustin's future. If they survived a week of family togetherness. On a ship.

"I'm sure it'll be great," Callie said. "What can go wrong?"

Emily shook her head. "Oh, Callie. After the mysteries we've read, you still have so much to learn."

The End

Acknowledgements

Writing a novel is a solitary occupation. One that suits my personality. But I do come up for air from time to time. When I do, I appreciate that family and friends are still there, ready to offer socializing opportunities. Until I duck back into my writing cave.

Thank you to my original critique partners, Joyce, Sharon, Beth, and Julie. You encouraged me to believe in myself when my writing was truly awful, and gently pushed me to improve.

Several years ago, I joined Mystery Writers of America and began carpooling to monthly meetings in Denver. The ride was often more educational than the program. In particular, short story master R. T. Lawton gave advice and encouragement that propelled me to eventual publication in Alfred Hitchcock's Mystery Magazine. Other influential carpoolers were Donnell Ann Bell, Maria Kelson, Steve Pease (AKA Michael Chandos), and Barbara Nickless, who have amazing published works capturing praise and awards.

As always, thank you to my husband Leonard, who encourages my writing obsession, but also brings balance to life with fishing trips and travel.

About the Author

Catherine Dilts is the author of the Rose Creek and the Rock Shop mystery series, and several installments in various Annie's Fiction series, for a total of twelve traditionally published novels. Eleven of her short stories have appeared in Alfred Hitchcock's Mystery Magazine. After a career in environmental compliance for a global corporation, Catherine now gets to write fiction full-time. Most of her published works have a cozy mystery flavor. She is stepping into Indy publishing this year with her co-author daughter Merida Bass, with the Ninja Grandparent Placement Mystery series, and the YA science fiction Tapestry Tales series. https://www.catherinedilts.com/

www.ingramcontent.com/pod-product-compliance
Lightning Source LLC
Chambersburg PA
CBHW021144310726
48971CB00002B/480

* 9 7 8 1 9 6 7 5 7 8 1 2 2 *